A
GENTLEMAN
OUGHT
TO KNOW

JANE
ASHFORD

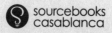
sourcebooks
casablanca

Published by Sourcebooks Casablanca, an imprint of Sourcebooks
P.O. Box 4410, Naperville, Illinois 60567-4410
(630) 961-3900
sourcebooks.com

Printed and bound in Canada.
MBP 10 9 8 7 6 5 4 3 2 1

One

CHARLOTTE DEEPING WALKED ALONG A COUNTRY FOOT-
path, partly shielded from the brisk October wind by a thorny
hedge. The month was almost over, and she was glad of her
warm cloak and thick gloves. Yellow leaves rustled at her
side, under scudding clouds, and wizened berries hung on
the branches. The air brought the scents of the waning year
and thoughts of endings. She told herself she was not lonely,
but she couldn't help wishing for her three best friends. Ada,
Harriet, and Sarah had been her constant companions since
they had met at school at thirteen. They'd been the sisters
she'd never had, and she missed them with a wistful melan-
choly that was unlike her. She was the acerbic one. Nothing
depressed her spirits.

A clutching briar snagged her cloak. Charlotte pulled it
free. Her friends were all far away and married now. She had
turned twenty. It was time to think of the future—a topic as
thorny as the hedgerow.

With only a flurry of hoofbeats as a warning, a rider hurtled into sight above the shrubs on her left, jumping bushes,
path, and all. More than a thousand pounds of horse surged
past a few feet from her nose, so close that it seemed gigantic.

Charlotte threw up her arms and jerked backward. Her
bootheel caught in the hem of her cloak. She staggered,
lurched, and fell flat on her back with a thud that drove the
breath from her lungs. Her bonnet tipped forward and covered her face.

"Oh my God!" exclaimed an appalled male voice. There

were subdued hoofbeats as the rider turned his mount. "Are you all right?" he called.

Charlotte concentrated on catching her breath. She knew she would, eventually, but the struggle was frightening. Her chest wouldn't work, which goaded her toward panic. That and the fact that one more step and the horse would have hit her, breaking bones at the very least.

Feet hit the ground nearby. Then two knees in riding breeches thumped down at her side, just visible from under the skewed brim of her bonnet. "Miss? Are you all right? Oh lord. Can I...? What shall I...?"

At last, Charlotte's lungs started functioning again. She drew in a welcome deep breath, and then another. She pushed back her hat and glared up at a figure silhouetted by the sun. "What the deuce did you think you were doing?" she asked.

The man drew back. He was holding the reins of a dancing, snorting hunter, who clearly objected to Charlotte's incursion into their ride. "I didn't realize there was a path along here," he said. "I was just hacking cross-country, you know."

She knew all too well. The area around the Deepings' Leicestershire home filled up with hordes of hey-go-mad young gentlemen as the foxhunting season approached each year.

"My friend Stanley Deeping told me the country was good in this direction."

"Oh, Stanley." The second of Charlotte's four brothers had the brains of a huge friendly dog. In her opinion.

"You know Stanley?" He seemed pleased by this fact.

"He's my brother."

"Oh." The sun-dazzled figure cocked his head. "You must be Charlotte then. Miss Deeping, that is."

His tone had altered. Charlotte didn't know what her brothers had told their cronies about her, but she doubted it was completely flattering. She sat up and adjusted her bonnet, insofar as that was possible. She suspected the back was irreparably crushed.

"Let me help you." He offered a hand.

"Is your hand shaking?" she asked him.

"What? No."

It definitely was. She decided to take it. He rose and pulled her to her feet in one smooth motion with an excess of casual strength.

Charlotte looked up and up. She was thought tall for a girl, but this man overtopped her by six inches. He...loomed. Though she didn't think he was doing it on purpose. He was bent forward, his forehead creased with worry.

Height was the only thing they had in common. He was well muscled, while she was often judged too slender. His hair was light brown, while hers was black. He had guileless blue eyes, and she an acute dark gaze. Handsome, yes, he was—very. A bit too much to be comfortable. And possibly well aware of it. She couldn't quite tell. He was probably around Stanley's age of twenty-six. She realized she was still holding his hand. She dropped it.

More than likely, he had the brains of a flea, Charlotte thought. Stanley didn't cultivate intellectual friends, while she was known for her sharp mind. It went with her sharp tongue and angular frame.

"I really am sorry," he said. "Are you all right? Shall I take you home?"

"Throwing me over your saddle like young Lochinvar?"

His eyes widened. "Who?"

"It's a poem. Never mind." It was foolish to quote poetry to Stanley's friends. Even Walter Scott.

"Oh, a poem." He said the word as if it explained any amount of strangeness.

"I'm quite all right," Charlotte added. "You should continue your ride." She wanted him to go. She needed to collect herself. Far more than should have been necessary, even considering the fall.

He looked uncertain. "I'm Glendarvon, by the way," he said. "Not a proper introduction, but I know your name, so…"

Charlotte searched her memory. She didn't think Stanley had ever mentioned anyone named Glendarvon. By the way he said it, she suspected it was a title. Her mother would know. She was a compendium of such information.

"It's too bad you don't have your horse. You could show me the best fox runs hereabouts." He said it with the air of someone offering a treat.

It never occurred to him that she wouldn't have a horse. Which was reasonable. Of course she did. In her family, it was unthinkable not to ride. The Deepings had been breeding racehorses and hunters since the time of Charles the Second. That racing-mad monarch had knighted her ancestor for his outstanding efforts. The family had grown increasingly prosperous because they didn't keep a racing stable themselves but rather sold to those who indulged in that expensive pastime. And the hunting season was her family's glory. Her father and brothers were all dead keen, even Cecil the dandy. And her mother enjoyed their happiness. "I'm sure Stanley will take you around," Charlotte said.

He nodded, not looking particularly disappointed. "Don't suppose you hunt."

She could have. She certainly rode well enough. But she didn't. Charlotte had no interest in being spattered head to toe in mud while chasing foxes who didn't deserve that level of organized aggression. In her opinion. She started to say so. But this topic was the subject of fierce arguments with her brothers, in a family that specialized in loud debates over the dinner table. She didn't care to begin one here, with a stranger.

"If you're sure you're all right?" he asked.

"Perfectly."

"Well, then I suppose…"

"Go on." Charlotte made a shooing motion.

Moving with loose-limbed grace, he mounted the horse.

"Do watch where you jump," she added.

"I will." He gave her a small salute and rode off.

Charlotte watched him go. He had an admirable ease in the saddle, but any friend of Stanley's *would*. He didn't look back. Why would he?

She resumed her walk but found her steps turning back toward home rather than onward. And when she reached the house, she went in search of her mother.

"That's Laurence Lindley, Marquess of Glendarvon," Mama replied when she inquired. "Stanley knows him from Eton. He's staying with us. He arrived this morning."

"Here?" asked Charlotte. Their house was spacious, but the family nearly filled it when they all were at home. It couldn't accommodate many of her brothers' cronies who came up for the hunting. They usually stayed in nearby inns.

"I thought we would put up a few of the boys' friends."

"The most 'suitable' unmarried ones?" Charlotte asked drily.

Her mother looked furtive. They resembled each other in the face, with dark eyes and angular features. Mama was smaller and more rounded, however. Ladies were supposed to be softly rounded, Charlotte thought. As well as sweet and biddable. And pure as the driven snow. She'd often wondered how these traits were to be reconciled. Biddable and pure could so easily conflict.

"You didn't take to any young men during the season," her mother replied. "I thought this would be an opportunity to become acquainted in easier circumstances."

"I've told you I don't intend to marry," replied Charlotte.

"You have." Her mother's tone had gone acerbic now. "A number of times."

"Yet you don't listen to me."

"Because it's nonsense. What else will you do? All your friends have married."

"I could help Papa breed horses. Henry doesn't wish to. He wants to be a diplomat. And Cecil is too fashionable to run the stables."

"And Stanley and Bertram?"

It was true that these brothers were deeply involved in the breeding schemes. And they were far better at it than Charlotte. Her liking for horses didn't stretch to the smallest details of their pedigrees and temperaments.

"You will be happy with a husband and family of your own."

As Mama was. And so she wanted that for Charlotte. But they were quite different people. Oddly, Charlotte thought she was probably most like her brother Cecil, despite her tepid interest in fashion. He would be horrified by the comparison, she thought with a smile.

"That's better," said her mother. "You have such a lovely smile."

No one seemed to realize how infuriating that remark nearly always was, Charlotte noted.

❧

Laurence couldn't believe the level of noise at the Deeping dinner table. Shouting seemed acceptable, even de rigueur. Passionate debates raged in several spots, competing for attention. The other two houseguests, old friends of Henry Deeping, had plunged right in, seemingly accustomed to the din. One of them pounded on the table now, rehashing a controversy from past hunting seasons with obvious relish.

He supposed it wasn't really shouting. Just lively argument. But Laurence had been reared by dutiful, correct, and very *quiet* people. Orphaned at four, the last of an eminent family line, he'd been put in the hands of subdued caretakers whose faces had continually changed. He'd scarcely had time to know one before they were gone. Later, when he came of age, his trustees had explained that they hadn't wanted him to become too attached to any caretakers, lest he be taken advantage of. They'd seemed to expect praise and gratitude for their efforts. Laurence hadn't provided them.

The kind of mayhem surrounding him now would have meant disaster in his early life. A voice somewhere deep in him cried, "Fire, fear, foes!" He didn't show that, of course. He'd learned very early to keep such feelings to himself. And since he'd attained his full growth and musculature, no one seemed to expect emotion of him, which made things easier. People who looked like him were not supposed to be anxious.

"Fop," said Bertram Deeping to his older brother Cecil.

"If you think being fashionable makes one weak, I am happy to take you outside and thrash you," replied Cecil.

"What, beat me senseless with your masses of fobs?" asked Bertram.

"With my punishing left," Cecil replied. "As you may remember from the last time."

Bertram grimaced. Then he laughed, which Laurence found inexplicable.

Laurence was still getting Stanley's brothers straight. They all had dark hair and eyes and a similar sharp cast of features. The eldest, Henry, was three years older than Laurence's twenty-five and seemed a pleasant, polished fellow. Apparently, Henry was set on the diplomatic corps as a path to make his way in the world. He was also, according to Stanley, a devil of a marksman, the envy of Manton's shooting gallery in London.

Stanley threw back his head and laughed at something his father said. The tallest and bulkiest of the four Deeping brothers, Stanley was the most open, accepting fellow Laurence had ever known. They'd met at Eton when Laurence first arrived, fresh from the strict, austere preparatory school he'd detested. Thirteen years old, Laurence had been wary and reluctant and nearly sick with nerves. And then Stanley had happened along, discovered they lived in neighboring counties, and greeted him with metaphorically open arms. Stanley had just assumed they'd be friends, with no guile whatsoever, and he'd guided Laurence to his quarters and the classrooms and past the potential perils of the place with kindness and unfailing good humor. Laurence would always be grateful to this least self-conscious of human beings.

Perhaps the third brother, Cecil, had absorbed all the self-consciousness available in the family, Laurence decided. Cecil was unmistakably a dandy. His waistcoat was bright enough to hurt one's eyes. And he couldn't wear all those fobs hunting, surely? The clatter would scare off the foxes. Yet, unlike many of his ilk, there was muscle under Cecil's exquisite coat and a hint of laughter in his eyes. "Puppy," he said to Bertram.

The youngest brother at eighteen, Bertram stuck out his tongue, earning a reprimand from his mother and ignoring it with all the exuberant bravado of his age. He seemed a bit unformed. Like Stanley, he was horse mad and involved in the Deeping breeding farm. Laurence had already discovered that those two could talk horses for hours. Literally. Fortunately, they didn't insist on it. Bertram didn't appear to have many other topics of conversation, however.

His gaze moving on, Laurence encountered the dark, sardonic eyes of Miss Charlotte Deeping, the lone daughter of the household. He'd nearly killed her earlier. He shuddered at the memory—the slender figure suddenly beneath his mount's hooves, falling backward. Catastrophe avoided by inches. Really, mere inches. He couldn't bear to think of it.

Miss Deeping's lips turned down as if she could read his thoughts. Which she couldn't, of course. Thankfully, that was impossible. She was a creature of angles, striking rather than pretty, dark and…spiky. The word came to him out of nowhere. It felt as if she had more spines than a hedgehog. Did hedgehogs bite? He wasn't sure. She looked as if *she* might.

Her dark eyebrows rose, and Laurence quickly looked away. He drank some wine and ate some of the excellent roast beef before continuing his examination of the company. Miss Deeping was one of only three ladies at the dinner table with eight men, which was unusual. The other two were his hostess, an older, softer edition of her daughter, and a sturdy square-shouldered lady of perhaps fifty. The latter had been introduced as Mrs. Carew, and she resembled their host, Sir Charles Deeping. Both of them had hair more dark-brown than black, and hazel eyes rather than the deeper brown of the rest of the family. Laurence hadn't quite figured out Mrs. Carew's position in the household. She'd said very little, but she did not have the air of a timid companion.

None of the ladies seemed bothered by the noise. Miss Deeping was self-possessed amid the cacophony of male voices. Her mother looked serene, focused on seeing that everyone got plenty of food. Laurence wondered if Mrs. Carew might be deaf. She simply ate with oblivious concentration. Then she looked up from her plate and said, "When we put him in with the mares, he had no more idea of what to do than a gelding."

Laurence coughed at this sudden eruption into the debate about breeding plans. No one else seemed surprised.

"Poor Dancer *is* dense as a bag of rocks," said Bertram.

"Ah, a kindred spirit, then," said Cecil.

Bertram threw a bit of bread at him, hitting Cecil square on the nose.

"Bertram!" barked Sir Charles.

Laurence's hand jerked at this voice of disapproving authority. He didn't wince. He'd stopped that years ago, but he couldn't help going still in apprehension.

Bertram dropped the piece of bread he'd been readying for a second shot.

His father gave him a stern nod.

Bertram made a face at him.

"Barbarian," said Cecil.

"Coxcomb," replied Bertram.

"I? You have no idea what you're talking about," replied Cecil in a lofty superior voice. "You've never been on the town."

"Well, I'm going to London next season, and I shall take the *ton* by storm."

"Ha!"

"I'll be the envy of the sporting set. You'll see."

"Yes, Bertram. I will." Cecil sounded sympathetic as well as unconvinced, and Laurence realized there was no real rancor in the brothers' banter. He was glad of it. The opposite would have been intolerable.

Dinner proceeded in the same vein. Some disputes were settled. Others had obviously been running for years and were more a game than issues to be finally decided. The second course was cleared away. The ladies departed. But there was no lingering over port in this household, where gentlemen expected to be up early and engaged in active sport. The bottle had only gone around twice before they joined the ladies in the drawing room.

Laurence had taken a few steps into the chamber when Lady Deeping appeared at his elbow. "Perhaps you would turn the pages for Charlotte?" she said.

Miss Deeping sat at the pianoforte, ready to provide some music. Though how anyone expected to hear it through the continuing roar of conversation, Laurence did not understand. "Of course," he replied, as good manners demanded. He moved to stand at the young lady's side.

Charlotte had watched her mother's maneuvering with resignation. "Do you read music?" she asked when the marquess was delivered to her like a neatly wrapped package.

"No, you will have to give me a signal when I am to turn the page."

She sighed. "I'll nod." She began to play.

"You are very good," he said after a while.

"I'm middling." Charlotte had been required to learn at school. She knew her ability was only average. Competent but not inspired, her teacher had said. At the time this had distressed her. She had grown to accept the fact since. "It doesn't matter because no one listens," she added.

"I'm listening," he replied, his deep voice simply sincere.

Charlotte was overtaken by an odd sensation, like a tingle running across her skin. More than a twinge, less than a shiver. It came with the idea that no man had ever said those two words, in that serious tone, to her before. She frowned. That couldn't be true. Yet when she riffled through her memories, she couldn't recall another occasion. She glanced at Glendarvon. His handsome face was blank of emotion. He'd meant nothing in particular. She nodded. He missed the signal. "Page," she said.

"What? Oh." Hurriedly, he turned it.

She played on. "You don't wish to join the discussions?" she asked. She could manage the pages herself. She usually did.

"I don't care for them," he answered tonelessly.

Too dull to be drawn in, she concluded. Charlotte

couldn't be interested in a slow-witted man. No matter how handsome.

"I apologize again for this afternoon," he said. "I have no excuse for my carelessness."

"You can't think of a single one?" Charlotte asked.

"What?"

Another small test failed. "My brothers would come up with whole lists."

"Of…"

"Excuses. Mostly involving my heedlessness in being in their way."

"You weren't in the way! I surprised you."

She looked at him. He'd sounded indignant, but his expression remained stolid. "Page," she said.

He hurried to turn it.

"Were you in London last season?" Charlotte asked. She thought she would have noticed if he'd shown up at any of the balls or evening parties. The marquess *was* exceptionally good-looking, and Mama would have made Stanley introduce him.

"No. I stayed home last year."

"Where is that?"

"A bit east of here. In Rutland."

"Ah." She waited for him to say something more.

He did not.

"Page," said Charlotte, feeling impatient. Conversation without sparkle was sheer hard labor. She'd plowed through enough such slogs during the season. She couldn't be bothered here in her home. A handsome face and athletic form were insufficient, she reminded herself. They might spark attraction. Well, they *did*, in this case. But disappointment would follow as the night the day.

She decided to make this her last piece of the evening. She doubted anyone would notice if she simply slipped away. Well, apart from Mama, who would scold her tomorrow.

Two

CHARLOTTE PICKED UP HER BREAKFAST TEA, SIPPED, AND coughed at the acid flavor of the brew. She looked up to find Bertram gazing at her, his dark eyes gleaming. "What have you put in my cup?" she asked him. She should have known to take care when she found only her youngest brother in the breakfast room. She shouldn't have turned her back to fill her plate.

"A spoonful of vinegar," he replied.

"Why?"

"You look so funny when you scrunch up your face."

"Are we four years old?" She and Bertram had shared a nursery for some years, as she had not with the older boys.

"No. You're twenty and I'm eighteen."

The latter was often worse than four, in Charlotte's opinion. Bertram was large enough to play serious pranks and still young enough to want to. "Beast." She pushed the cup aside.

Looking contrite, he fetched her a fresh one. After sliding a pot of raspberry jam in her direction, he said, "Can I ask a favor, Charlotte?"

"You put vinegar in my tea and then want a favor?"

"It was just a joke."

"It tasted vile."

"I'm sorry. But…would you speak to Papa for me?"

She raised her eyebrows in surprise. "About what? And why ask me?"

"He thinks you're the most intelligent of all of us," Bertram added.

"He does?" Charlotte experienced a moment of pure

gratification before wondering whether this was true. Bertram was in his coaxing mode. He might be exaggerating. He probably was.

"Also you're not afraid of him," her youngest brother went on.

"Are you?" She was surprised at that. Their father was not a tyrant.

"No. Not exactly. But when he doesn't listen, my tongue gets tangled and I make a muddle of things."

"What do you want from him?" Charlotte asked.

"I want to set up my own breeding line in the stables."

She should have known it would have something to do with horses.

"Stanley has one, and I have some very good ideas for crosses."

"Have you shared them with Papa?"

"I don't want him to steal them."

"Papa?"

Bertram shifted impatiently in his chair. "Not steal exactly. He just…if he thought my suggestions were good, he'd just make them without letting me…"

"Have the credit?"

"Show what I can do," Bertram corrected. "By the time the foals are born, everyone will have forgotten it was my idea. It's very difficult sometimes being the *fourth* brother."

She knew the feeling, more than he might realize. "All right. I'll ask him."

"You will?" His expression suggested that he'd thought she would refuse. "You're a good egg, Charlotte."

"But Papa doesn't think I know much about the stables," she pointed out.

"You could tell him you're impressed by me."

She gave him a look.

"I'm sorry about the tea," Bertram said. "I won't do it again." His hands closed into fists. "I really want to make my mark. I know I can do it."

"I thought you wanted to go to London and set society on its ear."

Bertram looked blank.

"You said so at dinner last night," Charlotte pointed out.

"Oh." He waved this aside, nearly knocking over the teapot with the sweep of his arm. "I was just twitting Cecil. That's the sort of thing he cares about. We can't let him get too full of himself."

"Why not?"

"It might get him into trouble, out there among the toffs," her brother replied, his tone only half joking.

There was more to Bertram than she'd realized. But then Charlotte had found that to be true with each of her brothers as they grew up. Henry had matured the most, becoming an acute, impressive man. But he was the oldest. Cecil's foppishness hid a keen wit. And Stanley, well, he was amazingly kind and unpredictably canny, though he would never be a thinker. "I'll speak to Papa today."

"You're the best." Bertram stood and came over to give her a hug.

⁕

Entering the breakfast room just then, taking in this scene of familial affection, Laurence received smiles from the two youngest Deepings. As Bertram straightened and wished him a good morning, Laurence felt a twinge of envy. No one had ever hugged him in that easygoing way. Amorous embraces were not the same. Here, simple warmth was obviously a common occurrence, as characteristic as the Deepings' loud debates. And it was ridiculous to resent this. He didn't. He wouldn't. That would be unacceptable.

Laurence felt as if he'd strayed into an alien land and was fleetingly sorry he'd come to visit the Deepings. He could have been calmly settled at some comfortable inn for the hunting season, where all was organized and…impersonal. This last word startled him. He dismissed it. He would be polite. Good manners got one through most things. Showing nothing of these thoughts, he said "good morning," sat down, and started to pour tea.

Miss Deeping held up a warning hand. "It isn't in the teapot?" she inexplicably asked her brother.

"No, it was just your cup."

She waved Laurence on as if nothing unusual had been said.

Conversation with this young lady was like ice-skating, he decided, a pastime he had not fully mastered. One would be gliding along, beginning to feel confident on one's feet, even graceful and exhilarated. Then an unseen bump would trip one up. The skates would slip. There would be flailing and clumsiness and then the inevitable tumble into disaster.

Miss Deeping offered him a plate of muffins. She wore a gown of peach muslin today. The warm color flattered her pale complexion, and ruffles softened her angular frame. He wouldn't have thought her prone to ruffles. Wondering why she compelled the eye, he reached for a muffin.

"Enjoy your breakfast with my favorite sister," Bertram

said and went out. Laurence dropped the muffin. Fortunately, it landed on his plate.

"All my brothers think that very amusing," she said.

Under her sharp gaze, Laurence felt that sensation of wobbling skates.

"I am his *only* sister," she added.

Of course. He knew that.

"So *favorite* is hardly a compliment."

She spoke as if to a small child. It was becoming annoying. "Obviously," he replied.

Miss Deeping blinked.

Should he have said something more flattering? But he couldn't think of anything. "What was in your cup and not the teapot?" Laurence asked.

"You noticed…"

"Obviously," he repeated.

She eyed him as if reconsidering something. "Bertram put vinegar in my tea."

"He what? Why?"

"He thought my reaction would be amusing."

"I don't imagine you were amused."

"No."

And yet a few minutes later, they had been laughing and hugging. Laurence didn't understand this family.

"Brothers play pranks," Miss Deeping said, as if this explained all.

"I wouldn't know. I haven't any."

"Sisters?" she asked.

He shook his head.

"None at all?"

"My parents were killed when I was four."

"Killed?"

Laurence was appalled. He never said it that way. And certainly not to a near-stranger. He was an expert at deflecting questions about his family. Yet here was a slip, like those skates again and the sensation of flailing. She was waiting. Laurence reached for one of his usual evasions, but he found himself saying, "They were murdered."

Miss Deeping's dark eyes widened. Her mouth fell a little open. He had thoroughly startled her. Laurence realized he had wanted to. And he took a surprising degree of pleasure in his success, even though he was also bewildered by his errant impulse. Regrets followed in a concerted rush. Why had he told her?

A rumble of voices heralded the entrance of Stanley and the two other houseguests. The room filled with boisterous young men debating where they would go shooting today and what birds they were likely to flush. Miss Deeping's dark eyes remained fixed on Laurence through this conversation, and he found her gaze unsettling. He was sorry to have attracted her attention. And yet he wasn't. The mixture was confusing.

❦

All the young men in the house went out shooting soon after breakfast. Charlotte, seeking out her father to fulfill her promise to Bertram, thought of nothing but Glendarvon's revelation. Murdered! How had that come about? Her mind bubbled with questions.

Her father was in the offices attached to the stables, where he could almost always be found at this time of day.

The Deeping farm stretched over broad acres, with space set aside for mares and foals, young horses being trained, stallions at stud, and older animals lazing in retirement.

"Good morning, Papa," Charlotte said as she entered.

Her father looked up from an account book and smiled at her. "Charlotte."

"May I speak to you for a moment?"

"Of course."

She sat in one of the chairs facing his desk. Knowing her father preferred people to come to the point rather than dance around it, she said, "Bertram was telling me he would like to start his own breeding line here. He is full of ideas, apparently."

He raised his eyebrows. "Why not bring them to me?"

Charlotte thought it best not to mention the issue of credit. "He said his tongue gets tangled when he tries. Perhaps he cares too much what you think?"

"Oh, is that it?" Her father smiled.

"I think it probably is."

"If he can't argue for his scheme, can he carry it out?"

"Well, those are two different things," Charlotte suggested.

"So you think I should agree?"

She hadn't expected to be consulted. "Me?"

"You are a good judge of people, I think. You have a keen mind."

His praise filled her with elation and led her to take a moment to think. "I would give him a chance."

Her father nodded as if this settled the matter. "Then I will."

Charlotte was immensely gratified by this sign of trust.

"How are you, my dear?" he added.

"Very well, Papa."

"You enjoyed your season in London?" Her father had not accompanied them to town, being busy with the stables.

"Yes."

"You've seemed quiet since you returned. Are you sad to be back at home after all the excitement?"

Charlotte shook her head. "But I do miss my friends."

He nodded. Ada, Sarah, and Harriet had visited the Deepings more than once over the years and charmed the whole household. "You must. You had their companionship for a long time."

She hadn't realized he'd noticed. But that was the way with Papa. He seemed immersed in his own concerns, but he missed very little.

"Your mother says you don't intend to marry."

"Oh, I was just putting her off. She will push young men at me."

"So you *do* mean to marry?"

"I suppose so. It seems the only choice."

"There will always be a place for you here," he said. "I will see to it."

"Like Aunt Carew?" Her father's sister had returned to her old home when she'd been widowed and now lived with them.

For the first time in this conversation, Papa looked doubtful. "Jenny loved the stables from the time she could walk over here."

Charlotte had always found this an incongruous name for her gruff relative. She could never quite call her *Aunt Jenny*.

"You don't, however," her father observed.

"I'm proud of our reputation and fond of the horses."

"But not interested in working at it like Jenny. And Bertram and Stanley."

"I'm sorry, Papa."

He waved this aside. "There's no need for that. Henry and Cecil aren't either. Each of you children must find your own way." He smiled. "I shouldn't say 'children.' None of you are that anymore."

They were not. And so they must find futures for themselves. Charlotte appreciated the scope her father offered. She'd seen families forcing their offspring into wretched mismatches. Or trying to. Her friend Harriet had been burdened with a grandfather like that. But the carte blanche was also a bit daunting.

"A passion gives life savor," he added.

Was he urging marriage after all? "For a husband?" wondered Charlotte. And then wished she hadn't spoken.

He shook his head. "Love is vital, of course, but I am speaking of some abiding interest or purpose." He gestured at the stables around him as an example. "A thing that lends importance to one's days. You should find yours, Charlotte. I think you are the sort of person who really needs it."

The observation shook her like a high wind. He was right. Charlotte marveled at her father's keenness. She longed for a sense of purpose. And she'd once had one.

She'd adored solving mysteries with her friends. The four of them had banded together to unravel some odd happenings at school, discovering they had complementary abilities. Some people had laughed at them. A good many people, actually. But later on, they'd uncovered a treasure hidden for centuries. Those had been triumphs! All her mental faculties had been alive and useful. She'd been so proud of their successes.

But that time was gone. Her friends were far away. Their lives had permanently diverged. She couldn't do it by herself. Could she? Without Sarah's head full of odd facts, Harriet's practical sense, Ada's flair and vision? Charlotte's talent had been—was—dispassionate analysis, charts, and methodical systems. Which were extremely useful, she noted. One might even say critical to figuring out solutions.

"What is it?" asked her father. "You went a thousand miles away suddenly."

"I was just thinking about what you said," she replied. Henry was about to begin a career in the Foreign Office. Stanley would take over the stables eventually, and Bertram would work with him. Cecil possessed his own ambitions. Charlotte had been comparatively aimless. Until the hint of a mystery had fallen into her lap this very morning. It seemed like fate.

"Ah," Papa said, looking flattered.

She could begin by making a few inquiries. Charlotte started to ask her father if he'd heard anything about the Glendarvon murders, then changed her mind. The marquess hadn't said it was a secret. But there'd been a moment when he'd looked stricken. She felt this was not information to be heedlessly shared. She would ask Stanley instead. He and Glendarvon were friends. Stanley would know whatever there was to be known. Charlotte rose, wondering if she could find her second brother.

She could not. And the entire day passed with no opportunity to speak to him privately. Stanley was a convivial fellow, rarely alone in the house. She hadn't quite realized how much he was liked. Watching him talk and laugh with Glendarvon and Henry's two friends, Charlotte found herself smiling not at Stanley's wit, which was uncomplicated, but at the good humor and acceptance he projected. If she ever had to confess an embarrassment, she would choose to tell Stanley, she decided. Just as she would take convoluted intellectual puzzles to Henry, social difficulties to Cecil, and... Well, Bertram would be helpful in plotting mischief, should she ever choose to do so.

The next morning, she finally tracked down Stanley in a loose box at the stable, with a mare's hoof in his hands. Stanley showed no surprise at her appearance even though it was unusual, saying merely, "Come and hold her, Charlotte."

She took the mare's halter, murmured to her, and stroked her neck while Stanley picked a small stone from under her shoe. It was a farrier's job, but Stanley never hesitated when there was a task at hand.

"Thanks," he said when he'd finished and set the hoof back on the ground. "What are you doing out here? Did you come to see the new filly?"

She hadn't, but she might have. It was certainly a reason he could understand. The last of the season's foals had been born a week ago, and Charlotte was well aware of the appeal of a baby horse. They walked together to the pasture where the mares and foals were kept together. Grooms walked among them, getting the latest generation of Deeping animals accustomed to a human presence and touch.

"That's her," said Stanley, pointing.

Charlotte followed his finger to the new filly, dark brown with a blaze of white on her forehead. She was playing a frisky game of peekaboo around her mother's legs, kicking up her tiny hooves with exuberant joy. It was contagious. Charlotte laughed. She recognized the mare as a good-tempered lady who had produced several champions. "She has nice lines."

"I knew she would." Stanley's voice held deep satisfaction. Breeding the perfect racehorse was *his* passion, no doubt about that. "So what is it?" he asked her.

"It?"

"You don't often come out here in the morning."

Stanley did notice things. It didn't do to forget that. "I wanted to ask you something," she replied.

Stanley merely nodded.

Best just to plunge in, Charlotte decided. "Your friend Glendarvon said his parents were murdered."

"He told you that?" Stanley sounded startled.

"Yes."

"He hardly ever tells anyone." Her brother gazed at her.

"He told you, apparently."

"Yes, but only after we'd known each other for years and had a bit too much to drink one night."

"So it's a secret?"

"Well…" Stanley's forehead creased with thought. "Not exactly. I mean, it's known. It was much talked of at the time, I believe. Glendarvon just doesn't mention it."

"What happened?"

"I don't know if I should speak about it."

"You can't betray any confidences, of course. I know you never would." Charlotte tried to keep her tone casual. "But he did mention the fact to me. And you say it was talked about."

Stanley frowned as if he was working this out. "Why are you interested?"

"I'm curious. It's a mystery."

"Glendarvon is not some lost bauble to be retrieved."

Charlotte struggled to remain calm and reasonable. "I'm aware of that, Stanley."

Her brother's frown deepened. Then he shrugged. "I don't know very much more. He was four years old. His parents were found dead in suspicious circumstances."

"What circumstances?"

Stanley shifted uncomfortably. "Circumstances that made it clear they'd been attacked."

"As if they'd tried to fight someone off, you mean?"

"This isn't really the sort of thing you should be thinking about."

Charlotte took this to mean it had been a gory scene. She didn't push for details. "Who did it?"

Stanley shrugged.

"The killer wasn't caught?"

"No."

"So no one knows who killed them?"

"This isn't like some pet crow stealing jewelry, Charlotte."

"I know that." It was a true mystery. She felt a distinct thrill.

"You mustn't stick your nose in."

"It all happened more than twenty years ago. I suppose there's nothing much to find." Unless people hadn't looked properly. Or added up the facts in the proper way.

"It's not your business."

"But if I could—"

"Glendarvon was there," Stanley blurted out, then looked sorry he'd spoken.

"What?"

"Never mind."

"He was there when his parents were murdered?"

"Forget I said anything!"

"I can't really do that." Charlotte gave him a sidelong glance. "I could ask him."

Stanley looked distressed and goaded. "Please don't."

"But, Stanley—"

"They found him when they found the bodies. That's all I know."

Charlotte felt a moment of horror. A four-year-old child had been nearby as his parents were being killed?

"I shouldn't have told you that," Stanley said.

"If you hadn't, I might have asked a very upsetting question," Charlotte replied.

"Yes! You mustn't mention anything about this to Glendarvon. Or anyone else, Charlotte."

She could see it would be difficult. Intrusive. Yet she knew curiosity would eat at her. Charlotte wished for her old friends more than ever. She could discuss anything with them without fear it would get out.

"Promise me you will not," Stanley demanded.

"I wouldn't, unless…"

"Charlotte!"

"I will not bring it up." She stepped away before he could insist on a stricter vow. She would keep her oath. But if Glendarvon ever broached the subject, she would not turn away.

Three

LAURENCE WAS NOT A COWARD. HE'D THOUGHT FOR A while, when he was quite small, that he might be. Because of the nightmares that had plagued him. But he'd learned through experience that he would fight back if he was attacked. Facing down bullies at school hadn't been terribly difficult, even before he'd grown too large for them to threaten. He hadn't served in the army, but he suspected he would kill if pushed to the limit. Called upon to protect an innocent, say. A child.

He could handle guns and shoot birds he intended to eat. He could tolerate firing on all sides, as was happening now on this second day of the Deepings' shooting party. He could career across the country in a mob of intrepid riders, jumping any obstacle that presented itself. Indeed, he was always more comfortable outside than in closed spaces. The din of conversation bouncing off walls, well, that was something else again. Walls could begin to feel as if they were closing in on him. Thankfully, the nightmares were a thing of the past.

"Good shot!" cried Bertram Deeping on his left. "You are the most complete hand, Henry."

His eldest brother accepted the praise with a grin. Henry was one of the best marksmen Laurence had ever seen, but he wasn't vain about it. He simply demonstrated excellence and made light of the admiration it roused. One of the dogs brought his kill and dropped it at Henry's feet. He reached down and ruffled her silky ears.

All the fellows at the Deepings' seemed good-natured

and easygoing. Laurence had seen none of the sneers and sniping he'd disliked in London during the season, not even from the dandy, Cecil.

Laurence had endured most of one season in high society because it was the thing to do. But he'd broken after two months and fled the hordes crammed into overheated rooms talking at the top of their lungs. It had felt like a sort of prison. The banter between the brothers was nothing like that. Something inside Laurence was relaxing in this pleasant company.

If he could feel as much at ease with Miss Charlotte Deeping, all would be well. But she was... What was the opposite of relaxing? Exciting, suggested an insinuating inner voice. Annoying, offered another. Dangerous, argued a third. No, that was silly. She was just a young lady, like the crowds of them he'd met at balls and evening parties in London.

Only she wasn't. Those girls had simpered and postured to attract his interest. They'd agreed with anything he'd said, sometimes before he'd finished saying it. They certainly hadn't...skewered him with a dark, measuring gaze and spoken to him as if he was dull-witted. That was why he'd let slip a bit of his history, Laurence decided. She'd goaded him. He'd wanted to shake her up. He'd succeeded. But he was concerned now that it had been a mistake. He'd caught the gleam of curiosity in her eyes. It had been like a sort of flame—a fire from which it was hard to look away.

"Is there something wrong with your gun?" Stanley called from his left side.

Laurence started. He'd been standing like a stock while the shooting went on around him. "No," he answered, raising his gun and looking for a target. None immediately presented itself.

He would see Miss Deeping at dinner that evening, Laurence thought. If not before. Had he ever felt such a mixture of anticipation and doubt? He couldn't recall another occasion.

∽

At the same moment, in a pleasant parlor in the Deeping house, Charlotte's mother said, "I have discovered that Henry's friends are both engaged. What a take-in." She vented her irritation on her embroidery, savagely yanking a thread through the canvas. The late-October sun streaming through the window illuminated her peevish expression.

"Didn't you do your research?" Charlotte asked, half teasing.

"I told Henry... Well, I might not have been clear."

"Or he might have realized I would object to being put on show like one of our horses."

Her mother ignored this. "There's still Glendarvon."

There definitely was, and he had become an object of fascination to Charlotte. As soon as she'd promised not to mention anything about his history, her mind had filled with questions. Had there been a robbery when his parents were killed? Did they have enemies? Who had investigated the crime? Surely they had found something? Had no signs been left behind? How would she ever make light conversation with him when her brain was occupied by this topic? Whenever one was ordered *not* to think of a thing, one immediately did.

"He is quite attractive, don't you think?" asked her mother.

Charlotte didn't want to talk about that. "I've had a letter from Cecelia," she replied as a diversion. "She and the duke will be arriving tomorrow."

"Here?" cried her mother. "We have no room."

"No, no, Mama. They are coming to an old hunting box near Melton Mowbray. I told you." Charlotte and her friends had grown close to Cecelia Vainsmede, now the Duchess of Tereford, during the season. They had been corresponding since it ended. "You remember, the previous duke left his estates all at sixes and sevens." Or as Cecelia liked to say, "afflicted by a surfeit of chaos." Charlotte continued, "They've come up to deal with one of his properties."

"Oh. Yes. Well, they will be a welcome addition to our society."

"They may be too busy for that. Cecelia's letter mentioned some problem there. I shall go and visit, see if I can be of help."

"What sort of help?"

"They may need to hire local people."

"The duke will join the hunting, I suppose."

"Perhaps he would like to borrow a horse."

Mama's lips quirked. "I'm sure your father would like to sell him one. Or two."

⤷

As the house party gathered to go in to dinner that evening, strong hands closed on Charlotte's waist, swept her off her feet, and swung her around in a wide circle. The skirts of her evening dress belled out in the air.

"Bertram, put me down!"

He did so, saying, "You are the best of sisters."

"Your only one, I know."

"You'd be the best even if I had dozens. Papa is allotting me three mares to cross as I wish. I am to take charge of the foals and train them."

"Oh, good." His happiness was palpable. She was glad for him.

"You are the best of *all* my family, Charlotte. I mean it. If there is anything I can do for you, you need only name it."

"I will keep that in mind."

∾

One didn't rescue a young lady from her brothers, Laurence thought. Did one? But Bertram had put Miss Deeping down, and they were talking quite amiably. No one else seemed to find his tumultuous greeting odd. Tumult was endemic to the Deepings, he decided. Miss Deeping must be accustomed to it.

They went in to dinner, and Laurence found the young lady in question was seated beside him. Last night she'd been placed by one of the other houseguests, and he wondered a little at the change. Had she requested it? Or perhaps the ladies were rotated through the overabundance of male diners? Her expression gave him no clue.

Platters emerged from the kitchens. Once again, the food was ample and delicious. Once again, the table erupted in debate. The Deepings did not acknowledge any rules of dinner party conversation. Everyone talked to whomever they wished, however distant around the table and as loudly as necessary to make their point. The din rose, words overlapping and bouncing off the walls. Laurence hunkered down and addressed himself to the succulent roast chicken.

"Charlotte knows," cried Bertram several minutes later. Laurence hadn't caught the beginning of this conversation. "Don't you, Charlotte?" the youngest brother added.

"I know many things," Miss Deeping replied. "But whether porcupines are related to hedgehogs is not one of them." She was cool and unmoved by the rowdy crowd. Laurence decided that if he ever had to enter one of these raucous arguments, he would try to bring her in on his side. "I think it doubtful," she added and continued cutting her portion of fowl into small precise pieces.

"They've both got spines," Bertram replied.

"Cats and horses both have pointed ears," said Miss Deeping. "But they are unrelated."

"That's not the same," her brother objected.

"I think it is, actually, Bertram," she answered.

He gave her a sulky look. "You might have just agreed with me. No one would have known the difference."

Miss Deeping seemed shocked at the idea of careless deception. Laurence liked her for it. "You could write a letter to the Royal Society and inquire about porcupine lineage," she suggested.

Bertram looked daunted. Miss Deeping returned to her dinner.

Laurence supposed she'd learned her impervious behavior during a lifetime of fraternal disputes. The noise that reduced him to uneasy silence was simply background to her.

If he'd grown up here, he'd probably be the same. Though he couldn't quite imagine it. He noticed that she'd turned to him.

"I am riding over to a house near Melton Mowbray on Tuesday to see some friends," she said. "Perhaps you would like to come along. You asked me to show you the best fox runs."

"You seemed uninterested in doing so," Laurence replied before he thought, and then clamped his jaw shut. How did she disconnect his tongue from his brain? He was more careful than this. Was he being affected by the freewheeling atmosphere?

"I was rather shaken up. From being ridden down."

"I didn't—"

"Nearly ridden down," she corrected. "I would be happy to show you about."

He looked at her. Those dark eyes were compelling. Deep. Not unlike those of a snake enchanting a rabbit. A what? Why had such a ridiculous image popped into his head? Still, he thought she had some hidden motive. And not just the usual interest of an unmarried young lady in a single gentleman. She was the least flirtatious girl he'd ever met. "I...er..."

"I don't know what my brother told you about me," Miss Deeping continued.

"Stanley said never to take your satirical manner as unkindness." Which had been reassuring and dismaying at the same time. Many people must have made that mistake if a warning was necessary.

She looked startled.

"And that there was no one he'd sooner count on in an emergency," he added.

Miss Deeping blinked several times, rapidly.

Surely those were not tears. He could not imagine Miss Charlotte Deeping in tears. She turned away for a moment. When her face was visible again, it showed no sign of emotion. But her voice was uneven when she said, "That was… decent of him."

Laurence accepted her invitation.

❧

Charlotte met the marquess at the stables after breakfast on Tuesday morning. She hadn't left the house with him because she didn't want to gratify her mother too much. Details of the expedition would certainly get back to Mama. And Charlotte would certainly be grilled about it. But not now.

Rolfe, a senior stableman Charlotte had known all her life, had her mare ready. As well as his own mount. He would be following along behind them for propriety's sake. "She's resty today," he said.

Charlotte set a hand on Stelle's satiny neck and received an affectionate nuzzle. "We'll give her a chance to stretch her legs."

Glendarvon came up, riding the same horse that had nearly killed her a few days ago. All seemed forgiven, however. The tall bay gelding greeted the party with spirited good temper. Charlotte was making use of the mounting block when her brother Henry emerged to join them, riding one of the freshly trained mares. She hadn't realized Henry planned to come, though it made sense as the Duke of Tereford was a good friend of his. It did put a crimp in her plan, however. Fortunately, another of their houseguests, Henry's crony, was mounting up as well. It seemed he, too, was acquainted with the duke.

She settled the long skirts of her riding habit, and allowed Henry to lead the way out. He took them down a lane that ran beside the paddocks rather than out the front entrance. His guest rode at his side, chatting, leaving Charlotte and Glendarvon to follow.

The marquess rode exceptionally well. She'd noticed his skill at their first encounter, but now she had the opportunity to observe details. An easy seat, light hands, an obvious bond with his mount.

"You ride very well," he said, as if echoing her evaluation.

"No child of my father is a poor rider," Charlotte replied. She might not be half centaur like Stanley or Bertram, but she held her own.

They came to a stretch of trail with no low branches or rabbit holes to endanger the horses. Henry and his friend put on speed. "Shall we give them a gallop?" Charlotte asked.

Glendarvon grinned. In unison, they gave the signal and pounded off. Rolfe came right behind. Any groom from the Deeping stables was a bruising rider, and none of their animals were slugs.

Exhilaration filled Charlotte as she leaned over Stelle's neck. The wind of their passage tugged at her hat. Her muscles adjusted automatically to the movements of the powerful creature beneath her. The hedgerow flew past. Glendarvon drew ahead with his gelding's longer stride, but she didn't care. Nor did Stelle. This was about the joy of movement, not a race.

They thundered on until their horses indicated they'd

had enough of a gallop. Slowing, Charlotte complimented her companion's horse.

"Ranger's a good lad," the marquess replied. "Stanley helped me pick him out at Tattersall's."

"I'm surprised he didn't try to sell you one of ours."

"I expect he'll manage that in the end."

"Yes?"

Glendarvon grinned again. He had an engaging smile. "He shows off his pets with nary a mention of selling. He just lets you see how good they are and leaves you to draw your own conclusions. It's masterful."

He noticed subtleties, Charlotte thought. Her first impression of him had been too narrow.

"You've been riding most of your life, I expect."

Charlotte nodded.

"It shows."

This simple statement was nothing like the florid compliments she'd heard other girls receive from London beaus. Perhaps for that very reason, it struck a strong chord. Charlotte felt herself blush.

Ahead of them, Henry had paused. He pointed across a meadow stretching down to a small stream. "There's a very good run down that way," Charlotte said, as her brother was no doubt telling his friend. "The foxes sometimes slip into the water and put the hounds off the scent. One wily old fellow likes to lure them into that thicket on the other side, then jump up a tree, run along a branch, and abandon the pack among the thorns."

"You know a good deal for someone who doesn't hunt," Glendarvon commented.

"When I was small, I used to come out and watch the foxes."

"Not the hunters?"

"The foxes were more interesting."

He looked at her. Charlotte felt his gaze on the side of her face. "More than the people?" he asked.

"Well, I saw people all the time."

"Um."

It was the sort of noise listeners made when they couldn't think of what to say to her. Charlotte was quite familiar with it. Still, she couldn't resist adding, "Foxes are also inhabitants of this place. Also there would be no sport without them."

"I suppose."

"And so the smarter they are the better, I would think. For the sake of sport, if nothing else."

He looked at her. His expression, never very readable, was even blanker than usual.

He thought she was odd, Charlotte concluded. Well, she was. She'd spent an entire London season trying to appear *not* odd, and she was tired of it. Let him think what he liked. Henry had moved on. She urged Stelle forward.

A little farther along, she turned the mare and put her to a hedge. Stelle gathered herself and jumped. They cleared it easily, moved across a grassy meadow, and took another stand of bushes on the other side. Stelle sailed through the air with exuberant ease. The others came after her a moment later.

"That was cracking," said Glendarvon when he caught up to her.

"And there was no one walking on the other side either."

"You'll never let me forget that, will you?"

"I don't imagine I will," Charlotte said, then saw that her answer implied they had a future before them. Which they didn't. Not a long one anyway. Not likely. A few weeks at most.

She turned Stelle, following Henry and his companion toward the road to Melton Mowbray. She'd arranged this outing with a purpose. It was time to get to it. She meant to interest Glendarvon in the idea of investigation. Surely this would lead his thoughts toward the mystery in his own past? Without breaking her promise to Stanley and simply *asking*. But how to bring up the subject without actually doing so? "You and Stanley were friends at school," she said.

"Yes."

"I had good friends at mine as well."

"Oh, ah, splendid."

"Sarah and Ada and Harriet. We solved mysteries together."

"Mysteries?"

Of course he was surprised. People always were. As if girls were devoid of curiosity and incapable of rational thought. "One of the maids was accused of stealing a ruby ring by this beastly girl," she added.

"Beastly?" he echoed with a slight smile.

It had been a schoolgirl word. Charlotte suppressed embarrassment. "The maid swore she hadn't taken it, and we decided to find the truth."

"You and Sarah and Ada and Harriet."

He remembered the names. She recalled the moment when he'd said he was listening. It seemed he actually did. Charlotte nodded, their gangling troop of fourteen-year-olds vivid in her mind. "We discovered the ring had been snatched by a teacher's pet crow."

"I beg your pardon. Crow?"

Charlotte nodded. "The ring was hidden in the bottom of the bird's cage, along with a number of other small lost treasures."

"However did you learn that?"

"We searched and analyzed and methodically followed a series of clues." This was important. It hadn't been luck. She wanted him to understand that.

"Didn't wring a confession from the bird, then."

She ignored the joke. "The crow did speak. A few words. It couldn't carry on conversations."

"And yet you managed to expose its villainy."

"Hardly that," replied Charlotte repressively. "Mere... acquisitiveness. Sooty just liked shiny things."

"As crows tend to."

He didn't seem to be taking her seriously. And his smile was threatening to divert her from her plan. He'd been so stolid before. She hadn't realized he possessed a smile like that—lazy, beguiling. What had she been saying? "Last year we unearthed a hidden treasure in Shropshire," Charlotte said. She should have started with that. It was much more impressive than the crow—the greatest triumph of her young life.

"Shropshire."

"On the estate of the Duke of Compton. It had been lost for *centuries*."

"Is this some sort of jest?"

"No, why would you say so?"

"It sounds like a boys' adventure tale."

"Boys!"

"Crows and buried treasure."

"It wasn't buried," Charlotte snapped.

"I beg your pardon."

Why did he not make the connection? She was good at solving mysteries; he had a mystery that marked his own life. The two cried out to be put together. But he was clearly not doing so. In fact, he had stopped paying attention to her when he came up near Henry on the crest of a low hill. All three men were staring down into the dip on the other side. Moving up to join them and following their gaze, Charlotte saw a house below. One wing had burned to the ground, quite recently it appeared. The rest of it—the main block—was singed and blackened.

"That is Lorne," said Henry. "Tereford's local property."

"What happened to it?" asked his friend.

"I don't know."

"A mystery?" asked the marquess, glancing at Charlotte.

She eyed him. Was this mockery? Would he dare? She gritted her teeth and urged her mare onward, losing sight of the damaged building as she descended. She heard the others coming behind her. They reached a stone wall and rode along it to an open gate. *Lorne* was carved into one of the gateposts. Charlotte turned her horse into an ill-kept lane.

She'd gone only a few yards when a tall thin man with dark hair and worn clothes stepped out from behind a bush and shouted, "Halt! Who goes there?"

Stelle, startled, threw up her head and danced back a step. Charlotte soothed her. "Hello," she said. "I am looking for my friends the Terefords."

"Can you prove you're their friend?" the fellow demanded.

"Can I...?" She examined him. He was a stranger, and his accent was not that of a countryman.

Henry moved up to her side. "Who are you?"

"Merlin," the man declared. "Guardian of the gate, repeller of enemies."

Behind Charlotte the marquess made a sound. Not quite a laugh. More of a choke. "*Repeller* is an awkward word," she said. "Perhaps you mean *repellent*."

Henry laughed at this.

"I must ask if you are carrying any incendiary devices," the man before them inexplicably replied.

"Any what?"

"Like a bomb?" asked the marquess. "In our pockets?"

"What do you know about those, eh?" This Merlin person glared up at them.

Charlotte saw a figure walking across the far end of the lane. Henry saw him, too. He waved and called, "Hello, Tereford."

The duke turned, looked, and began to walk toward them. He would clear this up. She turned to tell the man so, but he was gone.

"Hello," Tereford said when he reached them. "Welcome to yet another of my great-uncle Percival's debacles. There seems no end to them."

"Do you have a guard?" Charlotte asked him. "There was a man who tried to stop us."

The duke sighed. "Not voluntarily. Come along. Cecelia will be glad to see you." He strode away.

❧

As they followed, Laurence wondered how one involuntarily acquired a guard. The reasons that occurred to him were ominous, and seemed unlikely.

Near the house, they dismounted, and the Deepings' groom took charge of all their horses, saying, "In the shed over yonder?"

The duke nodded. "If you can find room. I daresay you can't. The stables were in the wing that burned."

"How did that happen?" asked Henry Deeping.

"No one seems to know. My money is on drunken carelessness."

"Whose?" Deeping inquired.

But the front door opened just then, and a lovely blond woman came out. "Charlotte," she exclaimed, hurrying over, hands held out, to greet Miss Deeping affectionately.

The latter introduced Laurence. "This is the Duke and Duchess of Tereford," Charlotte told him.

They exchanged salutations.

"Come inside," said the duchess.

Laurence followed the others in, trying to reconcile this polished pair with the state of their house. He'd expected to meet some country neighbors. The Terefords looked like denizens of the highest reaches of London society. Their clothes, manner, and rank all proclaimed it. Lorne, on the other hand, was shabby and small. It would have been even if the wing had not burned.

Then all at once he remembered the name. Tereford—this was the couple who'd caused a sensation last season. Hadn't there been something about a duel with a German princeling? Even he'd heard of it in his country home.

"We were stopped at the gate by the oddest man," Miss Deeping said as they walked into a shabby parlor. "He called himself *Merlin*."

The duchess sighed rather as her husband had when they'd mentioned the fellow to him.

"Oh!" Miss Deeping stopped short. "Sarah spoke of him in her letters."

"I'm sure she did," replied the duchess.

"The one who was in love with her husband's sister."

"Or thought he was."

"I wish I might have seen him before he shaved off his beard and cut his hair." Miss Deeping seemed to notice Laurence's confusion. "He was a kind of hermit at their property in Cornwall," she added. As if that helped.

Laurence looked around the room instead of answering. The furnishings were outmoded and rather dusty. It looked as if the place had been a fashionable hunting box perhaps half a century ago. Or earlier.

"There's no staff here at all," said the duchess.

"I can help you find people," said Miss Deeping.

"That would be splendid. I don't mind cooking, but there is so much else to do."

The duchess had been cooking? Laurence examined her and received a look bright with intelligence. It said she did not care if he found her unusual. She nearly dared him to. She led Miss Deeping to a sofa by the back window, and they sat side by side, leaning together like old friends.

"We have become superfluous," the duke said to the gentlemen.

That was obvious.

"Temporarily," Henry Deeping replied.

"I certainly hope so," answered the duke with a smile that said he was joking. "I was just looking over the grounds. Would you care to come along?"

There was no real choice, but Laurence didn't mind. He preferred the outdoors. The male contingent went back out and began to walk.

"So no one knows what happened?" Henry Deeping asked as they skirted the burned area.

"Beyond the fact of a fire, no," said the duke. "The caretaker—a term I use loosely—was at the village pub. Where he spent most of his time, it seems. When the alarm was raised, he staggered back here. And was no help to the neighbors in fighting the flames. He has departed."

Laurence was not surprised.

"They barely saved what remains of the house," Tereford added.

"And no sign of how it started?" asked Henry Deeping.

The duke shook his head as they left the ashes behind and walked over a stretch of unkempt lawn. "I feel sure it was carelessness. A candle left burning by a drunkard. A lantern kicked over in the stable as he left. We will have to rebuild. I had to send my coach and horses south."

His sort of equipage would not be exposed to the elements, Laurence thought. And the inns hereabouts were full to the brim with huntsmen and their horses. There'd be no place for the duke's carriage there.

"The one nag left here was a sad old creature," Tereford added. "The caretaker claimed him, and I let him go." A length of briar waving in the breeze snagged his immaculate coattail. He paused to remove it without ripping the cloth.

"How did the place come to this?" asked the fourth member of their group. Laurence tried to recall his name, but he'd forgotten.

"The previous duke, my great-uncle Percival, neglected his holdings," Tereford said. "Shamefully."

"He didn't come here to hunt?"

This earned a snorted laugh. "I wish I might have seen that. No. This place was purchased by an earlier duke. I don't think Uncle Percival was ever here."

They walked through the remains of a vegetable garden. Fronds of asparagus gone to seed straggled near a swath of rhubarb grown huge and woody. The berry bushes had been picked over by birds. Henry Deeping and his friend went to examine the fruits of a gnarled apple tree.

"You are in Leicestershire for the hunting?" the duke asked Laurence politely.

"Yes. Staying at the Deepings'. Stanley is a friend of mine."

"Ah yes, the Deeping stables. I suppose they could furnish me with a hunter."

"There is no doubt about that," replied Laurence with a smile.

"My wife will wish to stay until repairs are well underway."

"You do not?" Laurence didn't blame him. This place couldn't be comfortable. He felt an impulse of gratitude for the care his trustees had taken on his estate. Wrongheaded as they might have been about other things.

"I, too, of course," the duke replied, with something odd in his tone. "Glendarvon," he added. "That name is familiar."

With a sinking feeling, Laurence waited. The duke was young to have heard about the scandal of his parents' murder. And it was mostly forgotten by this time.

"Oh, deuce take it."

That seemed an odd reaction to the story. But the duke wasn't looking at him. Following the other man's gaze to a clump of trees at the back of the old garden, Laurence spotted a figure lurking there.

"No good deed goes unpunished," muttered Tereford. "Was it good, though?"

"It's that Merlin fellow," Laurence observed.

"It is indeed. His actual name is Oliver Welden, but he insists on being called *Merlin*."

Insisted? To a duke? "Was he really a hermit?" Laurence asked. Some great landowners hired men to play that part, he recalled. But that couldn't apply here.

"No. He is…something of a lost soul."

Laurence wasn't sure how to take this unexpectedly poetic response.

"We brought him from Cornwall," the other man added. "He wanted an escape, and I let myself be persuaded."

"Ah." What was one to say to that? He didn't know Tereford well enough to respond.

"Pah," cried Henry Deeping, spitting out a bite of apple. "They're wretchedly sour."

"Of course they are," said the duke. He moved on. "Do you suppose that was a kennel?" Tereford strode off to look at a ruined pile. Laurence followed.

❧

Through the parlor window, Charlotte and Cecelia watched them pass by. "Those two make quite a picture," Cecelia said.

Charlotte followed her gaze. The dark-haired duke had been called the handsomest man in London. The marquess was nearly as good-looking, if not so polished.

"Who is your friend?"

"My brother Stanley's friend," Charlotte corrected. "He is staying with us for the hunting."

"And riding out with you in the meantime?"

"With me and Henry and his friend."

"So your brother invited him to accompany you?" Cecelia arched a blond brow.

Charlotte didn't care to share her plan about the

marquess, an idea that had not borne fruit so far. "I am not flirting with him."

"Of course not."

A very superior abigail appeared in the doorway. Her curtsy somehow managed to convey outrage. "I fear we cannot offer refreshment, Your Grace. As there is none." She turned and walked out.

"My dresser is offended by the conditions here," the duchess said. "James's valet is taking it a bit better. He is in the village ordering provisions."

"I'll send over some helpers. Our housekeeper will know of people looking for work."

"That would be so kind, Charlotte. Thank you."

Charlotte vowed to consult the housekeeper at once. Lorne looked truly uncomfortable.

The gentlemen returned soon after this, and conversation became general. The duke was interested in the hunting that was about to begin. And Henry's descriptions of past years' runs engaged them all.

On the ride back to her home, the party stayed closer together, and Charlotte had no more opportunities to mention mysteries or investigations. It was vexing. She would have to think of some other way to get the marquess to confide in her.

Four

THE REST OF MISS DEEPING'S BROTHERS WERE IN THE stable when they returned from their ride, clustered around a loose box. Laurence found himself the object of a battery of dark eyes when he rode in next to her, dismounted, and handed his horse over to a groom. The Deepings seemed riveted by their arrival. Laurence felt like an actor without a play to perform. Henry Deeping and his friend arrived without attracting the same sort of attention.

"Has the new stallion come?" Miss Deeping asked.

This was an effective diversion. In the babble of response, Laurence gathered that the Deepings had purchased a scion of Eclipse's line and expected great things from this descendent of one of the ancestors of almost all Thoroughbred horses.

A resounding kick hit the wall of the loose box.

"He's settling in," said Stanley.

Laurence walked over to look at a magnificent chestnut stallion. He moved a little closer. The horse's neck snaked out. Its teeth snapped together inches from his arm.

"Dexter's not feeling at home just yet," said Bertram.

"So I see."

This brought the brothers' attention back to him. "Horses don't take to you?" asked Cecil.

"They know a man's character," said Bertram.

The stallion lunged and managed to bite off a scrap of Bertram's coat sleeve. The youngest Deeping swore mildly as he jumped back.

"Dexter does seem to be a keen judge," observed Miss Deeping.

"The Duke of Tereford may want a hunter," said Laurence.

This got their attention and, more important, diverted it from him.

"He has no stable though, over at Lorne. It burnt down."

"The whole place nearly went," replied Stanley. "He's come up to see about it?"

Laurence merely nodded. He somehow felt that the less he said the better at this moment.

"It's about time something was done. Lorne is falling to pieces."

"The duchess will lick it into shape," said Miss Deeping.

"The duke, you mean," said Bertram.

"No, Cecelia is the better manager. The duke always says so."

Having met her, Laurence didn't doubt it. He turned away from the ensuing discussion and went to change out of his riding gear.

And that would have been that, except the rest of the day was rather different from any in his visit so far.

First Henry, with whom he'd had very little conversation even on their ride to Lorne, invited Laurence to play billiards in the afternoon. And then Henry used the game as an opportunity to discuss various philosophical issues and how they influenced one's outlook on life, which put Laurence off his shots. By the end of the game, which Laurence lost decisively, he felt he had been very smoothly interrogated. About what, precisely, he had no idea.

Stanley, catching up to him as they went down to dinner, said, "So Charlotte invited you on a ride?"

"Er, yes."

"I hope she didn't play twenty questions the whole time?"

"What?"

"She's…inquisitive."

"She told me about a crow. And some buried treasure."

"It wasn't buried," said Stanley, as if this response was automatic.

"There actually was a treasure? I thought she must've been exaggerating."

"No. Charlotte doesn't exaggerate. She is extremely… tenacious though."

"Like a bulldog?" Laurence said, trying for a joke.

Stanley's startled stare told him he'd failed. Fortunately, they reached the others at this point, and Laurence was able to fade into the background.

He was not seated beside Miss Deeping for the meal, which was a relief and a disappointment. Watching her calmly cut her meat into symmetrical pieces while a heated debate about the best type of shotgun raged over her head, he found he missed her acerbic comments. He might have joined her in the drawing room after dinner, but Cecil the dandy drifted into his sights, saying, "Didn't see you in London last season."

"No, I didn't go up to town."

"Were there the year before though."

"Yes." Laurence had met Cecil in London, but the third Deeping brother had been very involved with his own set and had shown no interest in him.

"There wasn't much gossip about you."

"Me?" Laurence was startled to learn there was any. As far as he could tell, he'd made no impression at all on the *haut ton*.

"Beyond the old story, of course."

"Old…"

"Your parents," said Cecil Deeping almost apologetically. "I hear everything."

"Do you indeed?" This day was beginning to feel very long. And less enjoyable as the hours passed.

"No need to chatter about it, of course," the dandy added.

That was a relief. Though Laurence was also aware of a niggling desire to know exactly what had been said about their deaths. Not enough to ask, however.

"Gossip never dies entirely," the dandy added. "I suppose it's rather like ghosts in that."

"Shoals of spirits lurking about human society trying to whisper their scandal into new ears," said Laurence before he thought.

Cecil Deeping raised his quizzing glass to gaze at Laurence in apparent astonishment. "That's a rather dreadful picture."

Laurence could only agree and wish he'd said nothing.

The other man continued to stare at him. "Charlotte didn't really take," he said after a while, and seemingly out of nowhere.

"Well, I don't suppose I did either," replied Laurence.

This seemed to strike Cecil Deeping as a very interesting point. "You're a bit prickly, too, are you?"

"No, I am not." Witness the fact that he did not snatch the silly magnifier from Cecil's fingers and break it in half. "I am the best of good fellows."

"Are you?" The other man's dark gaze was not foppish, however he dressed.

"I try to be."

Cecil surveyed him, nodded, dropped the quizzing glass

to dangle on its chain, and turned away. Laurence wasn't sure whether to be offended or laugh. Neither, he decided in the end. Bland impenetrability was almost always the better choice.

Bertram Deeping simply threatened him as they headed upstairs to retire. "If you trifle with Charlotte, I will thrash you," he declared.

This time the laugh was uppermost for Laurence. This was becoming ridiculous. Also, he couldn't imagine anyone "trifling with" Miss Charlotte Deeping. She would cut them off at the knees. "It was simply a friendly ride," he pointed out.

"We protect our sister."

"You put vinegar in her tea."

"How do you know that?"

"She told me."

Bertram seemed to take this as both a betrayal and a portent. "If she likes you, well, that's all there is to it. But if she does not…" He glowered.

Wondering what Bertram thought he meant by "all there is to it," Laurence went to bed feeling almost as hunted as the neighborhood foxes.

᪶

As often happened when they were at home, Charlotte found Bertram in the breakfast room when she came down the next morning. The two of them tended to rise after Papa but before the other members of the household. She lifted the teapot and gave him a look. He waved a hand to indicate all was well, and she poured a cup. "You needn't worry about Glendarvon either," he said. "We set him straight."

Charlotte froze in the act of reaching for a muffin. "What?"

"Turns out we all spoke to him." Bertram seemed amused by this.

"All?"

"Henry, Stanley, Cecil. We compared notes."

Charlotte was speechless with outraged mortification or mortified outrage. The exact percentage of the two emotions was unclear.

"You can be sure he'll be on his best behavior after that." Bertram looked disgustingly pleased with himself.

"You…you… You're worse than Mama!"

"Eh? Does Mama dislike him?" He scowled. "If we'd known that…"

"No, she does not dislike him! On the contrary. She is always throwing men at me."

"Throwing?"

"You will stay out of my affairs. All of you. Do you understand me?"

"You're our sister. It's our job to protect you."

"From what? And no, it is not!"

"Yes, it is. You're a girl."

Charlotte grasped a muffin and launched it at Bertram. It hit him square on the nose.

"Hey!" He flailed at the missile, which had already fallen to the floor.

The Marquess of Glendarvon chose that moment to appear in the doorway. He hesitated when they turned to look at him, but then came in. Charlotte snatched another muffin from the plate and left the gentlemen to their repast.

Rushing back to her bedchamber, she fetched her cloak, bonnet, and gloves and slipped out a side door for a

walk—more of a furious stomp through the garden, really—
tearing at the muffin with her teeth as she moved. She contemplated the unconscionable interference of brothers, and
the impossibility of investigation under these circumstances,
and the unfairness of the universe, until her fuming was interrupted by the sound of hooves. If Glendarvon came charging
out of the shrubbery again, he was going to get an earful.

But the horse was riderless. It was Aspen, a mare from
their herd who should not be out here alone. Charlotte
moved toward her. Aspen whinnied and raced back the way
she'd come. Concerned, Charlotte followed.

❧

Rather than join the shooting party, Laurence had taken
a shotgun and headed off on his own—ostensibly to bag
some rabbits but actually to avoid Deepings for a while.
Miss Deeping had looked furious when she walked out
of the breakfast room. Not at him, he thought. Bertram's
glower had suggested a quarrel. But some of it might have
been aimed at him, left over from their last conversation.
Breakfast had been a trial.

Laurence strode through the countryside, not bothering
to look for rabbits, and gradually felt calm descend. The outdoors was soothing. Trees and grass and bushes rarely did
anything unexpected, and they never shouted. He was about
to turn back when he heard a female voice calling, "Hello? Is
anyone there?" It sounded as if she'd been asking for a while.

He hurried toward the sound and found Miss Deeping
lying flat on the ground slathered with mud. Her cloak lay over
a bush. He ran toward her. "What's happened? Are you hurt?"

A horse rushed between them. Laurence jumped back as it threatened to knock him over.

"Aspen, don't," cried Miss Deeping.

The horse shook her head and moved away.

"Rigel is caught in this fen," Miss Deeping said.

Coming closer, Laurence saw that she had her arms around a foal's neck, holding his head above a patch of mire. The rest of the little animal had sunk into it. They both looked weary. He put aside his gun and went to her.

"He can't climb out," she added. "And I can't lift him from here. I have tried. I daren't let him go to strip off so I can get into the mud."

"Strip off?" Surely she couldn't mean to undress?

"My skirts would drag me down," she said, as if explaining the matter to an idiot.

"You wouldn't really do that."

"Of course I would." The mare rushed up again, pounding very close. "Aspen is frantic," said Miss Deeping.

"Can you hold her? I will pull out the foal."

Miss Deeping nodded. Laurence shed his coat and knelt to take her place, getting a good grip on the small neck. "The mare has no halter," he pointed out.

"She knows me." Miss Deeping staggered to her feet; her skirts were already heavy with mud. "Aspen!"

The horse responded to her call, trotting over. Miss Deeping gripped a handful of her mane and leaned close to murmur in the animal's ear.

Laurence bent down, put his arms around the foal's torso, and heaved. The small animal struggled to pull his legs from the mud, almost slipping out of Laurence's grasp. The foal's frightened bleats made the mare neigh and dance.

The angle was no good. Laurence realized he was going to have to go in and push from below. He wondered about the depth. If he stayed right at the edge of this mud pit, he could get himself out again.

Keeping one arm around the foal's neck, Laurence struggled to toe off his boots. Miss Deeping came over to tug at them, and together they managed. She removed his stockings as well, not seeming the least self-conscious. Laurence clawed off his neckcloth and pulled his shirt over his head. Wearing only breeches, he slipped into the cold sticky mud, sinking at once to his waist. Unfortunately, his feet found no bottom.

He wrapped both arms around the foal and lifted. The little animal kicked and wriggled. One small hoof caught Laurence's ribs smartly. But he exerted all his considerable strength and managed to slowly raise the foal from the muck. His back emerged. Hocks, knees. Laurence heaved, feeling something pull in his back, and jerked the animal free, pivoting the little thing to lay him on his side in the long grass of the bank. This pushed Laurence deeper into the mire. Mud oozed up his chest to his neck.

The mare rushed over to nose her offspring. Laurence braced his forearms on solid ground and rested a moment.

"Give me your hand," said Miss Deeping. She had come back to kneel above him. She reached out.

"No! That might pull you in. Keep back."

Her arm dropped, and she retreated. Laurence took a deep breath, braced his palms on solid ground, and pushed. The mud resisted. He fought it, but not by thrashing. He knew better than that. Gripping sturdy tufts of grass, he pulled, easing his way along, bringing his legs gradually horizontal. When he was lying along the surface of the pit, he flexed his arms, slithering forward, inching his way out.

It took all his strength, but at last he was lying beside the foal, equally slathered with odiferous mud and almost equally exhausted. Or perhaps more. The foal twitched and made it to his feet, which was more than Laurence wished to do just now. The mare nuzzled her offspring protectively. The foal nosed in for a restorative meal.

Miss Deeping ripped up twists of grass and began to rub the foal down, paying no attention to her filthy gown. Laurence lay and panted.

"Thank you," she said.

"Of course." Did she imagine he could have walked away?

"I don't understand how they got out of the paddock."

Laurence had no answer to that.

"We'll give him some time to rest and then walk them back."

The foal's whole being was concentrated on warm milk. He seemed to have no trouble standing, however. Laurence was glad to see he wouldn't need to carry the little animal home.

The wind cut at his bare skin and soaked breeches, turning a brisk autumn day into misery. Laurence sat up. Then after a moment, he stood. Following Miss Deeping's example, he ripped up tufts of grass and used them to wipe off the mud as best he could. Miss Deeping made a sound. He looked up at her. "Did you say something?"

"No."

He scraped at the clumps of mud, not wanting to pull his clothes on over mud-slathered skin. He got a good deal of it. But he remained streaked with dirt from his neck to his bare feet. Starting to shiver, he sat to put on his stockings.

Pulling on his boots was unpleasantly gritty, but warmer. He stood again and donned his shirt, which clung to his damp torso. Miss Deeping came toward him, holding out her cloak. "You will need that," Laurence said. Her gown was wet and muddy all along its front.

"Less than you do," she replied.

Laurence shook his head, reaching for his hunting jacket. His valet was going to have a fit of despair. He pulled on the coat. Mud shifted wetly between garments. "Shall we go?"

Miss Deeping put on her cloak, pulled gloves over her muddy and no doubt icy hands, and grasped the mare's mane again. Aspen needed little urging to turn toward home. "Rigel must have gotten out somehow."

Rigel. Ah, that was the foal. He seemed well able to keep up with his mother. Laurence picked up his discarded gun and started off. His feet rubbed squishily in his boots.

They crossed a stretch of grass, a narrow band of trees, and a tiny stream. There was a lane on the other side. Aspen turned left of her own accord, the foal on her heels, and before too long, a gate appeared in the hedge. Miss Deeping went to open it. The Deeping place was closer than Laurence had feared.

The field on the other side was dotted with horses—older animals past their prime, Laurence observed. Miss Deeping led them across the paddock to another gate on the opposite side. There, another lane led them to a field holding mares and foals. They were spotted almost immediately. What seemed like a horde of people came running.

In the resulting babble, Laurence gathered that a new groom had left a gate half latched. Not the one they'd come through. Another. The foal had pushed through it, and his mother had gone after him. That was the predominant theory, at least. He was too cold to care much.

"Rigel needs a bath," declared Miss Deeping, cutting through the talk. "Warm water. And Aspen could use a rub-down. Blankets."

The group grew organized. The horses were led off. Laurence followed Miss Deeping toward the house.

"We're very grateful," said a voice at his side.

It was Stanley. Where had he come from? Laurence waved a dismissive hand, noting that the tips of his fingers were rather blue.

"It was lucky you were out walking together," Stanley said in a somewhat different tone.

"We weren't," said Laurence. "I heard her calling for help."

"Oh, did you?"

Was that skepticism in his tone? Laurence stopped to gaze at his friend.

Stanley blinked. "Right. You must be freezing."

"I am, rather."

"Your coat…"

"I hope my valet can clean it. The shirt's a dead loss, I think."

"You should go along and change."

"That is my intention, Stanley." Laurence walked on, not sorry that his voice had been rather sharp.

❧

In her bedchamber, stripping off her gown, the skirts heavy with soil, Charlotte thanked the maid who brought hot water. Her mind was full of admiration for the way the marquess had behaved this morning. He'd been quick and resolute. And strong, of course. She didn't think she could have rescued Rigel even if she had gone into the mud pit. Let alone gotten herself out. It had taken a set of powerful muscles to free the foal. And she'd gotten a full appreciation of *those*. The memory of him standing there in only his breeches like the statue of a Greek god, calmly stepping into the fen and then scraping at the mud afterward, warmed her far more than the steaming water.

And yet his bare feet had looked so vulnerable in the grass. The sight of them had touched her in the oddest way. She'd wanted to… She didn't know what. But she was aware the emotion wasn't gratitude for little Rigel's life.

She felt that, too, of course. And Glendarvon hadn't made a single complaint about the mud or the cold. Even when it was all over and a lamentation or two might have been understandable. He really was…something special.

"Tell the laundress I'm sorry about the mud," she told the maid who carried away her soiled clothes.

"Yes, miss. I'm glad the little fellow is all right."

Word had spread already. The Deeping servants took a strong interest in the breeding stock as all of them shared in the profits from the sales. "So am I," said Charlotte.

She put on a warm wrapper and sat in front of the fire. Perhaps her mother had been right, she admitted. It was far easier to get to know a man here at home than it had been at any event of the London season.

Five

LAURENCE STOPPED BY THE STABLES THE FOLLOWING afternoon to check on the foal's condition. He'd developed a proprietary interest in the little creature. However, Rigel seemed to find his concern nearly as irksome as imprisonment in a loose box with his mother. "We'll turn them back out into the paddock tomorrow," Stanley told Laurence. "There are no ill effects that we can see."

"That's good."

Rigel turned his back on them and applied to his mother for an early dinner.

"Huh," said a groom behind them. He was looking out the stable doorway at some sight that apparently startled him. Another stableman joined him and began to snicker. Laurence exchanged a glance with Stanley. They went out to see.

The Duke of Tereford was approaching, riding an exceedingly incongruous mount. "What is that?" Laurence asked.

"It's a mule," Stanley replied.

He'd recognized its breed. The question had really been what the extremely fashionable duke was doing astride a broken-down mule.

"That's Ridley's old feller, that is," said one of the grooms.

"I heard it died," said the other.

"Naw. I wouldn't have thought it'd take a saddle though."

"Don't seem exactly pleased."

The second groom snorted.

Laurence noticed Miss Deeping on the other side of the

stable yard. She'd stopped short to observe this unusual arrival. In the next moment, a side door opened in the house, and Henry Deeping came striding out. He was laughing.

The mule plodded up to the stable and stopped. The duke dismounted and held out the reins. "Perhaps you would take charge of this kindly but limited creature," he said to the grooms.

They jumped to do so.

"What the deuce are you doing?" asked Henry Deeping as he came up.

"The best I can manage," replied Tereford, showing no trace of embarrassment.

"How I wish I could draw," Deeping continued. "That picture would entertain the *ton* for an age. You would never live it down."

"I can only be thankful for your complete lack of artistic talent." The duke nodded a greeting. "Glendarvon. And Mr. Deeping. I believe we have met in London."

"Your Grace," said Stanley.

"The nonpareil on a swaybacked slug," said the elder brother. His eyes danced with unholy glee. "Oh, where is Rowlandson when you need him?"

"I've never been fond of satirical cartoons," the duke replied. "I'm sure the mule would agree." He addressed Stanley. "I am in need of transport. I sent my coach and team south as all the inns are full to the brim at this season."

"We might have housed them for you, Your Grace."

Tereford showed the first trace of chagrin. "I wish I had thought to ask you. Hello, Miss Deeping."

She had joined them. "Where did you find a mule?" she asked, clearly fighting a smile.

The duke sighed. "Merlin has been reconnoitering the neighborhood. That is his word, you understand. He came across a fellow with a mount for hire and made the arrangements without examining the, ah, object of the transaction."

"Your hermit rented you a mule."

"You have a succinct way of putting things, Miss Deeping."

Henry Deeping staggered about holding his midsection and laughing. Laurence thought the duke was taking this reaction better than he might have in his place.

"We can do rather better than that," said Stanley.

"I hoped you might. I would be happy to purchase—"

"We'll lend you something," Stanley interrupted. "And then we can see. There's a gig in the barn that's hardly ever used. It's a bit worn."

"No matter," said the duke.

"The Duke of Tereford in a shabby old gig," said Henry. "How the mighty have fallen!"

"Oh, do be quiet, Henry," said the duke.

The two men exchanged a look that spoke to Laurence of a long-standing friendship.

"And then some riding horses," Stanley went on.

"I have only a shed at present. No proper place to keep them."

"Ah yes. Just the gig, then. I'll show you." Stanley extended a hand to indicate the way.

The duke started to follow, then turned back. "Cecelia thanks you for the servants, Miss Deeping."

"She is very welcome."

The duke and the two Deeping brothers headed for the coach house. Laurence watched them go.

"Stanley will sell him twice as many horses in the end," Miss Deeping said.

"He is very good at what he does."

"He is, isn't he?" She walked past Laurence.

He followed her into the loose box. "Stanley said Rigel seems all right."

"He looks fine," she replied. "He has a strong heritage. His sire was a champion. And Aspen's as well."

"Do you know all the horses' bloodlines?"

Miss Deeping shook her head. "My father and Stanley and Bertram do. Aspen just happens to be a favorite of mine. She and my horse, Stelle, are sisters."

Bertram walked by the open stable door, checked when he noticed them, and came to join them at the loose box. He said nothing.

"Have you thanked the marquess for saving Rigel's life, Bertram?" asked his sister in an overly sweet tone.

"Eh?"

"It would have been a sad thing to lose him, would it not? Such a promising foal."

Bertram nodded. "It was well done. Thank you."

"I'm glad I happened by."

"Happened," repeated Bertram as if he didn't trust the word.

"Which horses will Stanley show to the Duke of Tereford, do you think?" Laurence asked Miss Deeping.

Bertram went on the alert like a hound catching a scent. "Tereford's here?"

"Looking for transport," Laurence replied.

"I should help." Bertram started out of the stable.

"Leaving me here on my own?" asked his sister, even more sweetly.

Bertram waved a dismissive hand without turning. The sound of his footsteps died away.

"Deft," said Miss Deeping.

Laurence shrugged.

"You are fortunate not to have brothers."

"It wouldn't be the same in my case. Sisters, now, that might do it."

❧

Charlotte looked this large, all-too-attractive sportsman up and down. "You pretend to be bluff and only moderately intelligent. That is, you try to do so. But it doesn't work, because you are neither of those things."

"It usually does work," he replied. "Nearly always, in fact."

She was surprised he had admitted his deception. "Really?"

"Very few people are as discerning as you."

Charlotte felt the blood rush to her face. Most compliments that young gentlemen offered were silly, even annoying. Like one of his earlier remarks, this was not.

"And I am many things that people expect me to be," he added.

"Such as?"

"I'm fond of sport. I can't make witty conversation. I do not have deep philosophical thoughts."

"What would deep philosophical thoughts entail?"

"Well, I don't know. Because I don't have them."

Catching the twinkle in his blue eyes, Charlotte burst out laughing. "I find your conversation satisfactory."

"Not excellent?" he asked, pretending disappointment. "Merely satisfactory?"

"You have quite enough wit to be going on with."

"With you. You're different."

Charlotte had long known that a handsome face was not enough to lure her. She now learned that when combined with a certain sort of mind, it was irresistible. She knew she should look away, but she couldn't. Warmth suffused her from head to toe. "How am I different?" she murmured.

"I am…still learning that."

She leaned toward him, drawn by a curiosity that was somehow softer than her usual inquisitions. "How do you intend…?"

Rigel began hopping around the loose box as if he was on springs. He bumped into his mother, bounced back, stumbled, then nipped at her tail and began to hop again. Aspen stepped forward and nudged Charlotte's shoulder. Charlotte put a hand on the mare's neck. "Yes, I know you would like to go outside," she told her. "Stanley said tomorrow."

Aspen looked back at her bumptious foal, then at Charlotte.

The marquess laughed. "Have pity," he said.

Charlotte smiled as she shook her head. "Not until I consult Stanley. He makes the final judgment."

The sound of hooves and rattle of harness heralded her brother's return. They went out to find Stanley leading a single horse harnessed to their older gig. Tereford and Henry sat in it. Charlotte went to explain Aspen's plight.

"I will go and see." Stanley bade the duke farewell and entered the stable.

"He gave you Trace," Charlotte said. This gelding had recently gone into retirement, though he was still hale and steady. He looked glad to be in harness again.

"And tempted me with some stunning hunters." As Henry had predicted, the polished duke looked incongruous in a slightly shabby gig, but no less assured. Charlotte wondered what it would take to overset the man. And then he drove that question right out of her mind when he added, "I've remembered where I heard the name *Glendarvon.*"

He was looking past her to the marquess, who had come out in her wake.

"My father knew yours, I believe."

Charlotte came alert as the marquess said, "Ah."

"He was consulted on the matter of guardians," Tereford went on. "I remember because he used the occasion to lecture me on a son's proper attitude and behavior. He had a great many opinions on that score. If your caretakers took his advice, you have my sympathies."

Glendarvon merely bowed in acknowledgment. The animation was gone from his expression.

Charlotte said nothing. But it did occur to her that carefully questioning the duke, at some later time, would not break her promise to her brother.

A groom brought out the mule and hitched its reins to the back of the gig. Henry climbed down. The duke nodded his farewells and drove off.

"Stanley has relented," said Glendarvon.

She turned to see her brother leading Aspen from the stable toward the mares' field. Rigel skipped along behind her, tossing his head and executing tiny leaps over tufts of grass. The foal's frisking warmed Charlotte through and through. She was so glad this bright spirit had not lost his life in cold, smothering mud. She smiled even as she blinked back a tear. Glancing at the marquess, she saw the same emotions in his face—elated, grateful, tenderly amused.

For the first time in the course of her prickly romantic life, Charlotte felt a whiff of danger.

~⚬~

Charlotte went to visit Cecelia the following afternoon, riding over alone through a brisk wind that loosed the leaves from the trees and whirled them in spirals around her. The air crackled with energy, making her mare dance. The first fox hunt of the season was not far off.

Arriving at Lorne, she found the shed empty and realized she should have sent word ahead. But when a boy came trotting from the house to take charge of Stelle, he told her the duchess was at home.

"James has gone off in the gig to speak to a builder," Cecelia said after Charlotte joined her. "He insisted on doing it himself."

Charlotte wasn't sure why her friend should think that worth mentioning. Cecelia's smile said it was one of those secret jokes many married couples shared.

"I had a letter from Sarah," she added. "She has found us a new tenant for our Cornish house."

"How did she sound?" Charlotte and her other friends had been worried about Sarah, whose impulsive marriage had not begun well.

"Quite happy, actually. The family seems to have come to an understanding."

"Oh good." They were exchanging the latest news about Ada and Harriet as well when movement outside the window caught Charlotte's eye. She turned to see a tall thin man striding across the far side of the garden. "Is that Merlin?"

Cecelia looked. "Yes." She shrugged. "He patrols the boundaries."

"Why?"

"For something to do, I think. He doesn't seem to have much of an idea about that."

"Does he make you uneasy?" Charlotte wondered.

"Not in the least. Perplexed and a little sad, perhaps. I don't see what's to be done with him."

"Are you required to do something?"

Cecelia shook her head. "But we brought him up here. At his request. And now he has set himself up in a tumbledown cottage at the edge of the property. Not a proper house at all. He lurks around the kitchen door at mealtimes just as he did in Cornwall. Fortunately, the staff you found for us are all very sensible. They seem amused by him."

"You want to help him," Charlotte observed.

"He's like…a task left undone." The duchess made a gesture to show that she knew this was silly.

"There isn't much call for a hermit."

"He has been a tutor and schoolmaster."

"I could ask if anyone in the neighborhood—"

"Both of which he hated, it seems," Cecelia interrupted. "I don't think teaching is his…talent."

Outside, Merlin suddenly jumped behind a tree and crouched out of sight. Wondering what had set him off, Charlotte rose and went to peer out. The gig came into sight, heading for the shed. "Does he hide from the duke?" she asked.

"He says he prefers to remain 'covert,'" Cecelia replied. "And no, I have no idea what that is about."

Tereford came in to join them a few minutes later. "Ah, scones. We are grateful for the cook you found us, Miss Deeping."

It had actually been their housekeeper, but Charlotte took the credit. She had questions for Tereford and was glad to see him in a good mood.

He sat and took the plate Cecelia handed him. "The builder can start reconstructing the stable next week," he said. "He has the materials available."

"He will have to clear out the cinders and ashes first," Cecelia said.

"He was aware. The ruins have attracted a good many local visitors, apparently. He thought the foundations could be reused as they are stone."

"Well done," said Cecelia.

Charlotte didn't understand her hearty tone. Nor the look they exchanged. It was another of those arcane marital signals. Charlotte let him finish the scone, well aware that hungry men were less amenable. Then, at last, she came to the point. "I was curious that your family knew Glendarvon's," she said to the duke. "Did you meet his parents before they were murdered?"

"What?"

She had managed to startle the most polished man in London. Charlotte almost felt she should take a bow. "You didn't know? He told me they were killed when he was four years old."

"Good lord," he said.

Cecelia looked both shocked and bewildered.

"I mentioned them when I was there about the gig," the duke told her. "My father was consulted about his guardianship."

"After they were killed?" asked Cecelia.

"It seems so," said Charlotte.

"Should I apologize?" wondered the duke. "I could tell him there were moments when I would have been happy to see my father murdered."

"James! That isn't funny."

"It isn't. I beg your pardon. Both your pardons." Tereford turned to Charlotte. "He told you about this? How did it happen?"

"I thought you might have heard." She didn't feel it was right to share the details she'd gleaned so far.

Tereford shook his head. "I only remember that my father used the occasion to lecture me on my shortcomings as a son. And the importance of a proper guardian." His lips turned down. "He did not see the irony in the fact that *he* was my preceptor. And yet I was everything he detested. So what did that say about his abilities?"

Cecelia reached over and squeezed his hand.

"The dead past," said the duke with a nod. "But murdered!" He shook his head again.

"It must have been talked of," said Charlotte.

"Undoubtedly. Twenty-odd years ago."

She needed older informants, Charlotte decided.

"You're interested in Glendarvon's history?" Cecelia asked her. Her blue eyes were acute.

"It is a mystery," Charlotte replied.

"And you find those fascinating."

"Yes," she said, which was true but incomplete.

"Well, I know nothing about it," said the duke.

"I wonder if Lady Wilton might," said Charlotte. The duke's irascible grandmother was an expert on society scandals. And she was certainly old enough to remember a twenty-year-old tale. Or a half-century one, for that matter.

The Terefords were staring at her. "You are not fond of Lady Wilton," said Cecelia.

"Well, no, but…I suppose you write to her now and then. Since she has become a relative."

"Not very subtle, Miss Deeping," said the duke.

"No," said his wife. "Really, Charlotte, I would have expected a more devious approach from you."

Charlotte saw that she'd amused them. "Harriet was always better at that," she admitted.

"You miss them."

Her friends' absence was an acute pain suddenly. She nodded, throat tight.

Cecelia looked sympathetic. "I will mention Glendarvon in passing. When I write. But only once, mind. I'll not rouse her…inquisitive impulses."

Charlotte nodded, in complete agreement and very grateful.

‿

Laurence rode back toward the Deeping house after an invigorating gallop down country lanes and a subsequent wander that looped through field and forest. The wind had blown the cobwebs from his mind and nearly stolen his hat. His horse had reveled in the movement as much as he did.

His thoughts had been just as active, circling around his

last conversation with Miss Deeping. He sometimes pretended to be duller than he was. This was true. It was a useful ploy for avoiding conversations he didn't wish to have. But the thing was, he didn't admit it when challenged. He simply looked blank and waited until people gave up. Assumptions took over. Prejudices reigned. A large, bland, muscular gentleman who was fond of sport was not expected to have brains. His few good friends gradually learned he wasn't a dunce, but they didn't talk about it. Why would they? They weren't silly tattlemongers. Yet when Miss Deeping had challenged him, he'd given up his ruse at once. He'd even been rather pleased that she saw through him. Pleased, Laurence thought. He examined the idea with wary curiosity. Yes, pleased.

He'd also told her things he hardly ever shared. He couldn't recall when he'd last mentioned his parents' murder, except to her. He'd made a fetish of keeping to himself, and he was comfortable that way. He always had been.

What was it about this particular young lady? He'd met prettier girls, a good many with sweeter dispositions, even some with more sprightly wit. Many had seemed determined to please him, whatever that might require. They'd hovered around him. Laurence had a flash of memory. At a certain London ball, he'd been surrounded by a bevy of debs, and they'd seemed to be vying to reflect his preferences. It had been an…assault of enthusiastic agreement.

Other men seemed to find this enjoyable. Right and proper, even. To Laurence it had seemed empty, perhaps because he was putting on a bit of an act himself. He hadn't been intrigued at all.

And now, suddenly, he was. Because… He groped for a reason. Miss Deeping was pleasant to look at. She was intelligent. She was treasured by her family, which was telling. But none of that seemed enough.

She was wholly herself, Laurence realized. She didn't hang back to see what he might want before she spoke. She didn't hope to please him first and foremost. Quite the contrary! She didn't give a fig. Laurence found he was smiling. Miss Deeping said what she liked. And she listened to the answers, hearing what lay behind the words. It was exhilarating and a relief.

More than that, she was brave. She navigated the bedlam of the Deeping dinner table without blinking an eye. She'd recovered in a moment when he'd nearly ridden her down, an actual brush with death. And look at how she'd gone after the mired foal. She was intrepid, he thought. *Intrepid*. The word vibrated in his mind. She was the sort of woman he could…more than admire. She offered the chance of a real connection.

With this thought came an unsettling surge of longing and fear. Connections broke, smashed by fate. Feelings overwhelmed, then turned to dust and ashes. The quiet life he'd created was…workable. He wasn't ready to let that go.

As if a treacherous fairy had summoned her, the subject of his musings appeared around a clump of trees ahead, mounted on her charming mare. Miss Deeping saw him at the same moment. There was no avoiding her. If he jerked the reins and turned to flee, he would only encounter her over dinner later and have to explain his rudeness.

"Hello," she said when they came closer. "Wandering about by yourself again?"

"As are you," Laurence replied.

"I've been visiting my friend Cecelia. You didn't care to join the shooting this morning?"

It wasn't an accusation. He didn't have to justify his choices. "I felt like a gallop."

The path back to the Deeping stables turned right ahead. They both took it, riding side by side.

"It is good to get the kinks out," Miss Deeping said.

"Yes." Laurence began to compose another bland sentence—a comment about the weather—when a flicker of movement distracted him. "What the deuce is that?"

"What?"

"There's someone in that tree." He pointed.

Charlotte turned to look. A figure stood on a branch in the middle distance, one arm hooked around the trunk for balance. Not a boy playing pirates; this was a man. She squinted. "It's Merlin."

"Who?"

"The man staying at Lorne with the Terefords."

"Ah, the one who talked of incendiaries at the gate."

"Yes. I can't recall his real name." Sarah had put it in one of her letters, but Charlotte hadn't paid attention.

"Oliver Welden," the marquess responded. At Charlotte's surprised look, he added, "The duke mentioned it."

"And you remembered."

"It's no great feat. What is he doing in a tree?"

"Cecelia told me he patrols the boundaries of their land."

"As well as guarding the gate. Why? Does he expect an attack?"

"She said he doesn't know what to do with himself."

"All right, but why do *that*?" The marquess gestured at

the figure in the tree. Apparently seeing he was exposed, Merlin climbed down and disappeared.

"I wonder if he's 'touched in his upper works' as Cecil would say."

"You fear he's a madman?"

"No. I imagine he needs a purpose, and he doesn't know where to find one." The words had popped out. And they'd sounded uncomfortably wistful.

"Up a tree seems an odd place to look."

He was dismissive. The Marquess of Glendarvon had no idea what it was like to have no purpose. He had an estate to care for, an established place in the world, all manner of options spread before him like a banquet. "Where would *you* look?" Charlotte asked.

"I suppose the duke could find him a position."

"Some place to shove him into and forget about him?"

Glendarvon raised his eyebrows. "Is this Merlin a friend of yours?"

She had sounded furious, Charlotte realized. And she hadn't really been speaking of Merlin, whom she didn't know at all. The point had hit much closer to home. "No."

Mortified, Charlotte urged her mare forward. His mount responded to the change in speed, coming up to Stelle's side just as the path narrowed between two stands of blackthorn.

The horses jostled like a crowd trying to push through a doorway. Charlotte and the marquess were pressed together—shoulders, upper arms. She felt the hard muscle of his thigh against her knee. His leg pressed hers where it was bent in the sidesaddle, as if urging it to open further. Charlotte gasped as a bolt of heat went through her body. Every inch of her was suddenly aware of him in an entirely different way, her body brought to tingling life. She looked up, startled, and met a searing blue gaze. Clearly, he felt it, too. Fire seemed to pass from his eyes to hers. She was leaning forward, drawn irresistibly, falling into inevitability. Mere inches, and they would be locked together in a...

Stelle nipped at his gelding, making her annoyance at this obstruction plain. Ranger's head jerked away from her teeth, having no room to shy.

Glendarvon frowned. Not in anger. Charlotte knew that. Perplexity, frustration, anxiety? She thought she saw all those and more. One of his powerful hands brushed her cheek even as he reined in his horse with the other. "Ranger," he said. "Get back."

His gelding responded, sidling backward. His hand fell away. Charlotte's mare walked forward.

And the moment passed. The pall of normality descended like a cloak to be swathed around her. She might have thought she'd imagined the whole thing, except that she was breathless. And the memory of his touch still filled her reeling senses. He was coming up beside her again. What did one say after a passage like that, when everything and nothing had happened? When the universe had swung out in a wild arc and back again?

"Awkward bit of path there," he observed.

One pretended nothing had occurred, apparently. But he had sounded shaken, and he was looking everywhere but at her. "Yes, I'll tell Bertram to see to it," she replied. She realized where they were. "There's also a hole. Careful." His gelding was nearly on it. Charlotte leaned over and grabbed a rein to stop him. "The ground drops off just there," she added. "The long grass makes it hard to see." She let go of his rein.

"Ah yes." He guided Ranger around the declivity.

"I'll remind Bertram about that as well," Charlotte said. "It was supposed to be filled in."

"Thank you. Ranger might have had a fall."

"You don't mind that I stopped you?"

"Should I?" He looked at her finally. The fire had not gone out of his blue eyes. It was merely banked. She could still feel it.

"If you were a dull bluff sportsman, you would be quite annoyed at the interference. Of a female, at that."

"Would I?"

"I think we both know you would."

The brush of mutual understanding was a touch of another kind, as heady as the press of his knee. Perhaps even more so. Charlotte took a deep breath and strove to gather her disordered senses. She pulled Stelle to a stop. "You should go on ahead."

He paused at her side. Not particularly close. And yet it felt as if he was.

"If we arrive back together, one of my brothers is likely to observe us," Charlotte added. "Without a groom or any other chaperone."

"Ah."

"And I'm rather tired of their unsolicited opinions."

The marquess touched the brim of his hat and, astonishingly, did as he was told.

Six

THIS WAS THE SORT OF LEICESTERSHIRE VISIT LAURENCE had imagined, he thought, as he rode with a group of young men to call on Stanley's neighbor and see his pack of foxhounds. Shooting, hunting, a bit of mild indulgence as the bottle went around in the evening, that had been his vision. Strenuous and restful at the same time. He'd known, in a general way, that Stanley had a sister, but he hadn't thought she'd figure much in their activities. From casual mentions, he'd expected her to be standoffish, even perhaps spinsterish, a despiser of the marriage mart and all its ways.

She was those things, partly. But the image they'd conjured in his mind was miles from the reality. Charlotte Deeping…shone with a kind of quicksilver glow that only gradually came into focus. Once it had, though, a man could scarcely look away. And after their encounter yesterday, he couldn't stop thinking about her. What would it be like to hold her in his arms? To see those sharp eyes go soft with desire? She'd reacted to his accidental touch. What had she felt?

He burned to know. And why not find out? There was no impediment. Of course, Laurence would not trifle with any female, especially not with his best friend's sister. But if he was ready to take a step toward marriage… And there his train of thought stopped dead. He thought of introducing her to the mausoleum of a house he was supposed to call home. His spirits sank into the depths.

They turned into the drive of a substantial brick house

and rode around the side to the back premises. Along with the stable, an extensive kennel stood there. Barks and yips made the presence of dogs obvious.

A short rotund man of fifty or so came out to greet them. Stanley introduced him as Frederick Fraling, owner of the estate and master of the local hunt. They dismounted, and this florid gentleman took them in to see the hounds. The animals fawned about him with obvious affection and respect. "Ripe and ready, aren't you, my beauties?" Fraling said. "They know the time of year as well as you do," he told the visitors.

They admired the pack and talked of the first runs, which were only a few days away. Fraling knew every inch of the surrounding country and was free with advice about how to get over it in the best style. "This will most likely be my last hunting season for a while," said Henry Deeping. "I shall be posted abroad next year."

"Get permission to come home," suggested Fraling.

The eldest Deeping son smiled at him. "I don't think the Foreign Office will see hunting as grounds for leave."

"They should," declared their host, only half joking it seemed.

When the party came out of the kennels, a young lady appeared from the house and invited them in for refreshment. Stanley Deeping presented his guests to Miss Felicity Fraling, and they followed her inside. Her relationship to Fraling was clear in her round face and buxom form, Laurence thought. Her blond hair and creamy skin came from her mother, whom they met within. The warmth of her personality seemed all her own.

As they enjoyed ale and cider and more speculation about the coming hunts, Laurence became aware of a current passing between Stanley and the daughter of the house. He was soon convinced there was interest on both sides. How deep or serious, he could not tell. It might be mere childhood friendship or light flirtation or something more. It was certainly enough to make him curious.

"Miss Fraling seemed very pleasant," he said to Stanley when they had started back to the Deeping estate.

"She is."

"I suppose you've known her a long time."

"All her life."

"So long?"

"She is only seventeen," Stanley said.

"Indeed? I would have thought older." Miss Fraling had seemed an assured hostess and well-informed about her father's affairs.

"Because she's so sensible," his friend replied.

"I suppose that was it," Laurence said.

"We mean to be married."

"Really? You have an understanding?"

"We have silently agreed to have an understanding."

Thinking this was a subtle distinction for Stanley, and more curious about the topic than he might have been just a week ago, Laurence said, "How do you know?"

"What?"

"If it's silent, how can you be sure?"

"I just am," said Stanley.

He certainly seemed so. "Well, I wish you happy."

Stanley nodded. "I haven't spoken because of her age, but next year, I shall. She will be just the sort of wife I need."

The final word struck Laurence as prosaic. "Need?" he repeated.

"She is well able to do her part to run the stables and the household."

This didn't seem quite sufficient to Laurence. "And you like her, er, personally."

Stanley turned in the saddle to look at him. "Of course. That was the first consideration." He stared. "What has gotten into you? You don't expect poetical flights from me, surely?"

Laurence shook his head. His friend had never been eloquent.

"And yet?"

"What?"

"I feel there is an *and yet* involved here," said Stanley.

"No. I haven't anything to say. It's just…I wonder what Miss Fraling expects."

"*You* do?"

"Don't young ladies have…romantic notions?" Laurence had heard that a fellow was supposed to offer compliments and express tender sentiments. Plays and poems and novels were full of such stuff.

"Felicity isn't like that," replied Stanley. But he frowned.

Charlotte Deeping wasn't either, Laurence thought. Seemingly. But who could say what she might require in wooing? If wooing were in question. Which it was not. And there was the "and yet" Stanley had mentioned.

"You think Felicity would like some flowery language?"

"I don't know." Laurence had an inspiration. "You could ask your sister. For the female point of view." There was no harm in gathering information. For possible, but highly unlikely, future reference.

"Charlotte!" Stanley burst out laughing. "I don't think so."

"Why not?"

"She is the least romantic creature on earth. She dissects compliments as if they were scientific treatises. I overheard a fellow in London tell her friend Harriet Finch that she had eyes like stars. Charlotte asked him if he meant huge orbs of pulsing fire. And how was Harriet to take *that* comparison?"

Laurence laughed.

Stanley smiled, too. "He didn't find it amusing. He wandered off as if he'd taken a gut punch."

He could imagine the scene. Vividly.

He was still enjoying the picture when he noticed Stanley was examining him. "So I wouldn't advise you to offer glib compliments to Charlotte," he added.

Pulling back, Laurence said, "We were speaking of you and Miss Fraling."

"Were we?"

"Yes. Because of our conversation about your future."

"And yet you brought Charlotte into it. Why was that?"

"I didn't."

"You did, my lad. You're making us all wonder a bit, you know."

"I only said…" *A bit too much*, Laurence thought.

"I have no objection in principle," Stanley went on. "But…"

Laurence waited.

His friend took his time, seeming to grope for words. "Charlotte's not an…ordinary sort of girl." He made a quick gesture. "She's my sister, and I love her, like all my family. We all look out for her, of course. But she isn't…" He paused, frowned, shifted in his saddle. "Felicity, now, she's so easy to talk to. I don't say she parrots my opinions. I wouldn't want that. But she can disagree in quite an…agreeable way. Charlotte's more likely to cut a fellow down. And enjoy it, too. She has a sharp tongue. You may have noticed. She's said she'll never marry."

It was one of the longest speeches he'd ever heard from Stanley, and it made Laurence wonder. Had his friend been keeping a close eye on them to protect Laurence rather than his sister? Did he think Laurence had no chance of interesting her? "Never marry," he repeated, without meaning to speak aloud.

"Shouldn't have said that," Stanley muttered. "What's the matter with me? Oh lord, I don't know why I began this. I don't know what I'm even talking about."

Partly out of pity, and partly for his own reasons, Laurence pointed to a hedge beside the lane. "Is that one of the 'regular raspers' Mr. Fraling warned us about?"

Stanley looked profoundly relieved. "Yes. The ground falls off steeply on the other side, and your mount will lose its footing if you're not prepared. One of the older foxes knows it, too, I'd swear. He slips through there at every opportunity."

Laurence turned to pass this observation along to one of their companions, and hunting once more took over the conversation.

❧

"I think we should organize a small dancing party," said Charlotte's mother as they walked through the garden, cutting blooms for the vases in the house. "The young men will like that."

"They only care about hunting at this time of year," Charlotte replied. "Or any time of year, some of them."

"Nonsense. After the first few hunts, they will want some diversion. And with a dance, we can entertain the duke and duchess with more than just a rowdy dinner. It is only a matter of recruiting partners from among the young ladies of the neighborhood."

Charlotte was not well acquainted with this group, as she had been off at school for so long. Also, the local crop of girls was just young enough to have been outside her ambit. "Are you using the lure of the Terefords to make social connections?"

Her mother gave her a severe look. "I don't need a lure, Charlotte. I visit with all the prominent families hereabouts. You might have too if you had come home for your school holidays more often instead of going off with your friends."

"Are you angry with me, Mama?"

"No, of course not." Her mother sighed. "It is just that you are the only girl in my mob of boys."

"And I haven't acted enough like one?"

"You have been yourself."

"And so very insistently," murmured Charlotte.

This roused a small smile. "I want you to be happy. You like dancing."

She did, and she was good at it, which was always helpful. Charlotte had a sudden vision of partnering the marquess. Perhaps even for a waltz? It was an intriguing idea. She wondered if he danced well.

"And there are your brothers to be settled," her mother went on.

Charlotte pointed a finger at her. "Aha, you have your eye on some prospects?"

"Don't point. It's rude."

Charlotte shook her finger teasingly. "But you do."

"Felicity Fraling would do very well for Stanley," her mother admitted. "She is the daughter of the local master of the hunt. A very sensible girl and loves the country."

"She sounds dull."

"Not in the least. Just because people don't like the same things you do doesn't mean they're dull. She's pretty, too. And I have seen signs of interest on both sides." Her mother nodded. "I think they will make a match of it, but it's just as well to give them opportunities to pursue the matter."

"You like her," said Charlotte.

"I do. Which is important to me, as Stanley's family will be living here with us, you know. Helping manage the stables."

"Ah." It came to Charlotte that she would prefer not to be here at that point. It was familiar and pleasant to have Mama as mistress of the house. An…understudy younger than herself was a different story. "Bertram will want to stay as well, I suppose." Her home would become crowded in the next few years.

"He will stay involved in the breeding program, I'm sure," replied her mother.

"Another family here would be quite a few," Charlotte said.

Mama acknowledged this with a nod. "I do have my eye on a decent house nearby, but I'm not sure we can afford a second residence."

"Who do you have in mind for the others?" Charlotte asked. Planning matches was amusing, as long as they weren't for her.

"No one specific. Henry should make diplomatic connections with his marriage, obviously. A young lady who knows her way around society and the court. There's no one like that around here."

Charlotte shook her head. "He and Tereford are friends."

"That's right. And the duchess will know all sorts of eligible young ladies. Another reason to invite them."

"And then there's Cecil," said Charlotte.

"I'm not sure what Cecil will decide to do with his life."

"Since he can't be a dandy forever?"

"It is not a profession," replied her mother firmly.

"Some seem to think it is."

"Well, they are mistaken," declared Mama. "It is far too expensive."

"Has Cecil been spending too much?"

"I don't think that's any of your business." Her mother looked uncomfortable, which was rather an answer in itself.

Charlotte let it go, though she filed away the information for later consideration. "Bertram is too young as yet," she said instead.

"He is. Although…"

"Ah. Another neighbor?"

Her mother made an equivocal gesture. "Caroline Proctor is only sixteen, and so it is not to be thought of for a while. She is horse mad though. And she is an only child who will inherit a small holding nearby."

"Which would give Bertram something of his own," Charlotte concluded. And perhaps some other place to live.

"Yes, but I am not counting on it in any way. That is years in the future."

"I must make the acquaintance of these girls."

"You won't say anything!"

"Of course not, Mama. I am the soul of discretion. When shall the dance be?"

"Oh, have I won you over?"

"Now that I know about all this intrigue? Yes." Of course, Charlotte said nothing of waltzing with Glendarvon. She continued to think about it, however.

"In two weeks, I think," said her mother. "It won't be anything grand. Just an informal hop."

Which probably meant no waltzes, Charlotte thought with regret. Then she realized the youth of the local young ladies would have ruled them out in any case. Still, dancing was dancing. "Let me know what I can do to help," she said.

Her mother gave her a surprised smile.

"I *do* like to dance," Charlotte added.

❧

Late that afternoon, Laurence walked out to the field where the mares and foals were kept. He was leaning on the fence, watching the grazing mothers and gamboling offspring, when he caught movement in the corner of his eye and turned to find Miss Deeping approaching the other side of the paddock. She checked when she noticed him, and they both stood still for a moment. Laurence might have laughed at the way their reactions mirrored each other if he hadn't been shocked by how the sight of her affected him. From one moment to the next, it was as if the landscape reeled and rearranged itself with her at its center.

He was drawn around the corner of the fence to join her.

Only then did he realize he needed something to say. She would think him a tongue-tied fool.

Fortunately for him, just then the foal they'd rescued together leaped straight up in the air. As he came down, Rigel kicked backward with his hind feet, then bounced off across the grass as if his legs had springs inside.

They both laughed. Their eyes met, sparked, and veered away toward the horses. "It seems there's no need to be concerned about *him*," said Laurence.

"I don't suppose he even remembers the fen," she replied.

Laurence recalled every single thing about it. "Where does his name come from?"

"Papa uses stars for the male foals and trees for the females. Rigel is the brightest star in the Orion constellation. One of the hunter's feet, I believe."

She sounded confidently knowledgeable. Watching her gaze at the horses, Laurence was certain she understood much more about them than he did.

"He says mares are steady, with their feet on the ground, and stallions are fiery, with their heads in the clouds," she continued. "I pointed out that this was not always true. Temperaments differed on both sides. But he claimed it was more likely than not, and at any rate one had to have a system for naming."

"Yet your mare is named Stelle."

"She wasn't bred here. Papa brought her in to strengthen the line. And she and I took to each other."

Her tone was warmly affectionate, without reservation. Laurence wondered if she ever spoke of humans that way. Under what circumstances would she apply it to him, for example? That would be a rare pleasure. "Do you prefer horses to people?" he asked before he thought.

She turned to gaze at him. "Is this a trick? My answer revealing my social ineptitude?"

"No. Why would I want to do that?"

She looked at him. "To demonstrate your superiority. And my limitations."

The idea was offensive in principle. But more so that she would think him capable of such behavior. That was surprisingly hurtful. Even in their short acquaintance, she ought to know him better. "You have been too lately in London," Laurence replied. His tone had been icy. But he could not call the words back. He didn't wish to.

A pause followed. Laurence kept his eyes on the field. His jaw felt tight.

"I beg your pardon," said Miss Deeping then. "You don't play such games."

"Is that what you call them?" He felt only partly mollified.

"Not I. Some seem to. In London, as you say."

"I have observed."

"*You* have?"

"Is that so surprising?" Laurence asked. Did she think him oblivious, or immune to sour mockery?

"No. Well, yes. You are…"

He raised his eyebrows and waited.

"A nobleman. Established in the world."

"Not in the world of the *haut ton*."

Miss Deeping considered this answer. Laurence found he was holding his breath. He longed for her good opinion, he realized.

"But you are in control of your own fate," she said finally.

A derisive snort escaped him. "Are you joking?" he asked.

She blinked, as if remembering things he'd told her. She

looked at the horses, took a step away as if to see one of them better.

It was the first time he'd seen her at a loss. Laurence found he didn't like it.

"In a general way, perhaps I do prefer horses," she said finally. "As a class. Individually, I care much more deeply about people—my family, my friends from school, a few others."

"And would do anything for them," Laurence said. He'd heard it in her voice, though he hadn't meant to say so. He'd been busy wondering how to become one of these privileged few.

Miss Deeping flushed, still not looking at him. "Not *anything*," she replied lightly. "Ada wanted us to learn how to fight with daggers. I refused."

"Because…"

"I didn't see how we could acquire any degree of skill. And even if we had, bouts at close quarters are never a good choice for a female. There is the matter of relative strength, you know."

She really was the most amazing creature.

"Pistols are a much better choice if a weapon is required," she went on. "And we had a tutor available for those."

"Tutor?"

"Henry," she said, as if the answer should have been obvious.

Her expert-marksman brother. "Did he teach you?"

"Of course."

As if there couldn't have been any question. Henry Deeping couldn't have resisted, Laurence acknowledged. She was irresistible. "And you became a crack shot." He had no doubt.

"I did rather take to it," she replied, only a little smug.

"I'd like to see you shoot against him."

Miss Deeping shook her head. "I never bested Henry. He is peerless. But I am…rather good. Better than any of my friends."

Her small smile was delightful. She was altogether charming. She looked at him, then away. Laurence realized he was staring in mute admiration.

"I must go in," she said. "It's nearly dinnertime."

He turned to walk with her. "I shall take an interest in Rigel's future career."

"Perhaps you should buy him."

"Do all Deepings sell horses?"

"When a chance comes along," she said with a smile. "But I was joking. I don't know what Papa plans for Rigel."

"Shall I ask?"

"That is entirely up to you, my lord."

She left him standing by the paddock, feeling as if all his faculties had been turned inside out and reorganized.

Seven

HER LIFE HAD GONE ALL TOPSY-TURVY, CHARLOTTE thought as she rode out of the stable yard a few days later on her way to Lorne. Cecelia had sent word that Lady Wilton had answered her letter, and Charlotte was eager to hear what she'd said. More than eager. It had become a matter of urgency to find out more about the Marquess of Glendarvon.

Charlotte set her jaw as she jumped Stelle over a hedge and cantered across a frost-touched meadow. There was no getting around it; the man had rattled her. When she'd encountered him at Rigel's paddock, she'd hardly known herself. She hadn't felt so clumsy and self-conscious since she'd first arrived at school nearly ten years ago, a wild girl more comfortable with horses than people. The marquess had touched on a sore point there, with his unexpected question. How had he hit on just that point?

Her school friends had liked her despite the rough edges. More than liked: they'd supported and encouraged her, and Charlotte had gained assurance. She'd discovered her analytical, impatient, sharp-tongued self. She'd never looked back.

Until now.

First, she'd been shaken by the shock of desire at his touch. That had been…interesting. But then she'd been reduced to a ninny who didn't know what to say. No, that was too harsh. Charlotte encouraged Stelle's impulse to leap over a stream, chopping off the head of a withered weed with a swipe of her riding crop as they passed. She would never be a ninny. Something had shifted though, the world realigned.

Was this what had happened to Ada and Harriet and Sarah, a change that had taken them away one by one? Until their bonds had…not broken, but thinned with distance and distraction. Charlotte didn't doubt her friends' happiness or begrudge it. But she was not prepared to be similarly afflicted and made into someone else. She was herself. She would remain herself.

She gave Stelle her head in a gallop that took all her attention.

"Lady Wilton answered my letter immediately," the duchess said when they were settled in the parlor together. "And her comments about Glendarvon are along the lines of 'you don't know who you're dealing with.'"

"Why?"

Cecelia handed over the letter. "James's grandmother could write sensationalist broadsheets. Her style is quite reminiscent."

"It's long," said Charlotte, fingering the sheaf of pages. She began to read. "A grisly scene," she exclaimed after a moment. "Knifed repeatedly. A sea of blood."

"What did I tell you?"

Shaken, Charlotte read on. The hammering from the builders working on the new stables outside was the only sound in the parlor as she went through the letter. And then she came to a passage that made her blood run cold. She looked up to stare at Cecelia. "This says Glendarvon was shut in a wardrobe in the very room where his parents were killed."

Cecelia nodded soberly.

"He was only four years old!"

Her friend grimaced.

"And he was right there?"

"Apparently."

"That is…" Charlotte couldn't imagine anything more dreadful.

"Horrifying," said Cecelia. "Barbaric."

Charlotte had to breathe a moment before she could go on reading.

When she finished, she returned to various parts and reviewed them. "So the previous Marquess of Glendarvon and his wife were killed in their own home in a horrible way."

"As you told us," replied the duchess.

"Society was aghast, and everyone wondered what he might have done to cause such an attack." Charlotte shook her head. "That seems vastly unfair."

"Which gossip never is, of course," said Cecelia drily.

Charlotte acknowledged her point with a nod. "Lady Wilton reviews the known history of Glendarvon's family and finds no 'whiff of criminality.' What a phrase."

"She was clearly disappointed."

"But then there was his wife," Charlotte went on with a wry glance.

"Isn't it curious how often the woman is blamed?"

They exchanged a look full of ironic understanding.

"But I don't understand Lady Wilton's point about the marchioness," Charlotte said.

"Because it consists of guesses and innuendo and has no basis whatsoever?"

"Her family was not known. She was a dreadful match for 'poor' Glendarvon. She might have had some connection with the troubles in France." Charlotte looked up from the page. "I don't see why Lady Wilton came to that conclusion."

The duchess made a dismissive gesture. "People were blaming everything on France in those days. With the guillotine and so on."

"This is very sloppy reasoning," said Charlotte, tapping the letter with one finger.

"It is Lady Wilton. Reason rarely constrains her."

"Due to gross incompetence at every level, the villain responsible was never found," Charlotte read. "It was undoubtedly a madman. Fortunately, he didn't range through the countryside on a killing spree." She looked up. "Killing spree?"

"Broadsheets," Cecelia replied. "Scandalmongers."

"She suggests at the end that you stay away from Glendarvon," Charlotte added, pointing at the offending words. "As if he was contaminated somehow by his family tragedy. That's outrageous."

"And typical of Lady Wilton."

"We shouldn't have asked her."

"I didn't *ask*," Cecelia replied. She gestured at the letter. "And that is precisely why. If she knew we were interested, she would be full of questions."

"You shouldn't mention Glendarvon to her again."

"I shan't. But what are *you* going to do?"

Charlotte had been wondering if she could ask the marquess about his mother without breaking her promise to Stanley. She knew the answer was probably no. "I?" she said.

"I know you, Charlotte. You find mysteries irresistible."

She couldn't deny it.

"That letter made me uneasy," Cecelia went on. "Does it seem quite right to dig into the man's past without his knowledge? Particularly when it is so painful?"

"The murders are public knowledge, and he mentioned them to me himself." Charlotte knew she was hedging.

"Yes." The duchess frowned. "I don't like feeling we might rouse up long-forgotten gossip."

"No." That would be most unfortunate.

"Glendarvon is not a lost treasure."

"Isn't he a victim of injustice?"

The duchess considered this. "Misfortune, certainly. Injustice, I don't know."

"Killers should not go free. Glendarvon should have the satisfaction of seeing the murderer brought to book."

"Each thing you say makes me more uneasy," the duchess replied. "We are talking about a very dangerous person. Or persons."

"Naturally, I would take care in any inquiries."

Cecelia looked more doubtful. "What could you find after all these years?"

"There's no way to know that until—"

"If Glendarvon wished to learn things, he would investigate himself," Cecelia interrupted.

People didn't always know how, Charlotte noted. On the other hand, she'd observed that a surprising number didn't *want* the truth.

"I think you should forget about this matter," the duchess said. She held up a hand at Charlotte's sound of protest. "But if you will not, you should ask him outright, not go behind his back."

There was much in what she said. She was going to have to retract her promise to Stanley, Charlotte decided. Because she really needed to know all about the marquess. She did not look forward to Stanley's reaction.

A clatter from the entry made them both turn toward the parlor door. It opened to reveal a male figure covered head to toe in soot. He held up a lump of it. "Look what I've found in the remains of the fire," he said.

It was Merlin, Charlotte realized when he spoke. She was curious about the fellow who had observed her from the branches of a tree.

"A cinder?" asked the duchess.

"What? No." He rubbed the grimy object on the sleeve of his coat. Bits of soot fell to the floor, and Cecelia made a small distressed sound. "It's jewelry," Merlin added.

Charlotte offered a napkin.

"Wait," said Cecelia.

But Merlin had already put the grimy thing onto the snowy linen, and Charlotte had begun to rub it clean. "I think it's a ring," she said.

"I knew that," said Merlin.

"Yes." Charlotte set aside the now filthy napkin and held the piece up. Gold glinted in the sunlight from the window. "Is that a sapphire? It's so large."

The duchess extended her hand. Charlotte put the slightly misshapen ring into it, and Cecelia held it up. "It looks real," she said.

She should know, Charlotte thought. She had all manner of jewels. "I wonder how it came to be in the ashes?"

"I don't know, but if you want to investigate *this* mystery, I give you carte blanche," replied Cecelia with a significant glance.

"I found it," objected Merlin. "And brought it to you. I didn't have to do that. I am the one who should investigate."

Looking into the burning green eyes in his soot-streaked

face, Charlotte recognized a kindred spirit. Here was some-one who longed for a purpose and had now found one. He would not have the chance snatched away. She had a good deal of sympathy for the outrage in his expression.

"My friend Miss Deeping has experience in this area," said Cecelia. "She uncovered a treasure that had been hidden for many years."

Charlotte found her friend's earnest tone suspect. Cecelia wanted to shift her from Glendarvon's case to this one, she thought. Cecelia imagined that a bit of evidence in hand would divert Charlotte. Cecelia was mistaken.

That did not mean she wasn't interested in the ring, how-ever. "My friends and I discovered it," she corrected. "More than one mind is helpful in unraveling mysteries." She stood. "We can look together," she told Merlin. "Show me where you found the ring."

⁂

The first hunt of the season gathered at the master's home early on a Tuesday morning in November. The harvest was in, and the fields were as bare as the trees. The sky held scud-ding clouds, but Laurence didn't think they would drop rain. A chilly mist drifted over the ground, which would help hold scents for the hounds. Picking up the excitement of the group, Ranger danced a little beneath him. Cecil Deeping's mount offered to take offense, and Laurence moved away. All the Deeping brothers had turned out for the hunt, for their own enjoyment and to show off the products of their breeding farm. They could certainly be proud of the horses they'd raised, Laurence thought. They were beauties.

Mr. Fraling's hounds milled about in front of his house under the control of the huntsman and his whippers-in. Riders continued to join them until the group numbered about twenty. Miss Felicity Fraling supervised a cadre of servants offering cups of wine.

At a signal from the master, the hounds moved off. The horsemen followed behind through a gate and into a field. The pack drifted this way and that, noses to the earth, examining a patch of woodland, a thicket, and a small ravine. At the end of the latter, their cries signaled the scent of a fox, and the hunt truly began, thundering off in the wake of the racing pack.

This was what Laurence loved—pounding along with riders all about him, Ranger's hooves throwing up clods of damp earth, the cries of the hounds urging them on, the wind of passage on his face. He relished knowing that at any moment he could be presented with a challenge—a declivity to fly over, a fence or a thicket to jump, a narrow turn to negotiate or take a spill. Often there would be no sight of what lay on the other side of a leap. The risk to life and limb was real, and split-second decisions made the difference. Hunting tested one's physical prowess and judgment and reflexes as well as the bond with one's horse. It was all out, a matter of instinct and experience with no time for thinking. He leaned forward and gave himself over to the melee.

They hurtled across a stubbled field and into a patch of small trees. The ground dropped off in the middle of it, and Laurence leaned back to help Ranger balance as the gelding sank onto his haunches to scramble down. On the other side, they splashed through a stream, sheets of water rising under dashing hooves. The pack lost the scent for a bit, but they sniffed along the banks until they regained it and set off up a hill and over, into a thorny crevice, and up a steep bank.

This fox clearly knew how to make them pay for chasing him. Indeed, in the first sight Laurence got of the animal, he seemed to be looking back over his shoulder and laughing as he lured them into a stretch of marsh where hooves raised a storm of muck and left them plastered from head to toe. Laurence received several dollops of odiferous mud right in the face. Like the slaps of a taunting duelist, he thought.

Dripping with mud, the hunters lunged and slipped up the opposite side, only to confront a stony ridge that was not jumpable, though the hounds poured over and down. They rode along it for a little distance until a cattle track appeared, then descended and galloped across the field below. On the other side, they were brought up short by a great thorny thicket. The horses had to circle this, giving their quarry an even larger lead.

In the end, the fox escaped, going to earth in a den that obviously had a labyrinth of tunnels and entrances. Laurence imagined that he twisted through these and ran out somewhere well away from the hounds, who were busy digging at the hole where he'd disappeared. This fox was long gone. As the afternoon was waning, and a sharp wind had risen, the huntsman called the dogs off and gathered them to head back to Fraling's house.

Laurence didn't feel cheated. Quite the opposite. He preferred it when the fox got away. It seemed more sporting. He'd heard, in fact, that a number of huntsmen purposely avoided kills. An experienced, wily fox made for adventurous hunts, like the one today.

The Deeping party returned to the house, wet and chilled

and happy. A can of hot water in Laurence's room was very welcome, as were dry clothes and a mug of ale. He went down to dinner well satisfied with his day. As a crowning touch, he found he was seated next to Miss Deeping once again.

"A good day out, I heard," she said.

"Yes." Laurence dug into his dinner with gusto. He was starving.

"Your quarry slipped away though," Miss Deeping said.

Laurence repeated the theory about conserving worthy vulpine opponents.

"Ah. I agree with you. We won't discuss it here though. It's liable to cause too much shouting."

Laurence had no trouble going along with that. The racket of fierce debate was already rising. He thought on how odd it was that a din in a dining room unsettled him while the raucous shouts of the hunt did not. The latter felt exciting, but arguments seemed a thing to avoid if at all possible.

A gust of wind rattled the casement behind them. "We're in for a storm, I think," said Miss Deeping.

"It'd be a prime night for the Wild Hunt," said her brother Bertram, who sat on her other side.

Miss Deeping glanced at him, looking surprised.

Having just taken a large bite of roast beef, Laurence could only look inquiring.

"Your friend Miss Moran told me all about it," Bertram went on. "And when I say *all*, I mean far more than any normal person would know, or want to." He stabbed his fork into a potato and conveyed the whole thing to his mouth.

"What is it?" asked Laurence.

"You haven't heard that legend?" Miss Deeping asked.

He shook his head. Bertram chewed with full cheeks.

"It's an ancient story," she continued. "My friend Sarah Moran did make a study of it when we were at school. From old tales and chronicles."

Bertram swallowed. "That girl is keen as any foxhound. Only with books." He shook his head.

Miss Deeping smiled. "She is. And as Bertram has brought it up, I will tell you what Sarah found."

Her brother muttered something about a big mouth. Laurence didn't know if Bertram was referring to his sister's friend or to himself. Laurence didn't care, really. In either case, he got the pleasure of hearing Miss Deeping talk.

"The Wild Hunt is a horde of supernatural huntsmen led by Odin or King Arthur or Gwyn ap Nudd or some other figure," she began. "The head of it depends on the local origin of the story. They course across the sky with a great howling noise on stormy nights and come roaring down to earth to hunt souls. If you are out in the dark and caught by them, you may be given the choice to join in. If not, or if you refuse, you are hunted. They will run you to exhaustion."

"And then take your soul?" Laurence asked.

Miss Deeping nodded. "It's said that once they do, you become one of their fearsome hounds—huge and jet-black and horrible, with eyes like saucers. Or sometimes they're white with red ears. Those are Welsh, I think."

"Red ears," muttered Bertram. "That's tosh. Who ever heard of such a thing? No breed like that on earth."

"The huntsmen are dark looming figures," Miss Deeping went on. She seemed to be enjoying her tale. "Difficult to make out except that they are gigantic and hideous."

"If you can't make them out, how can anyone tell they're hideous?" asked Bertram.

"I suppose it is a feeling," replied his sister. "A *frisson* of terror."

"A what?"

"So that one just *knows* they are ghastly looking," she added. Her tone was portentous, but with the hint of a laugh. Laurence enjoyed it mightily. She clearly had a good deal of experience in winding Bertram up. It was as good as a play.

"Ghastly," muttered Bertram. "Of course. Why not?"

"Would you ride or run?" Laurence asked.

"Ride, of course," said both Deepings, unsurprisingly.

"They're mounted on great black horses, or sometimes black he-goats," said Miss Deeping.

"There, that just shows you what bunk this is," said her brother. "No goat could carry a man. Let alone one who's 'gigantic and hideous.'"

"They are magical goats," replied Miss Deeping.

"Large ferocious magical billy goats," added Laurence, meeting her dancing eyes. He elicited a snort of a laugh, which gratified him immensely.

"Well, that's just stupid," said Bertram. "Who would have magical *goats*, of all things? Goats are the least magical creatures in the world."

"You don't think their eyes are eerie?" asked Laurence. "With the horizontal pupils?" He had once been stared at by a goat for several minutes and had found its gaze unnerving.

"They are odd-looking," Bertram conceded. "But that doesn't make them supernatural."

"I've never seen another animal with eyes like that though," said Laurence. "Have you?"

"Well, some horses have similar eyes," replied the youngest Deeping brother. He paused, fork suspended. Gravy dripped from the hunk of beef on its tines. "Not usually so pronounced though." He frowned. "Not sure how I'd stay atop a goat. Hold on to the horns, maybe?"

"People claim to have seen the Wild Hunt," said Miss Deeping. "There are various stories from different parts of Europe."

"With goats?" asked Bertram.

"There must be, but I can't remember," she admitted. "I would have to ask Sarah."

"She'd probably know right off," Bertram replied. "She does nothing but read."

"That isn't true. She does all sorts of things."

"When she visited here, every time I came across her she had her head in a book."

"Perhaps she was simply avoiding your stilted conversation," said his sister.

Bertram looked startled. And then worried. And finally hurt. He filled his mouth with roast beef instead of answering.

"Or perhaps the young lady is shy and didn't know what to say," Laurence suggested. The look he received from Miss Deeping warmed him through and through.

"She is rather shy. She told me once that she prefers books to people because books never require one to be witty."

"Which is a rather witty remark," said Laurence.

"She is much more acute than she thinks. Or she was."

Laurence had a sudden fear that her friend Sarah was dead. But surely she wouldn't speak of her so lightly if so?

"Since she married, she's become much more assured," added Miss Deeping, alleviating his worry. "Well, she had to." Her tone implied a story there.

"You can't talk to a book," said Bertram, still stuck on the previous point.

"You *can*, I suppose," said Laurence.

"If you wish to be thought queer in your attic."

"The conversation *would* be one-sided," said Miss Deeping.

"Yet you could win every point in a dispute," said Laurence.

"What dispute?" asked Bertram. "You're talking nonsense. Both of you."

Laurence supposed they were. Yet it was very pleasant nonsense. He felt he could go on tossing frivolous remarks back and forth with Miss Deeping for the foreseeable future. They flowed effortlessly. It was a delight he'd never experienced before in his life.

"Except for the silent disapproval," she added, ignoring her brother.

"There would be a good deal of silence," Laurence agreed. "But disapproval? How would the book express it? Who's to say?"

"*I* am," said Bertram. "I say you should start making sense."

"But nonsense is more fun," said Miss Deeping.

Meeting her twinkling brown eyes, Laurence wondered if he was losing his heart to this spiky young lady. He thought it very likely that he was.

Eight

THE FOLLOWING AFTERNOON, WHILE THE HUNTERS WERE out again, Charlotte received word that a man had come to the stables inquiring for her. "For me?" she replied. "Not for Papa or my brothers?" All sorts of people brought inquiries to the Deeping stables, but they didn't come to her.

"He asked for you particularly, miss."

Curious, she went out to see who it was and found Merlin leaning on the fence around the training paddock, where grooms were working with the young horses. Apparently, he had an aversion to walking up to doors and knocking on them like a civilized caller. "Will you come inside?" she asked him.

"I prefer to stay outdoors in full view of everyone," he told her. "I won't make that mistake again."

"What mistake?"

"Going off with deceivers," he muttered.

Was he referring to her? She'd given him no reason to call her deceptive. Charlotte decided to ignore this remark. She pulled her cloak closer. It was a brisk November day when a cheery fire was welcome. And standing about outside was not.

Merlin pulled the ring he'd found in the ashes from his pocket. It had been more thoroughly cleaned. "I took this to Leicester and showed it to a jeweler there," he told her. "He said it's a real gem and worth a good deal of money."

"The Terefords allow you to carry it around?"

He glared at her. "Why shouldn't they? I found it. It's mine."

Charlotte started to tell him that wasn't really true,

since he had discovered it on the duke's property. And so it belonged to Tereford, unless the owner of the gem surfaced to try to claim it. Merlin wouldn't like hearing that, however. Obviously. She decided to let the point go.

He moved the ring so the sapphire caught the light, flashing blue. "Nobody's doing anything about this," Merlin complained.

"I have been thinking about it," Charlotte replied. "That ring was either lost in the stables or hidden there."

"By that fellow who was watching over the place?" asked Merlin. "The duke sent him packing."

"If it had been him, he would have dug it out and taken it away," said Charlotte. "But we should speak to him, find out who has lived at Lorne in the past." She had asked Cecelia, but the Terefords had no information on this topic. The previous duke's records were chaotic.

"His name's Horton. He went off to his sister's. I asked at the pub."

"Well done," said Charlotte. Merlin did seem intelligent.

"The villagers think he set the fire." At Charlotte's sharp look, he added, "Not on purpose. He's a terrible drunkard, seemingly. Clumsy and careless with it. Likely to have knocked over a lantern or some such thing."

"Ah, I see."

"He told the duke he never did, of course."

"Were you there when they spoke?"

"I overheard."

"Oh, were you lurking?" asked Charlotte.

Merlin looked nonplussed.

"You lurk fairly well. Though the tree was a mistake. Far too visible and with nothing to duck behind."

He eyed her uneasily.

"Can you find out where Horton's sister lives? I would ask, but that might be too noticeable."

He nodded.

"You can be devious, I imagine. We don't want to scare him off."

"I reckon I can."

Riders appeared at the turn of the lane. The hunters were coming back, spattered with mud from head to toe. The horses looked very ready for their stables and oats.

"Idiots," muttered Merlin.

"You are fond of foxes?"

He gave her an incredulous look. "Foxes? They're vermin. I had a few chickens in Cornwall until the foxes got at them. Slaughtered the whole lot for fun as far as I could see. Left bits of them scattered all over the garden to taunt me."

"Then why do you call the hunters idiots?" Charlotte asked.

"They should just go out and shoot the foul things. Lie in wait with a gun outside their dens and eliminate them efficiently. Without all this show." He snorted. "Red jackets and pampered hounds and hunt balls. It's nothing but a way to puff off their wealth."

Charlotte turned to watch the approaching hunters. She hadn't seen them in quite that way. Her family supplied costly horses trained for the hunt.

"A diversion for bored idlers," Merlin added. "Like most pursuits of the so-called aristocracy. Look at those fools. *They* won't be cleaning all that mud off their clothes."

That was certainly true. "I don't think shooting all the foxes is a better idea," she said. Stanley raised a hand in greeting, and she waved back. "Sport can be a healthful pastime." She turned back to find that Merlin was gone.

❧

Guiding his second-best hunter through an open gate, Laurence saw Merlin slip away from Miss Deeping and slither around a corner of the stable. He wondered why the two of them had been huddled together by the fence. A former hermit, current lost soul, and all-around sneak seemed an unlikely companion for a young lady. She looked around as if uncertain where he'd gone and then walked away toward the house.

He was in no state to go after her, being sweaty with exertion and shedding bits of mud. And he had no reason to, besides a growing desire to follow along whenever he saw her. Like some sort of overgrown puppy, he thought with a mixture of amusement and mortification.

He was not seated next to Miss Deeping at dinner that evening, and he found that a great disappointment. Laurence supposed in this crowd of young men, he could not expect to monopolize the daughter of the house. But he missed her sprightly presence and exhilarating conversation. With her at the other end of the table, he was reduced to rehashing details of the day's hunt with one of the other visitors.

When that topic was exhausted, he turned to his other side. Cecil Deeping sat there, raising his quizzing glass to examine the guest talking to his father, a newcomer who had arrived to fetch a horse he'd purchased.

Feeling a little impatient with this dinner, even disgruntled, Laurence said, "Do you know that quizzing glass is annoying?"

"Of course."

Laurence blinked at this ready response.

"It's meant to be annoying," Cecil went on. "Or intimidating. Or flattering. As I choose. It is an instrument of social manipulation."

"Like an orchestra conductor's baton?"

"Ha! Very good. I like that. I shall steal it. You won't mind, will you? Being the best of good fellows."

"The..."

"You said you were."

Laurence recalled their earlier conversation and was reminded that Cecil's intellect was sharp, however foppishly he dressed. "Right."

"The glass is also simply necessary," Cecil added. "I'm very nearsighted. I can't see across a ballroom without this thing." He gestured airily with the quizzing glass. "It is all a colorful blur."

Surprised at the confidence, Laurence said, "I don't suppose you would want to wear spectacles."

"I don't suppose I would." Cecil grimaced. "The picture I would present."

"Not fashionable."

"Not remotely. Good lord, I'm seeing it now. Between an exquisitely tied neckcloth and a perfect haircut—spectacles!" He shuddered.

"They might be more convenient for walking in the street, say," Laurence pointed out.

"I would rather be run down by a speeding carriage." He smiled. "A high-perch phaeton with a cracking team, of course."

"The modish way to die."

"You aren't quite the clod you sometimes play, are you?" asked Cecil.

Of all the brothers, he was most like Miss Deeping, Laurence decided. They were both acute observers.

"Which is a relief since…" Cecil broke off.

"Since?" Laurence prompted.

"Since I am sitting beside you at dinner," replied the other man lightly. "Do you like to dance?"

"Are we going to do that next?"

Cecil smiled. "Not today. My mother is planning a small assembly."

"Ah. Well, I do like to dance. Mostly. Not the quadrille."

"Complicated," said Cecil.

"Devilishly."

"This will be an informal hop for the neighborhood. No quadrilles."

"That sounds pleasant," said Laurence. He would have an opportunity to stand up with Miss Deeping, he realized.

"Does it?"

"I think so. I suppose it's not your sort of thing."

"Why do you say so?"

"You are accustomed to grand London occasions."

"I am," Cecil replied. "But I do other things, too."

He was an intrepid hunter, Laurence recalled. He'd seen Cecil take a five-barred gate with complete insouciance. Even more of a feat if his vision was imperfect.

"I wonder if I can convince Mama to add a waltz or two," Cecil mused. He tapped his chin with the quizzing glass. "Probably not."

Laurence's vision of holding Miss Deeping in his arms wavered and collapsed. "No?"

"The young ladies hereabouts are rather young. Their families wouldn't like it."

"Ah."

"Disappointed?" Cecil asked.

His dark eyes were sharp. No need for the glass at this distance, Laurence thought. "I just got the knack of it last season," he explained.

"Knack?"

"Not stepping on anyone's feet or risking collisions."

"It's the oddest thing," said Cecil. "But I don't believe you."

"You don't think I can waltz?" Laurence felt unreasonably piqued.

"On the contrary, I suspect you are very good at it."

A roar of laughter from Cecil's other side made him turn, and allowed Laurence to avoid answering. Which he appreciated because the other man's tone had been unsettling.

Several seats down, Bertram Deeping balanced a fork across his nose, weaving back and forth to keep it from falling off. Cecil raised his quizzing glass to watch. "I can't even suspect him of being a changeling," he murmured.

"A...?"

"A substituted fairy child would be less...boisterous, don't you think?"

The fork tipped and tumbled. Bertram caught it and stuck it into a potato on his plate.

"I do hope he will decide against a season," Cecil muttered.

"Because you'll be ashamed of him?" Laurence asked.

Cecil turned to stare at him, the quizzing glass hanging

free. His dark eyes had gone cold. "Because he won't like it," he answered. "And I shall be forced to…punish people who mock him."

There was no hint of a joke in his tone. In fact, Laurence felt a twinge of apprehension. This was not a man to cross.

"He also has dreadful taste in waistcoats," Cecil added as if his tone had never gone icy. "Sometimes I think he chooses them just to watch me wince."

"I wouldn't be surprised. He likes to keep things lively."

"He does that. Tereford's grandmother mentioned your family the other day. In London."

"What?" Laurence blinked. The man had shifted the conversation completely without a change in tone.

"Lady Wilton. Have you met her?"

"No." He'd never heard of her. Why should she be talking about his family?

"I have a good many correspondents in town," Cecil Deeping added. "I hear all the news."

"How splendid for you."

The other man took no note of his sour tone. "This was no great matter. Merely a passing…sneer. But I thought you might like to know."

He didn't like it. Quite the opposite. He wondered if his own mention of the past—so unlike his usual reticence— had roused ancient gossip. From Miss Deeping to Tereford to his sneering grandmother. The idea disturbed him. He hadn't said it was a secret, but he hated to think of them rehashing the old tales.

The ladies rose to leave the table. After a round or two of port, the gentlemen went to join them in the drawing room. Laurence looked for Miss Deeping at the pianoforte, but saw her sitting with Mrs. Carew on the side instead. He was surprised when the older woman beckoned. He'd scarcely spoken to her during his visit.

"Very good work with Rigel," she said when he joined them. "He's a promising lad."

She spoke of the rescued foal as if he was a person.

"Good bones, fine configuration, temperament seems lively. He'll race well, I daresay."

"My aunt is a seeress when it comes to horses," said Miss Deeping.

"Seeress," snorted the older woman.

"You have an uncanny ability to predict their futures."

"Nothing uncanny about it. I've been around the stables all my life. Well, except when I was married." Mrs. Carew shook her head. "Not such a good judge of men. Eddie didn't stay the course."

❧

"My uncle Carew died quite young," said Charlotte. She watched Glendarvon's reactions to her crusty relative. Aunt Carew was a kind of test. Many people didn't know how to take a woman who said whatever she liked and cared nothing for a man's opinion unless he was an expert on horses, which Glendarvon was not, in her aunt's terms.

"I'm sorry," said the marquess.

"Not still mourning him after thirty years. And if a fellow is going to die of consumption, he ought to be a poet or some such thing, don't you think? Pale and languishing. Eddie was a bear of a man. But it took him down all the same. A scourge, that's what it is."

"Consumption is a terrible disease," said Glendarvon. "So you think Rigel will win races?"

He had clearly understood Aunt Carew's true passion.

"Not saying he'll win," her aunt replied. "You never know what the lineup may be. Or the conditions on the day. And so on. But he'll put his heart into it, I'd say."

"Perhaps I should offer to buy him," Glendarvon said with a smile.

He had a positively melting smile, Charlotte thought. And he didn't seem to know it, which was a point in his favor. She disliked fellows who wielded smiles like weapons.

"We won't let him go," said Aunt Carew. "We don't sell foals." She gave Charlotte a sidelong glance. "And I don't say that because I think of them as my children."

"Henry said that, not me," Charlotte pointed out.

"You found it amusing," said her aunt.

She could not deny it.

"And Henry is not as wise as he thinks he is," added Aunt Carew.

"I'll tell him you said so," Charlotte teased.

"You may do so with my blessing." Aunt Carew turned back to the marquess. "We train our horses before we let them go," she told him. "Gently. Properly. We can't control what happens to them after they are sold." She glowered. "Though if we hear of any mistreatment, you may be sure we take steps."

"Good for you," said Glendarvon.

Charlotte's aunt eyed him as if evaluating *his* configuration, then turned to her to say, "Are you going to play for us tonight?"

"I think perhaps people have had enough of my feeble efforts," Charlotte replied.

"Don't be wet. You do well enough. And a bit of music is always pleasant."

"How can I refuse such an effusive request?"

As always, her aunt was immune to irony. She recognized it. She wasn't heedless. She simply didn't care.

"Allow me to escort you," said Glendarvon, standing as Charlotte did. She might have pointed out that she hardly needed support to cross a room. But she rather liked having him at her side. And then she began to feel self-conscious. Which led to annoyance and nearly edged toward despair.

This shifting of emotion was exhausting. She hadn't lost her wits. When she and the marquess talked with other people, she could toss remarks back and forth with ease. More than ease. Delight. It was as if they formed a team, lobbing conversational gambits. Very exhilarating. But when they were alone, the glib words ran dry, and some other sort of perception took over.

How did he become so very *present*? The sense of him at her side was like the heat of a hearth fire beating on her skin. She wondered that everyone wasn't staring at the conflagration. The short walk to the pianoforte seemed both endless and instant.

"Has anyone ever mistreated one of your horses?" he asked.

Charlotte looked up at him and saw concern in his blue eyes. Was he always to be unexpected? She'd anticipated some comment on her aunt's gruff manner. "Only one time that I know of," she answered.

"What happened?"

"My father went and brought her back."

"So easily?"

"Not at all. He was threatened with a horsewhip, I believe. The...person was very fond of the whip." She sat at the pianoforte.

"Blackguard," said Glendarvon.

"Yes."

"I hope your father thrashed him."

"I don't know exactly what he did. But the mare came home, and the man didn't find it easy to buy blood cattle after that."

"He ought to have been put to pulling stagecoaches," said the marquess. "For a driver who was free with the lash."

Charlotte was surprised into a laugh. "What an odd idea."

"Why? It's a punishment to fit the crime," Glendarvon replied.

He was indignant, she saw. His sympathies had been thoroughly roused by the mare's fate. She met his burning gaze and fell into it. The feeling was as heady as several glasses of champagne. She felt slightly dizzy.

"Hop it, Henry!" declared Bertram.

Charlotte came to earth with a jolt. The crowd around them included some acute observers. Not Bertram, but...

"What would you like to hear?" she asked Glendarvon.

"Eh?" He seemed as distracted as she'd been.

She moved her hands on the instrument's keys. "Music?"

"Oh. It's all the same to me, I'm afraid. I haven't much of an ear." And yet he leaned on the pianoforte, gazing down at her, showing no desire to go. "Unless perhaps a waltz?"

"A waltz?"

"Your brother Cecil told me there's to be a dance."

"Yes."

"But with no waltzing, he thought."

"The neighborhood mamas wouldn't like it," Charlotte said. "Most of the girls in the neighborhood aren't officially out."

"And so I've found something to regret about the last London season," he replied.

"What?"

"That I did not go to town, so I missed my opportunity to waltz with you."

The heat in his eyes and his tone left Charlotte breathless.

Nine

MERLIN SHOWED UP AT THE DEEPING STABLES AGAIN TWO days later, once more lingering outside near the paddocks. When Charlotte came out to speak to him, he told her he'd gotten word of Lorne's former caretaker Ned Horton. "He's hanging about an inn in Leicester," he told her. "Spending the money the duke gave him on drink."

"We should go and speak to him," Charlotte replied. "I'll order a gig." She did so, and then went inside to gather her things for the eight-mile journey. She left a note for her mother rather than attempt explanations.

When she returned to the stables, the gig was harnessed, and Merlin was sitting in it. He did not climb down to hand her up. Nor did he take the reins, leaving that to her. This suited Charlotte as much as it surprised her.

They were passing out of the stable yard when Glendarvon appeared on his horse Ranger. There was no formal hunt today, but the gentlemen visiting the Deepings did not let that stop them from seeking out some form of sport. It seemed the marquess had chosen a ride. He raised a hand in greeting, and when Charlotte did the same, he moved to ride beside the gig. "Where are you off to?"

"Things to do," replied Merlin before Charlotte could speak. "Nothing to concern you."

Laurence turned to stare. The man's tone was curt, verging on offensive.

"Be off and kill something," Merlin added. "You lumbering types are good at that."

Verging no more, thought Laurence. Had he annoyed this fellow without knowing? He couldn't remember doing anything to deserve contempt. "I beg your pardon?" he said.

"Here now," said Miss Deeping at the same moment.

It was odd for her to be going off with Merlin, just the two of them, Laurence realized. He wasn't jealous. That would be foolish. But he was curious, and irritated at Merlin as well.

"We are driving into Leicester to see the former caretaker of Lorne," answered Miss Deeping. "We want to see if he knows any more about the fire."

"So you see, nothing to do with you," said Merlin.

Laurence ignored this. "Tereford thought the man most likely caused it himself," he said. "Some clumsy accident."

"I know," said Miss Deeping. "But Merlin found—"

"Do you intend to spread the news all over the neighborhood?" the latter interrupted. "Because that does not seem sensible to *me*."

His rudeness was going beyond amusing. Laurence glanced at Miss Deeping to see if she felt it. She seemed lost in thought. Wondering what Merlin had found, Laurence said, "I will join you."

"This is not some pleasure jaunt," said Merlin. "We don't need you."

His effrontery apparently knew no bounds. "I have an errand in Leicester," Laurence replied. Which was seeing that Miss Deeping had a proper escort and assistance should she need it. He did not trust Merlin to notice or step up to help.

"You are welcome to ride with us," she said. When it looked as if Merlin would object further, she added, "This is my gig." The fellow set his jaw and subsided. Laurence rather enjoyed that.

Unfortunately, the lane narrowed then, leaving no space for him to ride beside the vehicle, small as it was. He spent most of the journey trotting behind them, watching the backs of its passengers. They did not seem to be saying much.

Reaching the town, their party turned twice into lesser streets before the gig pulled up at an inn, the Tattered Crow. Merlin jumped down before it stopped completely and went inside, leaving Miss Deeping to deal with the horse and gig. Which she was well able to do, Laurence thought, but that was not the point. He dismounted and led Ranger over to add his efforts to hers.

When they returned from settling the animals, they found Merlin beside the horse trough. His hand was twisted in the coat collar of a stocky untidy man, and Merlin was shoving the fellow's head into the water. The man heaved and twisted and came up gasping. "What the devil's wrong with you?" he asked. "Let me go!"

Merlin gave him a shake, keeping hold of his coat. Their companion was stronger than he looked, Laurence decided. "This is Ned Horton," Merlin said. "Former caretaker of Lorne."

"We would like to ask you a few questions," said Miss Deeping with perfect composure. "Shall we go inside?"

"You don't want to do that," replied Merlin.

He was still rude, but probably right, Laurence thought. The inn looked like a low dive. Not a place Miss Deeping would be comfortable. Or not a place in which *he* would be comfortable seeing her, perhaps. He silently admitted it was more the latter. She seemed up for anything. "The bench?" he suggested. There was a wooden seat under a tree at the side of the yard.

Merlin gave his captive a shove toward it.

"Lemme go. You got no right to maul me about."

"I am associated with the Duke of Tereford," replied Merlin.

Laurence liked that. Associated, indeed. He doubted Tereford would put it that way. Merlin was shameless. But it worked. This Ned Horton slumped onto the bench and sulked. Water dripped down his face. He swiped a hand through his sodden hair. "Got no call to push me about," he muttered. He gave an exaggerated shudder at the cold.

"We just have a few questions," said Miss Deeping, settling at the opposite end.

"If you was to buy me a drink or two," Horton began.

"No more drinks," said Merlin. "You're half-sprung as it is."

"Not nearly half," said Horton, with a glint of humor in his rheumy eyes.

"Well, we shan't be giving you any more."

Merlin was rude to everyone, Laurence noted. Regardless of rank or degree. One needn't take it personally. Though a time might come when he did.

"We were wondering who lived at Lorne in the past," said Miss Deeping.

"There's been nobody there but me for years," Horton replied.

"How many years?"

"I dunno."

"Playing ignorant won't do you any good," said Merlin.

"I ain't playing anything! You're a right rudesby, you are."

"Five years?" asked Miss Deeping. "Ten?"

She was utterly assured and not to be diverted, Laurence saw. There seemed no end to the facets of this fascinating young lady. And all of them were intrepid.

"Six, I reckon," said Horton sullenly. "Before I was thrown out like a load of garbage."

"The duke gave you a hundred pounds," said Merlin. "That'd set you up all right, if you weren't drinking it away."

Miss Deeping made a calming gesture. "Who hired you originally?" she asked Horton.

He squinted at her. "Originally?"

"When you first started at Lorne."

"Oh, that was years back. I was naught but a lad."

"And hired by?"

"The stableman who worked for old Mr. Cantrell." Horton pulled his sleeve across his running nose.

Charlotte knew *Cantrell* was the duke's family name. This must have been some relative of the previous incumbent.

"A dreadful creature he was, old Cantrell," Horton went on. "All yellow-like, and wrinkled as a prune. Lord knows how old. No teeth to speak of, and you kept thinking the tip of his nose would meet up with his chin when he talked. Some fools in the village claimed he was a wizard. On account of how he looked and his carved devils."

"His what?" Charlotte thought she couldn't have heard him correctly.

"The house was full of heathen idols," Horton continued. He grimaced. "The old man begrudged us every cent of our wages. Getting paid was a rare trial, I'll tell you. And then he laid out piles of blunt for outlandish foreign statues. Horrible creatures with staring eyes and too many arms. I wouldn't go beyond the kitchen for fear of them dark fiends."

"I'm sure they were not devils," said Charlotte. "Perhaps they were foreign deities?"

"Heathen altars," Norton insisted, contradicting his claim never to have gone beyond the kitchen. "It was a scandal." He shuddered, but with a hint of enjoyment. "They're all gone now," he added. "And good riddance to them."

"Where did they go?" asked Glendarvon.

Charlotte preferred to do the questioning herself. But she did wonder the same. There was no sign of such items at Lorne now.

"I dunno," said Horton. "I didn't *want* to know about that heathenish trash."

Charlotte suspected he knew more than he realized. She decided to back up a little, while noting that they should look over what remained at Lorne to see if there were any signs of these items. She was sure Cecelia wouldn't mind. She'd probably already begun an inventory. "So old Mr. Cantrell was living at Lorne for a long time?" she asked.

"Long as anybody could remember." Horton scratched at his armpit. "I recollect now. Somebody said the duke was his cousin. The old duke, that would be. Not this present one." Horton looked bitter.

"And then Mr. Cantrell died," said Charlotte.

"Had to, didn't he?" answered Horton. "We all come to it, and he weren't no wizard after all. In the end."

"And his household dispersed."

"They what?"

"His servants left," Charlotte clarified.

"What else were they supposed to do?"

Charlotte wondered if one of them might have hidden the ring in the stables before they were turned out. But why would they? It was easily portable.

"*You* stayed on," said Merlin. His aggressive tone was not helpful.

"Somebody had to look after the place. The stableman died the year before Cantrell. And there was two horses to care for."

"How did you manage—" Merlin began.

"But what happened to the, er, idols?" Glendarvon repeated at the same time.

"The old man's nephew came snooping around," said Horton. "Well, he said he was his nephew. I never thought he was. He wasn't near old enough, for one thing."

"What was his name?" asked Charlotte.

"He didn't give it to *me*. He brought a wagon and went off with all the foreign bits. We was all glad to see the back of them."

"What did he look like?"

"A toff." Horton scratched again. "And a hard man. Who didn't want to be bothered with questions."

"So he asked you to stay on at Lorne?"

Horton looked furtive. "He left a bit of money for upkeep, like. Everybody else was gone. I stayed."

"For years," Merlin pointed out. "A 'bit of money' wouldn't cover that."

"He sent more." Horton looked aggrieved. "Never more than a pittance, you understand. And not regular."

"Enough to keep you in drink, it seems," said Merlin.

Horton glowered at him.

"Where did the payments come from?" asked Charlotte.

"Out of the air, far as I could tell," replied the man grumpily. "I'd walk into the stable…"

"Drunk from the pub," put in Merlin.

Charlotte made a slashing gesture. She really wished Merlin would keep quiet. As the marquess was doing, surprisingly. "Do go on, Mr. Horton," she said.

"After a companionable evening," said Horton sulkily. "And there'd be an envelope lying on the table."

"With no letter or address?"

He shook his head.

"So you just assumed it was this nephew who'd sent it."

"Who else would it be?"

That was a good question. Charlotte made a note to ask Cecelia if there was any record of the estate having sent money. "Did old Mr. Cantrell have regular visitors?" she asked.

"There weren't nothing regular about him," Horton responded, clearly thinking he'd made a joke. When no one laughed, he muttered, "Nobody wanted to visit the likes of him."

This was taking them no closer to the enigma of the ring. "About the fire," she began.

"I never set it! They're liars who says I did."

"I expect it was an accident."

"There weren't no accident," Horton insisted. "I went off to have a drink as usual. And when I came back, the whole wing was aflame."

"How much had you drunk before you left?" Merlin asked.

"Naught. To speak of."

"Are you ever sober?"

"You can be damned," muttered Horton.

Charlotte considered for a moment, then came to a decision. She gave Merlin a signal. He frowned. She nodded more emphatically. Slowly, reluctantly, he took the ring from his pocket.

"Have you ever seen this?" she asked Horton as he showed it.

"Eh? What's that? I didn't steal nothing!"

"I am not accusing you. We have been trying to find out more about this. It was found in the ashes at Lorne."

"*I* found it," declared Merlin. He glared as if she'd said something offensive.

"I don't know nothing about that," Horton said. "I've never seen it. I didn't put it there."

"May I look at that?" asked Glendarvon. Charlotte started. Engrossed in her questions, she'd nearly forgotten he was there. Now the sense of his presence came flooding back in a flutter like feathery wings in her chest. She turned. The marquess was staring at the ring in consternation. He looked pale.

⁓

Laurence gazed at the object Merlin held. It was a gold circle with a large blue stone, partly deformed by heat. A curve of the design had sent a jolt through him, and now he couldn't look away from the jewel. He held out a hand.

Merlin scowled at him. After a long moment, the man handed it over.

Laurence turned the piece to look at every angle. It

was somewhat misshapen, but the decorations carved into the gold were disturbingly familiar. His innards tilted and dipped. A wave of dizziness passed over him.

"What is it?" asked Miss Deeping.

He hardly dared put it into words. Why was this happening? Why was the past rising again when he had so thoroughly buried it? He didn't want to speak. But her dark eyes drew him out. "This…resembles a missing family heirloom," he said finally. "Part of a set of sapphires. The ring has been gone since…for more than twenty years."

"What?"

"I can't be absolutely sure." He must be wrong, Laurence thought. How could it be? This made no sense. And yet on some deep level, he knew he was right. "I would have to compare it to the rest."

"More than twenty years?" repeated Miss Deeping.

He gazed into her eyes and saw she understood the implications. Though his throat was tight, he couldn't stop the words. "My mother used to wear it."

"And…afterward, it had disappeared?" Miss Deeping asked.

She didn't mention his parents' deaths before Merlin and Horton. He was grateful for that. "The timing is not clear." There had been much else to think about, and he had been a child. But he didn't think the ring had been seen since the murders. Shaken, he pushed the thing away. Merlin snatched it back.

"I never saw it before," repeated Horton. "It has nothing to do with me. You can't say it does."

Miss Deeping turned to him. "You're certain you didn't see it at Lorne? A guest wearing it, perhaps? When they came to the stable for their horse?"

"Never in my life. I swear it."

Merlin slipped the jewel into his pocket again. Laurence felt both relief and regret to have it out of sight.

"Very well," said Miss Deeping. "I think that's all for now, Horton."

"All of what?" The man looked from one of them to the others.

"The questions. Thank you for your help."

Horton seemed equally bewildered by the thanks and the idea that he had been helpful. At a push from Merlin, he lurched to his feet.

"Get on, then," said Merlin.

Horton walked away. At the door of the inn, he paused to frown at them, then disappeared inside.

"We should see if the ring matches the Glendarvon jewels," Miss Deeping said then.

Laurence was battling internal upheaval. A memory of his mother's hand with just such a ring on it had flashed before him, rousing sadness, fear, disbelief. He felt nearly ill with the mixture. "I must be mistaken," he managed.

"I expect you are," said Merlin. "And you're not getting the ring away from me with some wild story. Be sure of that."

"There's no question of—" began Miss Deeping.

"It's worth a great deal of money," Merlin interrupted. He glared at Laurence. "Why would your family heirloom be in the ashes at Lorne? Eh, answer me that!"

"That is the puzzle," said Miss Deeping.

"It wouldn't be," said Laurence. Partly he longed to examine the ring more closely, and partly he never wanted to see it again.

"Your home is not too far from Lorne, is it?" asked Miss Deeping.

Laurence visualized the map. He hadn't noticed the angles before. The duke's shabby property was much nearer to his estate than the Deepings' house. "No." The word felt comprehensive, denying all manner of things.

"We should make a visit and compare the jewels."

"You're thinking he set the fire?" asked Merlin. When they gaped at him, he added, "He claims the ring's his."

"And has been missing for many years," replied Miss Deeping.

"We've only his word for that. Maybe he dropped it when he was burning down the stables."

The accusation was too ridiculous for outrage. And Miss Deeping was gazing into Laurence's eyes. Her expression was warmly sympathetic and inquiring. Laurence shook his head to try to clear it. "I did not burn Lorne," he said.

"Of course not," said Miss Deeping. "But if the ring is what you think, that is extremely curious. We must verify the connection."

Laurence was shaking his head even harder well before she finished. He wouldn't. He couldn't.

Miss Deeping's calm logic overcame every hesitation. She didn't argue. She simply reasoned her way forward like an inevitability. And somehow it was decided that they would undertake an expedition to his house and make the comparison, even though Laurence was reluctant and Merlin offensive.

Laurence followed the gig back to the Deeping house in a daze. How had a simple morning ride turned into a fiasco?

❦

Handling the reins, Charlotte acknowledged that this was the opening she'd been looking for into the mystery of the murders. As well as being exceedingly interesting. And she had not broken her promise. She had not asked. A way had dropped into her hands. Literally. Stanley couldn't say that was her fault.

She glanced back at the marquess, riding behind the gig. She was sorry to see him so uneasy. But the ring existed. It would not go away. Surely it would prey on his mind if he didn't find out more about this mystery?

They reached home by three in the afternoon. Glendarvon dismounted in the stable yard and left his horse to the grooms, striding away as if pursued. Charlotte watched him disappear in the direction of the garden and thought she would look for him there in a bit. "Perhaps I should take the ring," she said to Merlin as they stepped down from the gig.

He put a protective hand over his pocket. "No! You won't cut me out of this investigation. I'm the one who found it."

He seemed fixated on that fact. "I only thought..."

"No," Merlin repeated. He glared at her.

Charlotte abandoned the subject. Leaving Merlin to skulk off, she went inside to remove her bonnet and cloak. A maid was at her bedchamber door almost immediately. "Mrs. Deeping says can you come down," the girl said. "There's a visitor."

Charlotte was glad to hear it. Her mother couldn't scold her for going off to Leicester in front of a caller. Downstairs, she found Cecelia sitting in the drawing room with Mama. "There you are," said the latter, impatience clear in her tone. Charlotte greeted her friend and sat down.

"James couldn't bear to miss out any longer," the duchess

said. "He's gone off with Henry and the others to buy a hunter."

"Oh, good. I'm sorry I wasn't here when you arrived."

Her mother rose. "Please excuse me, Your Grace," she said. "I must speak to the cook." With a fulminating glance at Charlotte, she went out.

"Are you in your mother's black books?" Cecelia asked with a smile.

Charlotte nodded. "But I can't be sorry. I have so much to tell you, Cecelia!" She plunged into the story of her expedition to Leicester.

Cecelia was wide-eyed when she had finished. "Heathen idols? We haven't found anything like that at Lorne."

"They were all taken away by this nephew apparently. Do you have any idea who that might be?"

The duchess shook her head. "We had no communications about Lorne. I don't think he can be a Cantrell. Perhaps he is connected to the old man's mother."

"And was secretive because he had no right to his possessions?"

Cecelia shrugged. "Perhaps. We found no will." She frowned. "But how did this ring get to Lorne? Assuming it is Glendarvon's lost heirloom."

"One good question among many," Charlotte replied.

"I don't know of any connection between the families."

"There's a great deal to be learned."

"But how?"

"Step by step, piece by piece," replied Charlotte. "That is the way of puzzles. We will begin by checking the ring." And whatever else she could discover at the place where the murders had occurred.

"Well, you are not going to Glendarvon's house without me," Cecelia replied.

"You wish to come?"

"Of course I do!"

Charlotte was always glad of Cecelia's company, but in this case, her friend's presence would also make the arrangements much easier. Her mother would not object to an outing with the duchess.

"When is it to be?"

"Wednesday. When there is no hunt being held."

"Splendid." Cecelia looked blank. "Ah, I have no carriage or riding horse here." She frowned. "I don't believe I have ever had that problem before. How horribly spoiled I am."

"We will use ours," said Charlotte. "We can come to Lorne and fetch you. And Merlin."

"Oh, is he to come?" Cecelia smiled. "Of course he is."

"As he continually points out, he found the ring. He seems to think that makes him the center of this endeavor."

"We really must find some suitable occupation for that man."

Charlotte wondered if such a thing existed. She was glad it wasn't her task to find out.

Ten

THE PARTY THAT SET OUT FOR LAURENCE'S HOME EARLY in the morning on Wednesday was even larger than he'd expected, especially since he hadn't actually invited anyone. He'd never hosted guests and certainly never held a house party at his estate. It wasn't a jolly place.

He might have given grudging approval. He didn't recall. His thoughts had been a bit jumbled since his sight of that damaged ring. Odd snippets of memory kept surfacing and then dissolving like rising smoke. His nights had been disturbed, though he couldn't remember any details from the dreams that brought him surging up, heart pounding.

Here he was, however, riding beside the Duke of Tereford, who was mounted on his new hunter. Ranger had taken a dislike to the gelding for some reason, and they proceeded in an uneasy truce, broken by occasional snaps of equine teeth. Henry Deeping was on the duke's other side. Laurence was glad of that because the two men were friends and kept up an amiable flow of conversation. Beyond Henry was Cecil, who had discovered their purpose and inserted himself into the group so smoothly that Laurence couldn't quite remember how it had happened. A carriage followed with Miss Deeping, the duchess, and Merlin. Merlin hadn't wanted to borrow a horse. With another man, Laurence might have suspected a desire to flirt with the ladies, but Merlin had never shown any signs of that. Perhaps he was unused to riding and didn't care for four hours on horseback.

Laurence's home was on the eastern side of Rutland,

nearly to Lincolnshire and north of the famous Burghley House. It had been decided that they would stay the night. By somebody. The look Mrs. Deeping had given Laurence when this was announced had worried him. She had suspicions or expectations, or both, and she clearly had not been convinced by their story that the Terefords wished to learn more about the neighborhood of Lorne. At least he had been able to send a groom riding cross-country to warn his housekeeper of the visit. She would have skinned him otherwise. He wondered what the staff thought of this unprecedented occasion.

The day was fine, though with a sharp wind. The Deepings and the duke chatted as they navigated a tangle of lanes, Cecil simply bursting with savoir faire. Laurence chimed in often enough to be sociable, he thought. His mind kept drifting off—to the ordeal ahead, to Miss Deeping and what she might be thinking, to the hazy reaches of the distant past.

They topped a small rise just after noon and started down into the shallow valley that held his estate. The house was visible in the distance, and Laurence felt a mixture of regret and anxiety rise in him. As they drew near, he tried to see the place as a stranger would—Miss Deeping, for example. It wasn't ancient. His great-grandfather had married an heiress and used her magnificent dowry to pull down the old Glendarvon home and build a new one of pale stone with a grand columned entry. Unusually, its two wings jutted out from the central block at a slant. A school friend had compared the resulting shape to open arms welcoming visitors. Laurence hadn't been able to agree.

The building and its grounds were well-kept. He'd learned

careful management from his succession of guardians. There was no wall around the property. A band of trees marked the boundary of the gardens, mostly bare at this time of year.

Laurence drew ahead as they rode down the drive, and by the time the carriage pulled up, he had opened the front door and stood ready to welcome the whole party. The housekeeper stood at his side, and he was aware of other servants observing from various vantage points and obviously brimming with curiosity. The ladies were attracting particular attention. His staff was likely speculating about these guests.

There was an organized bustle as they were conducted to their rooms and given a chance to freshen up. The party then gathered in the dining room, where an array of cold meat, fresh bread, and preserved fruit was set out with ale and wine.

"Are we going to get on with it?" asked Merlin, who stood at the edge of the group looking uncomfortable. When the others turned to look at him, he stared stubbornly back.

He was rude but right, Laurence decided. They had come on a specific errand. Everyone was wondering. They might as well get on with it. With a nod, he left them and went to the estate office at the near end of the east wing. He closed and latched the door, not caring to be observed even by such trustworthy guests, and walked over to the inner wall of shelves. When he pressed one of the carved rosettes, there was a click, and a section of shelves shifted. He pulled it open on silent hinges, revealing a locked iron door. This was the estate's strong room, where valuables were kept. Taking out a ring of keys that never left him, Laurence undid three locks, one after another. He then pushed a lever and opened the heavy door. Behind it was a fortified closet the width and breadth of his extended arms.

Metal shelves lined the three walls, rising to the ceiling well above his head. They held everything deemed too precious to leave sitting out in his house, along with the cash he kept on hand for unexpected expenses.

He picked out a smaller key on his ring and unlocked a metal box that sat on a shelf at chest level. He removed a velvet-covered jewel case, backed out, refastened the strong room door, and restored the office to its previous condition.

Carrying the case back to the dining room, Laurence found his steps slowing as he neared the waiting guests. His placid existence rested on *not* thinking about the tragedy of his childhood. It was the easier and more sensible course. Why dwell on what he could not change? Now the past threatened to rear up, and he was being pulled along despite a rising tide of reluctance. Why hadn't he refused this visit? He might have said he'd made a mistake about the ring. Miss Deeping would have been disappointed if he had, he realized. And he disliked the idea of disappointing her.

Still, when everyone looked at him as he entered the dining room, Laurence's empty stomach roiled. It was like facing a blind jump, he told himself. One had to gather resolution, lean in, and go. He set the jewel case on the table that held the remains of their luncheon and flipped it open.

A gold-and-sapphire necklace was spread out within, flanked by earrings and a heavy bracelet. The golden settings were ornamented by fanciful traceries. The gems glinted blue in the sunlight from the windows.

"Let us compare the ring," said Miss Deeping. She gazed at Merlin.

With his usual reluctance, the man took the piece from his pocket. He didn't seem to want to let it go, but he finally set it beside the necklace. There was a space for it, Laurence noted. The ring settled into a small depression in the velvet.

Everyone moved closer and bent over to look.

Laurence hardly needed to. The design was the same. There couldn't really be any doubt. This was the ring that had been missing for so long. Possibly—very likely—it had been taken from his mother's hand after she'd been killed. He swayed a little and stepped back to hide it.

"They look the same," said Miss Deeping.

"Any bit of jewelry might have a few curlicues," replied Merlin.

"This branch pattern is distinctive," she replied, pointing to a detail on the ring and then the necklace.

"It's mistletoe," said Laurence. His own voice sounded far away. "It's on our crest."

"That could be any sort of plant," said Merlin.

"Not really," replied the Duke of Tereford.

Henry Deeping walked over to the fireplace and examined the coat of arms carved into the mantel. "Here it is again," he said. "It looks the same."

"Well, and what if it does?" snapped Merlin. "What difference does it make? The ring has been lost for years. Nobody looked for it."

"They did, though," Laurence couldn't help but say. There had been succeeding inquiries, and the ring had become more prominent as the hopes of catching the murderer waned. "They even hired a Bow Street runner. More than one, I think." He had been a child and not really consulted.

"A what?" asked Merlin.

Laurence turned away, wishing he'd kept quiet. He didn't want to talk about this.

"The Bow Street runners investigate crimes for magistrates," said Miss Deeping. "Their headquarters are in London, but they respond to requests from around the country."

"This is a profession?" asked Merlin.

"A job, at any rate," said Cecil Deeping.

"They have a good deal of experience," said Miss Deeping. She was diverting attention from his unease, Laurence realized. He was grateful. "And a close relationship with the Home Office," she continued. "With more financial resources at their disposal than local people."

"How do you know all this?" asked the duchess. She looked amused.

"When I was younger, I thought...but of course no women are involved in the runners."

"They are paid to solve crimes?" asked Merlin.

"Not precisely," said the duke. "There is an informal agreement with the treasury. The government can use the runners as they think necessary, particularly for threats to national security and social disorder."

"Indeed?" Merlin looked fascinated.

"But anyone can engage them," said Miss Deeping. "One reports the crime, and the runners set to work."

"Most victims are expected to pay the expenses of the investigation and to offer a small reward for information as well," said Tereford.

"And your family did all this for a ring?" Merlin asked Laurence.

And here it was, the moment Laurence had dreaded since this process had begun. Miss Deeping and the Terefords gazed at him sympathetically. The others looked puzzled. The story had to come out. It wasn't even a secret. Only forgotten after more than two decades. Why couldn't it have remained forgotten? "You tell them," he said to Miss Deeping, and walked out.

❧

Charlotte's hand went out automatically. But he was gone.

She turned to find her brothers' dark eyes on her. She'd been surprised when Cecil joined this expedition. She saw now that both of them had come to watch over her. As if she needed supervision!

"What do you know that we don't?" asked Cecil. "And *why* do you? What's going on?"

"That ring disappeared when Lord Glendarvon's parents were murdered," she said.

"Murdered!" exclaimed Merlin. "By whom?"

"No one knows," said Charlotte. "It is a mystery."

Cecil looked appalled. Henry glanced at Tereford as if seeking corroboration. The duke nodded.

"So you see, it is more than a simple piece of jewelry," Charlotte added. "The murderer probably dropped it at Lorne."

Cecil's mouth fell open. Merlin's eyes narrowed. "That is a large logical leap," said the duke.

"It seems obvious to me," Charlotte replied.

"The tragedy occurred more than twenty years ago," Cecelia said. "Time for a good deal to happen to a ring."

"There was no sign of it, even though it was searched for. I think the killer had it."

"Killer!" exclaimed Merlin. "We are searching for a killer?" He sounded more excited than apprehensive.

"No, you are not," said Cecil. "Or *you* may be. I don't care. But not Charlotte. This is the outside of enough, Charlotte. You have no business—"

"*You* have no authority over me," she interrupted. She was tired of her brothers thinking they did.

"Mama and Papa will say the same when they hear about this."

"Going to tattle, are you?"

"This is not some childish prank." Cecil glared. "Don't be an idiot, Charlotte."

"I am not an idiot!"

"You don't have any business chasing murderers."

Charlotte saw that Henry and the Terefords agreed with him. They thought she should back away from the inquiry. Merlin was avid, but he was a chancy ally. More than ever, she wished for her school friends. They would understand.

"Perhaps we should return home today rather than lingering," said Henry.

"Absolutely," said Cecil. "We should go immediately."

Charlotte turned away and left by the same door Glendarvon had used.

She rushed through the house, taking turns when they offered, meaning to lose herself so she couldn't be hustled back to the carriage. The rooms were immaculately kept and richly decorated in the style of the previous century. It looked as if one of Glendarvon's forebears had furnished the place and little had been changed since. The stiff decor didn't seem to suit him. It was more like a museum than a home.

She came upon a housemaid dusting porcelain figurines

from a cabinet. "Do you know where his lordship has gone?" Charlotte asked her.

"To the old lord's room," the girl said. She gazed at Charlotte as if cataloging every detail of her appearance.

"Where is that?"

The girl turned to point.

Following her directions, Charlotte went upstairs and along a carpeted corridor. A door was ajar at the end. She paused to listen, but there was no sound. Walking up to look in, she found the marquess standing in the center of a tapestry-hung bedchamber. He was very still. His face was blank, his hands hanging loose at his sides.

"I never come here," he said. He seemed unsurprised by her appearance, as if they had agreed to meet at this moment. "My room is at the far end of the south wing."

She moved farther in and looked around. She couldn't help but be curious.

"All my father's personal things were taken away. I only kept..." He held up a heart-shaped locket, the gold chain trailing from his fingers. Charlotte wondered if he had taken it from his pocket or around his neck.

He opened it. Inside were two miniatures, a man and a woman facing each other. Charlotte wanted to look more closely, but she didn't wish to intrude.

As if he understood her wish, he handed the locket to her. Charlotte gazed at the small faces in the frames. The marquess resembled his father. They had the same light-brown hair and square jaws. The previous lord seemed to be another handsome large man who looked as if he belonged outdoors in the saddle. Glendarvon's mother was different. Her skin was pale, her hair raven-black. She was very beautiful in a fiercely elegant way. And the painter had caught a unique expression in the tiny image. Charlotte tried to define it. The phrase that came to her was wistful defiance. She wondered what had made the woman stare out so stubbornly.

"They hadn't had portraits done for the gallery before they were killed," Glendarvon said. "So this is the only image that…remains."

He was holding out his hand. Charlotte returned the locket.

He turned away and stood gazing at the wardrobe against the wall on the right.

A frisson of dread went up Charlotte's spine. "This isn't where…?"

"I was shut in that wardrobe when it happened," he said, nodding at the large cupboard.

"*That* one?"

He nodded. "I don't remember. Not really. Not very much. Only now and then, in a closed dark space, I will be overcome with horror. And…paralyzed with fear. I literally cannot move in those moments. Not until I fight it off." He blinked, grimaced, and turned his back on the wardrobe with a gesture of rejection. "I should not have mentioned that. I beg your pardon."

"No, you don't."

"What?"

"You do not beg my pardon for telling me something so intimate and…raw."

He gazed at her, the pain in his blue eyes diluted by surprise.

"Why haven't you gotten rid of it?" Charlotte asked fiercely.

"The…"

"You could have it taken away. Better yet, you could chop it to pieces." Charlotte walked over and kicked the wardrobe. "You could send for an ax right now."

"I…I didn't think of that. For some reason."

"Two axes," she suggested. "I'll help you."

A laugh burst from him. "Would you really? I believe you would."

"Of course I would! It would be a pleasure." Charlotte went to the hearth and hefted the fireplace poker. "Shall I give it a few preliminary bashes?"

He stared at her as if he'd never fully seen her before. Charlotte's cheeks grew hot under that marveling gaze. When he looked away, it felt like a loss. "I prefer never to come to these rooms or think of that time," he said.

"But doesn't that make it difficult to live here?"

"How could it be otherwise?"

"It's your home," Charlotte began.

The marquess walked over to the window and looked out at the sere November landscape. "It never has been that," he said. "Not that I can remember, at any rate. I care for the place, preserve it for the future. That's my duty, and all I can manage."

Gazing at his back, those broad shoulders and powerful limbs, the uneasy set of his head, Charlotte felt an aching weight of sadness. He had no home, at heart. How could he exist that way? She couldn't imagine emptiness where the sense of home should dwell. Feeling a sudden sharp longing to help, she set the poker aside. "If you could find the murderer—"

"That wouldn't change anything," he said.

"The person responsible would be brought to justice."

The marquess turned to face her again. "Which wouldn't bring anyone back."

"No. But it might be a clear ending. And new beginning." Charlotte didn't mention the deep itch to puzzle out the truth, the urge to solve the mystery. But she felt them.

"I don't think that's possible," he said. "It's been too long. And many people looked long and hard at the time but found nothing."

"Now we have the ring," Charlotte reminded him.

Glendarvon looked goaded and bewildered. "That damnable ring!"

"Why do you say that?" It was an obvious clue. A spot to pick at until the tangle started to unravel.

"It's brought everything back. I suppose they're all gossiping about my parents in the dining room."

Charlotte couldn't promise they weren't.

"I never had to endure much of that because I was so young," he went on. "But I heard about it later. The sensation sweeping across society, the wild rumors and cruel innuendos. My guardians only mentioned it in whispers."

"So an evil man's shadow lies over your whole life," said Charlotte.

He blinked at her and frowned.

"I said 'man' because that is most likely, I think."

"It *was* a man," said the marquess.

Charlotte watched his expression shift from surprise at his own words to bewilderment. "You sounded certain," she said finally. "What made you say so?"

"I...I heard a voice." He shook his head. "Did I? I don't know. But I feel I'm right." He pushed a hand through his hair. "Without any basis whatsoever."

Charlotte ignored the last sentence. "Perhaps there are other bits you can recall if you try," she dared to suggest. "We could piece them together to find the culprit."

"That…person is long gone. He may even be dead."

"Perhaps." Charlotte knew the mystery might never be solved. That would be frustrating.

"Why do you want to poke about in my lamentable history?"

It wasn't only the mystery, Charlotte realized. Perhaps it wasn't even chiefly the mystery. She wanted to help him. More than she'd wanted almost anything else in her entire life. And she thought shedding light on the thing he'd pushed away for so long might clear out a tainted place and make it new and clean. She wasn't sure how to say any of this without offending him. "If you knew the truth, you might find it easier to live here," she tried.

Glendarvon frowned.

"It wouldn't be better, but nothing would be hidden. You would have done all you could."

"You think I haven't done enough? That I'm a coward, perhaps?" His voice was stiff.

"Nothing of the kind! I think a task like this needs allies." The sort she'd had with her school friends, Charlotte thought. And he'd never had.

"That is why everyone came here? Tereford?"

"Oh no. They want to drop the matter entirely. Well, except for Merlin, but he doesn't count."

"They know it is hopeless."

"They think examining a murder is beyond my ability," she replied. And immediately regretted using that word. He didn't need to be reminded of the deaths.

He gazed at her. "Or that it might be dangerous?"

"I am very careful."

Laurence didn't think she was, actually. "*I* am careful," he replied. "*You* are intrepid." Far more than he was, he feared. She'd waved that poker like a warrior of old. It had been astonishing.

"And you think a woman shouldn't be?" she demanded.

Laurence hadn't realized dark eyes could burn so tempestuously. They ignited something in him. "Would you really have bashed the wardrobe?"

"Of course." She looked at the poker and raised her eyebrows as if offering to show him.

The idea made the weight of the thing less oppressive. Her bright presence in this room altered its grim atmosphere. "What do you propose we do?"

"Look for any connections your family has with Lorne," she replied promptly. "See if there is anything suggestive in its history. And—if you will—try to dig out more bits lurking in your memory."

He had always avoided doing that, Laurence acknowledged. It had felt perilous. But with Miss Charlotte Deeping at his side…perhaps possible? She made the world feel like a different place. He took a deep breath, and another. If they did this, they would have to spend a great deal of time together. Laurence nodded. He wanted more of her. Much more.

"You agree?" Her lips parted in amazement.

Such tantalizing lips, Laurence thought. "I do."

Her delighted smile thrilled him. She looked as if she'd been given a longed-for gift, which sent all his reservations flying. She stepped closer, holding out a hand. Laurence clasped it. Her fingers were warm and strong in his. She came nearer. He gazed down at her and lost himself in the depths of her eyes. Her lips parted as if to speak, or perhaps for something else. A shy invitation. He bent his head. She raised her chin.

And they were interrupted by a knock on the half-open door.

Laurence dropped her hand and turned to see his housekeeper standing there, looking scandalized at finding them in a bedchamber alone. "People are asking for you, my lord," she said. "And the lady."

"Of course," said Laurence. "I was just showing Miss Deeping…" He trailed off. Fortunately, none of his current servants knew the significance of the wardrobe. His guardians had pensioned off the staff of that bygone time.

"The tapestries," Miss Deeping put in. "I am interested in old-fashioned weaving techniques."

"Indeed, miss." She didn't sound convinced. Laurence didn't blame her, though he admired Miss Deeping's quick wit.

"We should go back to the dining room," he said.

They did so, to find his other guests waiting with varying degrees of impatience. He had no idea what to say to them. And no need to wonder, he discovered, as Miss Deeping took charge.

"You will want to return your family jewelry to safety," she said to him.

This did need to be done, and Laurence was glad to leave

with the velvet case. When he returned from the strong room, he found disputes in progress, nearly as loud as the Deeping dinner table and oddly shocking in his usually silent home.

First, Merlin had claimed custody of the ring as its finder, again. Miss Deeping wanted to take it, for reasons he now understood. "Since it is part of my family's heritage, I would be happy to pay you for it," Laurence said to Merlin.

The man glared at him. "You can't use your money to cut me out." He held one hand cupped over his waistcoat pocket, where the ring currently resided.

"Out of what?" Laurence asked.

"I intend to be part of the investigation."

"There is not going to be any—" began Cecil Deeping.

"Or simply do it myself," Merlin interrupted. "Yes, that's better. None of you need to worry about the matter. I will find out the truth, and then His Grace can give me a good recommendation."

"Recommendation?" Laurence looked around to see if any of the others understood this. None appeared to, Tereford least of all.

"To the Bow Street runners," Merlin said. He looked at the duke. "I'm certain he is acquainted with any number of magistrates and men high up in the government."

Tereford's wry expression admitted as much. Henry Deeping grinned at him.

"And he is eager to find me a position," Merlin added slyly. "Elsewhere." The man's smile was practically feral.

"You want me to recommend a devious schemer?" asked Tereford.

"I suppose those qualities would be useful for a Bow Street runner," said the duchess.

The Terefords exchanged a communicative gaze. Laurence found himself doing the same with Miss Deeping. Neither of them had counted on Merlin's active participation, he concluded.

"Seems reasonable," said Cecil Deeping. "No need for you to bother with all this then, Charlotte. We can head home."

The look Cecil received in response might have daunted a lesser man. Laurence was glad it was not directed at him.

And so began the second part of the argument. The Deeping brothers wished to leave immediately. Their sister emphatically did not. The Terefords seemed undecided, the duchess pointing out that they could scarcely make it back before dark. Merlin expressed a wish to stay, and then wandered out of the room. Laurence suspected he meant to snoop around the house in his new persona as a budding Bow Street runner, looking for clues that did not exist.

"Riding back today would be hard on the horses," said Miss Deeping.

Her brother Henry seemed moved by this argument, but Cecil offered a bland society smile and moved closer to his sister. "Let us go for a stroll in the gardens," he said to her.

"It's too cold," she replied.

"You like a bracing walk."

"I have already had a bracing carriage ride. I don't require any more air."

"We will move slowly. Just to clear out the cobwebs."

"What cobwebs are those, Cecil? Are you impugning Glendarvon's housekeeper?"

"Perish the thought! I spoke of inner cobwebs only."

"I haven't any of those," replied his sister.

"Ah, but I do." He took her arm.

Miss Deeping let him, and Cecil led her away. Laurence wouldn't have laid odds on him convincing her, however. They looked equally obstinate.

The rest of the party dispersed to their rooms, and Laurence wondered how he would entertain them through dinner and the evening that stretched ahead. It felt as if it would be very long. And loud.

Eleven

THE DUKE OF TEREFORD JOINED THE NEXT HUNT ON HIS new Deeping mount. As the hounds set off and the riders followed in a milling crowd, he felt a surge of exhilaration. It had been too long since he'd indulged in one of his favorite sporting activities. Marriage was of course a delight, but he was accustomed to bouts of hard physical effort, and he realized as he pounded across a stubbled field that he had been missing them.

"You and Titus seem to be doing well together," called Stanley Deeping. He had taken great care to match Tereford with a horse that would suit him.

"Splendidly," the duke replied. They came up to the hedge surrounding the field and sailed over it. Tereford laughed exultantly.

The terrain offered all the challenges one could desire, and the fox was wily, leading them on a merry chase. The duke soon suspected he was teasing the hounds, staying just out of reach and tantalizing them into thorns and mire. He rather admired that.

The hunters had slid down the side of a small ravine and were clambering up the opposite slope when sideways movement caught the duke's eye. A stone flew past, hurtling into the melee of straining hocks and hooves. It struck the head of a rider on his right. The man reeled at the blow. His mount stumbled at the unexpected pull on the reins, barely staying on its feet.

Tereford yanked at his own reins and urged Titus on with

his knees, turning to aid the fellow. It was Glendarvon, he found when he reached him. He looked dazed.

This sort of thing did happen. The mass of thundering hooves threw up all sorts of bits along with mud and sod, and hunters had been hurt by flying objects. Fleetingly, Tereford thought the angle seemed wrong. The stone—a rather large one—had whizzed in from the side rather than emerging from the mob galloping ahead. But there might have been a rider out of sight over there. He hadn't been looking.

There was no time to think about it. Glendarvon was woozy, bent over his horse's neck now, swaying, and other riders were coming up behind them, risking a pileup. Tereford needed to get him out of the way and then make certain he was all right. He reached for the other man's reins.

Glendarvon's horse snapped at Titus, who responded in kind, and added a sidling kick. They had never reconciled despite a long trek together to Glendarvon's home. "Do stop," said the duke. He grabbed for the reins again. Glendarvon's mount shied away.

Another rider pounded past them, shouting a question that was lost in the wind of his passage.

Tereford didn't wish to dismount. He would be in positive danger on foot. He urged Titus forward, leaned out as far as he could, fended off an attempted bite, and finally got hold of the loose reins. Glendarvon's horse tried to pull away. Tereford held him and, after a flurry of equine disputes, got the two animals headed up the ravine to a spot where the walls were too steep for riders. There, the duke got down. He secured the horses to separate saplings. Only then did he ease Glendarvon out of the saddle, sit him on the ground, and examine his injury.

The stone had glanced off the back of the marquess's head, where a lump was rising on his scalp. Fortunately, it had not struck his temple, which might well have been lethal.

Glendarvon muttered something. He raised a hand to his head and found the lump. "Ow!"

"Best not to touch it," said the duke. The wound wasn't bleeding, he noted. But the swelling was pronounced.

"What happened?"

"You were struck by a stone thrown up by the riders."

"Ah." Glendarvon blinked as if trying to get his eyes to focus. "Hurts."

"I am not surprised." The duke looked around. The last of the riders had passed. The ravine had gone quiet. He reviewed the countryside they'd passed through, departing from the master of the hunt's home and moving mainly south and east. "We should return to the Deepings," he said then. It was not too far, as well as being Glendarvon's lodging. Also he was not familiar with other houses in the neighborhood.

"I can go back on my own," replied the marquess. He appeared to be steadying.

"Nonsense."

"I don't want to spoil your hunt."

"There will be others."

"A stone." Glendarvon touched his head again. "Ow."

"Are you dizzy? Can you stand?"

"Of course." He did so, but stumbled upon reaching his feet. Tereford caught his arm and guided him over to his horse, which bared its teeth. "Ranger!" said Glendarvon.

The duke helped him mount up. "All right?"

"Perfectly," the other man lied. He raised a hand, then let it drop after fingering the bump on his head again.

Tereford climbed into the saddle, and they rode slowly side by side down the ravine to a flatter spot and over the side. Fortuitously, they came upon a lane going in the right direction and turned to amble along it. Even better, it was wide enough so their mounts could not reach each other and resume hostilities.

As time passed, Glendarvon sat straighter and looked more alert. "I've been struck by a spray of pebbles during a hunt," he said after a while. "But never anything like this."

"It was a rather large stone."

"Seems like it must have been a boulder, the way my head is pounding."

"I can imagine," said Tereford sympathetically.

"Piece of bad luck."

"Indeed."

Glendarvon's horse drifted toward Titus and shoved with his shoulder. "Ranger!" He slapped the horse's neck and guided him away. "I wonder why they dislike each other so much?"

"One of those unreasoning hatreds that arise from time to time," replied the duke. "No explaining them."

His companion turned to look at him. "Isn't there always a reason for hatred?"

"Usually, of course. But now and then, it is simply... instinctive." The duke shrugged. "In my experience."

Glendarvon shook his head, and then clearly regretted it. He raised a hand but managed to refrain from touching the lump on the back of his skull. "That track leads to the Deepings," he said then. "I recognize it."

"Good."

They turned onto the path, and not too long afterward came to a fenced paddock dotted with horses.

❧

Charlotte was out watching Rigel and the other foals frisking around their field. The youngsters had reached a tearing, tireless, bouncing stage that occasionally earned them a toothy reprimand from the mares. It was quite entertaining. She saw two riders approaching and recognized Glendarvon and Tereford. Surprised because the bulk of the hunt was still out, she walked over to the stable yard to see the marquess stumble and stagger when he dismounted. He gripped the saddle to stay upright. "What's wrong?" she asked.

"Nothing," he replied.

"That is obviously untrue."

"A small accident."

"Did you fall?" Charlotte automatically checked his horse for matching signs of injury.

"I did not!"

Charlotte looked to the duke, standing beside his mount as composed and polished as ever. She gave him a questioning look.

"He was struck in the head by a stone flung up during the hunt," Tereford said.

"In the head!"

"Don't fuss," said Glendarvon.

"I'll fuss if I like." Charlotte went over to take his arm. "Come inside. We'll send for the doctor."

"The doctor is completely unnecessary."

"Mama and I will be the judge of that."

"There is no need to bother Mrs. Deeping."

"She will certainly want to know."

❧

Charlotte led him off. They had both forgotten all about him, the duke noted. The moment they came together, the rest of the world became background. He didn't mind. He was more interested in the fact that their exchanges reminded him of the way he and Cecelia used to speak to each other before they were married.

Grooms were waiting to take the horses. Knowing there was no catching up to the hunt by this time, Tereford handed them over. Titus resided here for now, until Lorne had a stable again. The duke retrieved his old gig and drove off to the most dilapidated of the ducal properties they had inhabited so far.

Cecelia was at the writing desk surrounded by account books when he walked in, a familiar sight. "The builders say the stable will cost a bit more than they thought."

"As builders always seem to do."

She nodded. "And I think Merlin is quite serious about his Bow Street runner scheme. This morning he told me I should call him *Mr. Weldon*. When I expressed surprise, he said the runners wouldn't want an agent named after a wizard."

"Mightn't it be an advantage?"

"Mystical powers of perception?" Cecelia smiled.

As always, her smile went straight to Tereford's heart. He went over to drop a kiss on her lips, then urged her to the sofa, where they sat nestled together.

"Aren't you back early from the hunt? Not that I'm complaining."

"Glendarvon was hit in the head by a flying stone," the duke explained. "He was quite shaky, so I took him back to the Deepings."

"The blow was so serious? Is that common?"

"A good deal of mud and other bits are always thrown up. But this stone was rather large."

"It must have been to have stunned him."

The duke nodded. "And I thought the angle seemed odd," he said slowly. "It seemed to come from the side rather than the mob galloping ahead of us."

"You don't think someone could have thrown it?" Cecelia asked.

"What? No. Why would you say that?"

"Something in your tone. As if you were worried."

Tereford shook his head. "There must have been riders in that direction. I wasn't looking."

She nodded. "Well, I don't like the idea of missiles hurtling across the hunting field. I can't even ask you to take care, because how can one guard against a random accident?"

"An extremely rare one," he told her. "A bad fall is much more likely."

"Is that supposed to be reassuring? Because it is not."

"I am an expert rider."

"I know you are." She rested her head on his shoulder.

He pulled her closer. "What do you think about Glendarvon and your friend Miss Deeping?" he asked to pull her thoughts from accidents.

"They are quite taken with each other," Cecelia answered

without hesitation. "Though they don't quite know it yet. Perhaps."

"I begin to feel like Cupid, making matches wherever I go," the duke joked.

She raised her head and looked at him, a lovely smile playing over her perfect lips. "*You* making them?"

"Eros is a male, is he not?"

"I've always thought that very stupid."

"Have you?"

Cecelia nodded. "Women think far more about love and marriage than men do."

"I can't argue with that."

"A great many of them are fine archers, too."

"Not among the old Greeks or Romans, I suppose."

"Weren't there…" Cecelia frowned. "What were they called—Amazons—with bows?"

"I have heard that. But they were not matchmakers. From what I recall, they were far more likely to perforate a man in battle."

"A man trying to kill them."

"Indeed."

She nodded as if her point was proved. "Arrows aside, I think Glendarvon might do very well for Charlotte."

"Because?"

"Various practical reasons," Cecelia replied. "And also the way they speak to each other reminds me of our early days."

He looked down at her. "I was thinking that very thing not an hour ago."

"*I* noticed it days ago," she teased.

"Do you claim to be two steps ahead of me? As always."

"Not always," she answered with an impish grin. "Just… often?"

"But don't you think it is less so than last year? Or the years before that?"

Her expression grew serious. "Yes, James, I do." She laced her arms around his neck and drew him down for a lingering kiss.

৶৹

Laurence had a devil of a headache. He hadn't been in this much pain since he'd broken his arm falling from a tree at age twelve. And pain was worse when it was centered in one's head, he thought, though that probably wasn't true. The addition of muddled thoughts *was* worse though. Since the stunning blow on the hunting field, he felt as if things had been shaken loose in his mind. Ideas and emotions and memories wheeled through like a flock of birds flushed by a beater and fleeing in all directions.

The day was dragging. He hadn't wanted to lie in bed. Boredom seemed to increase the pounding in his skull. So he'd taken himself to a small parlor at the rear of the house. A cheerful fire burned there, and there were shelves of books. He found he was unable to read, however. It made the headache worse. He sat by the window and watched the horses graze in the paddock on the other side of the garden. The house was fairly empty as the other fellows were out in the field again.

The door opened, and Miss Deeping came in. She carried a tray. Laurence started to stand, but she shook her head. "I've brought you something," she said.

"How did you find me?"

"I have many sources of information." She set the tray on

a small table beside him. "This is willow-bark tea. It will help with the pain and is better for you than laudanum." She sat opposite him.

"And tastes horribly bitter, if I remember correctly."

"I've put some honey in it."

Laurence knew he had sounded sulky. He picked up the cup and drank some of the tea. It was indeed better than willow-bark concoctions he'd had in the past. He drank it. "Thank you."

"You're most welcome."

"I should not be fussing."

"A blow to the head is quite serious," Miss Deeping replied. "I've heard of a man who received one, insisted he was perfectly well, and then dropped dead the next day."

"What?"

"Which I'm sure will not happen to you," she added hurriedly. "The doctor said you would recover in a few days." She poured another cup from the teapot on the tray, added honey from a small pot.

Laurence drank it. "It is only a headache," he told them both.

"A wretched one, I expect."

She was very kind to have brewed him a remedy. And looked lovely in the sunshine slanting down from the window. His thoughts drifted off to the day they'd come so close to each other on the narrow path.

"I still don't quite see how this happened," she went on. "Earth and pebbles thrown up by horses' hooves would usually hit one face on."

"I suppose the stone bounced off a tree or some such thing." Her face held such bright intelligence, Laurence thought. Her form was spare but somehow more alluring than buxom curves. He was glad to be sitting here with her rather than galloping over the countryside after the hounds. That was surprising.

"Odd accidents do occur," she admitted. "Have you come here for a book?"

"I found I couldn't read." Laurence gestured at his head.

"I could read aloud to you," Miss Deeping offered, sounding more dutiful than enthusiastic.

"You're fond of that?"

"Not like my friend Sarah. I read to find things out. She devours any form of printed words and is happy to spend all day in a book."

"I am more in your camp."

Silence fell between them. Miss Deeping checked the small teapot and poured the last of the willow bark into his cup. Laurence picked it up and tried to settle his mind. The tea seemed to be taking hold. The pain was easing a little. He drank the last of it. "We should confer," he said. "We made a pact to dig into my history."

"Pact?" she repeated with a smile.

"What do you call it?"

"I like *pact*. But you need to rest."

"I'm wretchedly bored." The pain was definitely less.

"Well, I did have some thoughts," she said.

"What?"

"Do you know if there was any report by the investigators who looked into the murders?"

"No." He'd never tried to find this. That seemed strange to him now.

"We could look among your papers," she said. "And we

might try to speak to any of your servants who remember the…tragedy. Ask them about things that occurred around the same time."

"There are none left," Laurence replied. "My guardians pensioned off the staff." He grimaced. "I suppose they might have wished to go after what happened. I don't remember."

Miss Deeping nodded. "Perhaps some might be found? If pensions are being paid."

"Ah. In the estate records." Laurence had never looked. He had only looked away.

"Yes."

"I will send a note to my estate agent inquiring about those things."

Miss Deeping nodded. "Also…"

Laurence found her expression fascinating. "What else?"

"If you care to, sometime, we could examine the…process of that day."

"Process?"

"Exactly what happened, moment by moment, when your parents were killed."

His gesture of rejection was automatic. "I don't remember."

"Very likely not. But… We can discuss this when you are feeling better."

"No, go ahead. What do you mean?"

"Are you certain?"

Laurence hesitated. Was he? He wouldn't have thought so. But having this young lady at his side made facing the past at least conceivable. He wasn't sure why, but it was so. "Yes."

Miss Deeping examined him before speaking slowly.

"Sometimes, if one concentrates on small bits of a story, details come back."

"Bits. What does that mean?"

"Moments. Rather than the whole overwhelming tale."

He nodded, though he was still not certain what this would entail.

"You really want to…?"

"Yes."

"All right. Well, for example, that day, how did you get into the wardrobe?"

"I was put in," Laurence answered without thinking. He wasn't sure how he knew it, but he did. He had a flash of being lifted off the floor, squirming, and being thrust into darkness.

Miss Deeping nodded. "That suggests to me that there must have been some sign of approaching danger," she went on, still slowly. "Which gave your parents time to hide you. A sound perhaps? A threat of some kind?"

Laurence waited, but nothing came to him this time. He shook his head. "I don't know."

She nodded again. "Once in the wardrobe, you were afraid?"

"Angry," he replied at once. "I was shut in. I wanted out."

Miss Deeping gazed at him. Her dark eyes were steady and sympathetic. They seemed to support him, even as chaotic images and feelings surged through his brain.

"Then there were sounds," Laurence said. He closed his eyes, then immediately opened them again, not wanting to be in darkness. "Glass breaking? Shouting?" He shook his head. He couldn't specify. There was only a sense of mayhem whirling through his mind.

"Words you understood?" she asked.

"No." His parents had been cut up badly, but he couldn't have heard a knife. Could he? The idea made him shudder. "I was afraid then," he added. He trembled a bit now as the vivid, visceral sense of crouching in the bottom of the wardrobe, afraid to move, swept over him. "For ages," he said.

"What was for ages?"

"Hiding, waiting."

She reached over and put a hand on his. It felt like an anchor in the inner storm. Laurence clung to that feeling. "Then, after a while," she prompted.

"Silence." And the certainty of monsters in the dark. Slavering to hunt him down.

"But eventually the silence ended," Miss Deeping said softly.

"My nurse was screaming," Laurence replied. His voice sounded distant in his ears. "She was calling my name. I knew her voice."

"You wanted to go to her," Miss Deeping murmured.

"I had to beat on the door." Laurence heard himself say the words. It was almost as if someone else was speaking.

"So you were locked inside the wardrobe?"

"I...I suppose I must have been."

"To protect you."

He nodded. He knew, rationally, that this was right. It had still felt horrid to be trapped in the dark. But the alternative would surely have been worse.

"You were brought out of the wardrobe," she went on.

"The door opened. So bright. I couldn't see. A shadow swooped down." He was fairly certain he'd shrieked when hands had touched him. He didn't tell her that. "My nurse grabbed me and ran." He'd been clutched so tight, it was hard to breathe, Laurence remembered. The sharp memory tightened his chest. "She was sobbing, so I cried, too."

"Of course you did."

"She held my face to her shoulder. So I didn't see... anything."

"Good for her," said Miss Deeping fiercely.

Her hand still rested on his. She squeezed. The touch felt shockingly intimate. It spiked sensations through his entire body. Because he'd let her into memories that he'd shared with no one else, Laurence thought. Miss Charlotte Deeping now knew more about his scarred past than any other person on earth. And he didn't mind. He trusted her, he realized, and was overwhelmed by a wave of emotion. Trust was a rare gift in his life. He hardly ever managed it.

"Where did you go after that?" she asked softly.

"The nursery?" he guessed. He had no memories of that.

"No, I mean later. Did you stay on at the house?"

Laurence tried to think. His hysterical nurse dominated his thoughts. She'd been the foundation of his young life, and then she'd fallen to pieces. It had been as unsettling as the abrupt disappearance of his parents. He strained to recall a recovery, a return to normalcy, and could not. Had she gone away?

"The servants would have called for help," Miss Deeping said quietly.

"Yes." He shrugged. "I'm sure the house filled with people. I just don't remember."

"They kept you safely away from all that," she said.

Laurence had a flash of huddling in his small bed, miserable and rather hungry, with wild sobbing in the background. There were reasons for his refusal to think about those days. They contained nothing but misery.

"As they should have," she went on.

They should have, but did not—an oversight rather than cruelty. After all these years, he could understand the lapse.

"Someone stepped in to make arrangements," she said. "And to set an investigation in motion."

"My former trustees would know," Laurence said. It was good to think of something he could control. "I'll write and ask them."

Miss Deeping nodded. "It's brave of you to look back this way," she said.

"As I never did before?" he asked wryly. She must think he was a fool never to have asked questions.

"It is difficult to do alone."

"That's it." He met her eyes. "Dashed difficult. But with you helping me, I can manage."

She flushed a deep rosy red. Their gazes held. Their hands were still touching. Laurence felt a depth of connection knitting together between them, more profound than attraction, broader than convention.

The door to the parlor clicked. Miss Deeping pulled her hand away.

"There you are," said Mrs. Deeping, looking in and then entering the room. "I could not conceive where you had gone, Charlotte."

"I brought Glendarvon some willow-bark tea."

"I thought Daisy was doing that." Her mother looked back and forth between them. She made Laurence think of one of the foxhounds catching a promising scent. "I hope you found it helpful, my lord."

"Very. Thank you."

"We'll brew up another pot whenever you feel the need."

"You are very good."

"You can take the tray back to the kitchen," said the older woman to her daughter.

Miss Deeping rose and picked it up.

Laurence wished she would stay, but her mother obviously did not intend to leave them alone any longer. "Thank you again," he said.

Miss Deeping gave him a nod that seemed to hold great significance and departed. Her mother lingered, however. "We are so sorry about your accident," she said. "I hope you are feeling a bit better."

"I am."

"It is too bad that you are kept from hunting. Stanley said you are very fond of it."

Laurence nodded, becoming aware of a spark of sharp inquiry in his hostess's dark eyes. They hadn't conversed much during his visit so far, but he suddenly suspected she had been observing him the whole time. And that he might not have measured up to some exacting standard.

"There's little for a sportsman to do here at the house during the day," she went on.

She seemed to expect him to say something in particular. Perhaps a compliment to her hospitality? "It's exceedingly comfortable," he tried.

And disappointed her. Clearly. "What were you and Charlotte talking of?" she asked, with the air of a last-ditch effort.

Laurence's mind went blank. He couldn't tell her *that*.

Mrs. Deeping gazed at him, waiting like a schoolmistress with a dilatory pupil.

"Horses," he blurted out. "We pulled that foal from the fen, you know. Rigel."

"Horses," she repeated. "Of course, horses. No one talks of anything else at this time of year."

"You breed such fine ones," he answered.

She sighed and turned toward the door. "Ring if you would like more tea, Lord Glendarvon. *Daisy* will bring it."

Though he was sorry to have left her dissatisfied, Laurence was relieved when the lady departed.

Twelve

CHARLOTTE HAD EXPECTED HER MOTHER TO FOLLOW along as she returned the tray to the kitchen, but when she set it down, Mama was not there. She didn't see her again until the mail arrived later that day, bringing letters from two of her school friends. Mama dropped them on Charlotte's writing desk with a smile, saying, "I knew you would want to see these as soon as possible."

"Oh yes. Thank you." They came from Sarah and Harriet. Charlotte reached for a letter opener to slit the pages.

Her mother lingered at the door of her bedchamber. "This morning, when I came into the parlor, you and Glendarvon looked—"

"He was glad to have the tea," Charlotte interrupted. "He had a dreadful headache."

"And you kindly provided it." The irony in Mama's voice was unmistakable, making the point that medicinal tea and ministering care were not characteristic of Charlotte.

"I felt sorry for him."

"Ah."

"He is a guest in our house."

"Indeed."

"Do stop sounding portentous, Mama."

"Did I? So you took him tea, and then you talked of horses."

Charlotte couldn't help but look startled since their conversation had been about something quite different. Immediately, she knew she'd revealed too much.

"So he said to me, at least," her mother went on. "You discussed the foal you saved together."

"He's been very interested in Rigel since then."

"Naturally." Her mother gazed at her. "You do see that he could well be a serious suitor, Charlotte."

"I don't think—"

Her mother held up a finger to stop her. "He seeks you out. If he sees you walk by a window, he generally goes out into the garden to join you." She raised another finger. "He gazes at you during dinner, until he remembers he shouldn't stare. And then he looks self-conscious." A third finger went up. "He praises your intelligence and discernment to your brothers."

Charlotte hadn't heard that last one. A palpable thrill went through her. "Does he?"

"Yes, he does, my dear. And Cecil says—"

"I wish my brothers would mind their own affairs!"

"It is natural for them to want to watch out for you."

"It's more of a glowering hover, Mama. I don't do that to *them*."

"You didn't tell Stanley last season that Miss Grillon was mean-spirited?"

"That was different. I overheard her saying some quite cruel things. And then she behaved so differently when gentlemen were present."

Her mother waved this aside. "You have been spending a good deal of time with the marquess."

"We are investigating what happened to his parents."

Her mother could not hide a wince. "I think it is more than that," she said.

Part of Charlotte wanted to admit it. The desire that

flared up startled her with its strength. But she didn't want her family interfering.

"You seem to like him," said her mother.

Charlotte couldn't lie. So she said nothing.

"If you do, you should encourage him. Not put him off as you have others."

"I never—"

"Mr. Scrope."

"He was unctuous and a dreadful hypochondriac!"

"He was an exemplary young man. With a respectable fortune."

"He once talked to me about the symptoms of consumption for nearly half an hour!"

"He was kind and amenable."

"Without a single opinion of his own. Except that he must be sickening from something. It didn't do to disagree with *that*!"

Her mother hesitated. "I have sometimes thought you would prefer a man who was a bit…biddable. The way you like to plan and…investigate. You do tend to take charge."

Rejection shook Charlotte. "I want someone with a mind of his own."

"And does Glendarvon appear to have one?" Mama sounded doubtful.

Charlotte's instinct was to leap to his defense. But her mother would read volumes into that. "Or I would, if I was considering the notion of marriage," she added, retreating to her former position on this topic. She shifted in her chair. "I am not a shrew, Mama."

"Of course you are not. I didn't mean anything of the kind."

"My friends admired my planning and analyses. My charts, too!"

"That is rather different, my dear."

"Why should it be?"

"A gentleman and a friend are not the same."

"They can be the same person."

Her mother looked doubtful.

"You and Papa are friends."

"Well, yes. Of course. And no."

"What do you mean?" Charlotte felt a quiver of apprehension.

"Just that I would not immediately think of that word in regard to us."

"You don't think of him as a friend?"

"He is more than a friend. And also…" Charlotte's mother frowned. "Not less. That sounds wrong." She looked frustrated. "It's just that one doesn't talk to a man in the same way as a female friend."

"*I* do," said Charlotte.

"Ah," said her mother in an unfathomable tone. She considered for a moment. "You must allow that I know more of people—men—than you do. Simply through years of experience. You might want to consider my advice. Since you are inclined to like the marquess."

"I didn't say—"

Her mother's ironic look stopped her. "I certainly know *you*, my dear. And I can see how you treat him. You have not shown such a…preference before."

She wished she'd been more opaque.

"It's charming. And he has been taking an interest in your ideas and schemes."

Charlotte knew Mama didn't mean to be patronizing, but her attitude was clear. Mama had always thought her drive to solve mysteries was a girlish whim that would pass as she grew older. "We are working together on the matter."

Mama looked indulgent. "That is the sort of thing gentlemen say when they are flirting. They will claim an interest in things they don't give a snap of their fingers for. Or positively dislike."

Suddenly, Charlotte wondered if Glendarvon could be humoring her. Had he gone along with her wish to investigate as a gentleman in London might shower one with compliments or send bouquets? Had he fabricated the history he'd been telling her to seem interesting? She'd seen people do that sort of thing as well.

"Your father pretended to like dancing when we first met." Her mother smiled reminiscently. "He asked me to stand up with him at every opportunity. But you know I can hardly drag him onto a dance floor now."

"Papa lied to you?" Charlotte had always considered him scrupulously honest.

Her mother sighed. "You take everything so seriously, Charlotte. It wasn't really lying. Just part of the game of courtship."

"But if you relied on what he told you and then found it was just a ruse…" That would make Charlotte very angry indeed. But Glendarvon wouldn't use his parents' death in that way, she told herself. No one could. Yet a kernel of doubt niggled.

"We have strayed far from my point," said Mama. She sounded a bit irritated. "You like Lord Glendarvon. You have time and opportunities to become better acquainted. So you should make use of them to lead him along to a declaration. Rather than talk constantly of investigations."

"Lead him along," Charlotte repeated. "Rather like one of the horses?"

"Don't be prickly," replied her mother.

"But I *am* prickly."

"Because you insist on being so!"

"I don't *insist* on being who I am, Mama. I simply can't help it. I know you would like me to be different—"

"I wouldn't! I want you to be happy. Oh, I wish I hadn't said anything. Forget I did. We will just let things take their course."

Charlotte would not sit around and wait for *things*, she thought. She would find out the truth for herself. That was what she *did*.

❧

By dinnertime Laurence felt better. He'd been offered a tray in his room, but he didn't want to behave like an invalid. The sporting crowd here at the house and around the neighborhood would think him soft if he took to his bed after a mishap. More important, Miss Deeping would be at dinner, and if he had gauged Mrs. Deeping's rotational system correctly, that fascinating young lady might be sitting beside him.

His hopes proved true. She was there, and the sight of her filled him with elation.

The usual loud dinnertime conversation arose. Debates raged; good-natured mockery flew back and forth, and joking challenges were issued. As he listened, Laurence realized his attitude toward the din had changed. He didn't have to hide a wince at a particularly raucous exchange or laughing threat. He didn't worry that a bout of fisticuffs might break out at any moment. The longer he stayed among the Deepings, the more he understood how a lively family interacted, a process he'd never observed so closely before. He saw strong emotions were a natural part of it. Individuals grew angry, hurt, offended, and the world did not come to an end. They kept on talking, and after a while—days, sometimes—the matter was resolved. Or it died a natural death out of sheer triviality. The point was: topics were not forbidden, as they had been in the household where he'd grown up. The field was open to anything. Joys and triumphs were celebrated, too. He admired the result immensely.

Pleased with his insight, he tried to put it into words for Miss Deeping. But he quickly discovered the nurturing young lady of the afternoon had disappeared. His dinner partner was more like the acerbic girl he'd first encountered, after he'd nearly ridden her down. He couldn't understand what had happened. He hadn't done anything. "Is something wrong?" he ventured.

"There are many things wrong in the world."

That was sheer provocation. He recognized it. "So are you contemplating poverty and injustice?"

"Man's inhumanity to man," she replied.

"Ah. Some particular instance?"

"Deception," she said. "There is nothing more horrid."

"Not war? Or pestilence?"

"I'm not joking," she answered with a flashing glance.

He could see that. "Have you been deceived?" he asked. Since this afternoon when she seemed quite different, he wondered, but did not add.

"I don't know. Have I?" When he simply stared, she added, "There may be an attempt."

"What, right now?" Laurence looked around the table. Brothers on all sides. Was that the problem?

A question from another diner called for her attention.

"Have you offended Charlotte?" murmured Henry Deeping on Laurence's other side.

He turned to the oldest of her brothers. "I don't see how I could have. But she does seem…"

"Truculent?"

Laurence was surprised by the aptness of the word.

"I've known her all her life," Deeping pointed out.

Could he be a source of insight into a complicated young lady? "So you understand her?"

"I wouldn't go that far."

Miss Deeping had been drawn into an argument about riding zebras. She looked unlikely to free herself for some time.

"But if you would like a suggestion?" Henry Deeping asked.

"Please."

"Apologize," said Deeping.

"For what? I don't know what the matter is. And I'm pretty certain I haven't done anything wrong."

"Irrelevant," the other man replied.

"But…"

Henry Deeping raised a finger to silence him. "If you've done something—inadvertently, of course—you've asked pardon," he explained. "If you haven't, she will ask what you mean. You say you feared you had offended her, and then she may tell you what is wrong."

Laurence worked his way through this reasoning. It seemed shaky to him. "May?"

Deeping shrugged. "It's a chance, not a certainty."

That didn't seem enough. "She mentioned deception," Laurence added.

"Of which you are not guilty?"

"I am not." Laurence searched his conscience to be sure. He shook his head. He'd been more open with Miss Deeping than with any other person he'd ever known.

"If I got hold of a zebra, I'd soon have it trained to the saddle," Bertram Deeping declared. Loudly, for the whole table to hear.

"They're mean as snakes," one of the houseguests replied. "Friend of mine was in Africa and thought like you do. Tried to put his leg over one. The zebra got its teeth into his arm and would *not* let go. Like some sort of huge bulldog. Dragged him through a thorn thicket, ripped his shirt to shreds. Good section of his skin, too. He has scars."

"I have no better advice for you," said Henry Deeping to Laurence.

"Apologies have done the trick for you?" Laurence asked. "With your sister."

The other man considered. "About half the time. Particularly when I took her by surprise."

The zebra debate continued to rage. Bertram Deeping could not be made to believe that there was an equine-shaped animal he could not ride. He went through a lengthy catalog of all the mounts he'd mastered since childhood, with their quirks and rebellions, requiring Miss Deeping's corroboration on each example. Laurence let the noise wash over him as he pondered her brother's suggestion and devoured the excellent dinner before him.

"Tereford tells me you like fly-fishing," said Henry Deeping during a lull.

"Yes," Laurence replied. They had discussed that in passing during their first meeting.

"We're going to try for some trout tomorrow, if you'd care to come."

Knowing the other two men were good friends, this felt like a significant invitation. It was also welcome, since Laurence was tired of sitting around the house but his head wasn't up to a bruising ride in the hunting field. "Yes, thank you."

"You don't mind starting early?"

"Not at all."

"Splendid. We'll leave from the breakfast room at seven. I'll have the gear."

"What gear?" asked Miss Deeping, exercising her knack for rejoining a conversation from ambush.

"Glendarvon is going to join me for a bit of fishing," replied her brother.

She looked Laurence up and down. "Good with a lure, are you?"

She spoke with an inexplicable emphasis. "Fair to middling," he replied.

"Full of tricks to get them wriggling on your hook?"

The twist she put on the word *wriggling* was strange. Like a dare of some kind. Did she think fishing cruel? Laurence looked at her brother and got no help. Henry Deeping seemed as puzzled as he was. "Only the usual ones," he answered.

"Oh, the *usual*."

Obviously, she was unhappy, and Laurence found he

didn't like that at all. Could hardly bear it, really. "I would like to apologize," he said.

"For what?"

"I fear I may have offended you."

"Why do you think so?"

Laurence threw Henry Deeping a reproachful glance. The other man shrugged unhelpfully, leaving him to his fate. Miss Deeping was frowning. Here was that sensation again, Laurence thought, of sliding across the ice on wobbling blades toward disaster. "You seem…"

"Yes, how do I seem?" she demanded.

Challenge flashed in her dark eyes. They seemed to drill into him. Laurence suddenly felt as if everyone in the room was staring at him, waiting for his answer. He glanced sideways and saw it wasn't true. Except for Henry Deeping, who clearly was listening. Laurence searched for words, fairly certain that anything he said would be wrong.

"Prickly," said Henry Deeping with a teasing smile.

Laurence thought he was trying to help. But he hadn't. He'd made things worse. Miss Deeping's bared teeth were more a snarl than a smile. She would not, of course, bite. But she looked as if she'd like to. Laurence picked up his wineglass and drank.

"Where do I buy a zebra, Charlotte?" called Bertram Deeping from down the table. He made a broad gesture. "And how much will it cost? The fellows are going in with me on the price."

"I haven't the slightest idea."

Laurence would have subsided at her cutting tone, but Bertram appeared unaffected. "Come, you must have some notion," he said. "You're always full of odd facts and fancies."

"Am I?" Her voice might have cut glass.

"Like that guff about the Wild Hunt." Bertram looked around the table. "Hounds with red ears," he told the others.

"Guff?" repeated his sister.

Laurence decided Bertram Deeping was the bravest man he'd ever met.

"If you know that, you must know where to get a zebra," the youngest Deeping added.

Or perhaps he was simply the most oblivious, Laurence thought.

"That does not follow by any system of logic in existence," replied Miss Deeping.

"Hoity-toity," said Bertram. "Surely you can take a guess?"

"Say, what about Astley's Amphitheatre?" asked one of the houseguests.

"I don't think they have zebras," said another.

"Perhaps you should go to Africa and fetch one," said Miss Deeping.

"That would take ages," replied Bertram as if it had been a serious suggestion.

The dispute went on without any sign of resolution, even after Mrs. Deeping rose and took the ladies away. At that point, Laurence turned reproachful eyes on Henry Deeping. "Apologize," he said sarcastically.

"I swear I've known it to work," the other man said.

An oblique approach was wrong, Laurence saw. He should just get Miss Deeping to tell him what was wrong. They'd talked so openly before, surely she would. Perhaps whatever had irritated her had nothing to do with him. He would find out, as soon as he found a proper opportunity—not surrounded by a vociferous crowd.

❦

Charlotte did *not* go down to the breakfast room at seven the following morning. She was awake, however, and very much aware that Glendarvon was meeting her brother there and leaving the house for some hours. At one and the same time, she longed to see him and did not wish to give him the satisfaction. Dinner had been a strain. Whenever they spoke, she'd found herself listening for false notes. How could she ask him if he was pretending to be interested in the investigation in order to attach her? He would say he wasn't—whether or not it was true. And it sounded odiously vain. What if he was *only* interested in the mystery and not her at all? That was a startlingly lowering reflection.

When she did go down an hour later, she found a group of hearty gentlemen stoking their bodies for another day of sport. Bertram was regaling them with a dream he'd had about riding a zebra through Buckingham Palace to demonstrate his prowess to the king.

"The creature would bite him," said one of their guests. "And then where would you be?"

"Beheaded for treason," suggested another with grim relish.

"I'd keep the beast well in hand," protested Bertram.

"I'm telling you that you couldn't," responded the font of information from last night.

Charlotte resisted saying that Bertram and his exotic mount would never have gotten into the palace in the first place. She knew there was no use applying logic to errant nonsense. She ate her breakfast in silence instead.

One of the maids came in with a folded sheet of paper

and handed it to Charlotte. Opening it, she found a few lines from Cecelia, saying that Merlin had been injured and would like to speak to her as soon as it was convenient. Charlotte snorted at the polite wording. She'd wager a good deal of money that Merlin had demanded her presence immediately, with no thought of her convenience. Still, this was curious. She changed into her riding habit, had Stelle saddled, and rode over to Lorne.

She expected to find Merlin in the house, but when she arrived, Cecelia told her he'd insisted on staying in his hut. "Which is ridiculous," her friend added. "He can't get about on his own."

"What happened?"

"He fell out of a tree and broke his leg."

"Oh no."

"The doctor set the bone and said it will heal with time. But, clearly, he must stay here and be looked after."

Cecelia sounded irritated, and Charlotte didn't blame her.

"He is the most stubborn creature," the duchess added. "And he is wild to speak to you."

"I wonder why."

"You will have to ask him. I can send a maid with you. I'm afraid I am very busy this morning. There are problems at the London town house and elsewhere."

"How many houses does the duke have?"

"Far too many! I think we must sell some properties despite James's reluctance." Cecelia turned back to stacks of papers on her desk, and Charlotte left her to them.

She declined the maid's company. A chaperone hardly seemed necessary in these circumstances. Mounting the horse again, she followed Cecelia's directions to a small run-down cottage across two fields from Lorne.

"Who is it?" shouted Merlin when she knocked.

"Charlotte Deeping," she replied.

"Finally! Come in, come in."

She pushed the door open, a little leery about what sort of place she would find. The interior was all one room with a pounded dirt floor and no windows. A lighted lantern showed a large hearth at the back with a small fire burning in it, a table and chair, and a low bed on which Merlin reclined, one leg splinted and raised on a pillow. She was somewhat surprised to see the place was quite clean.

"What took you so long?" the man demanded.

Charlotte decided to ignore this. "How did you fall?" she asked. He had seemed quite at home in the tree when she'd seen him.

"A trap was laid for me," he replied. "A branch I always stand on was sawn nearly through."

"What?"

"I'm certain of it. But you must go and make sure before the villain can make off with the evidence."

"Villain?"

"Did you not hear me? Go at once and find the fallen branch so we can verify the saw marks."

"But that would mean—"

"At once!"

Seeing he would not let go of this point, Charlotte said, "Tell me where."

He did so. Charlotte mounted Stelle again and followed his directions to the tree in question. She knew she'd found it by the recent pale scar on its side, rather high up. The break did look suspiciously smooth. She got down to search for the fallen branch and found it not too far from the trunk. The end was not jagged except at the very bottom. She ran her fingers over the wood. The rest did indeed appear to be sawed.

She dragged the branch over to her horse. It was too large for her to carry. Stelle objected at first to towing it along, but Charlotte managed to soothe her. They proceeded slowly back to Merlin's hut.

"Do you have it?" he called when they arrived.

"Yes."

"Bring it in."

"I don't think it will fit."

"Nonsense," declared Merlin.

Gritting her teeth, Charlotte maneuvered the bushy limb through the low door. It filled much of the room.

Merlin sat up, leaning forward with no thought to his injury. "There! Do you see? That has been sawn almost through."

"I think you are right."

"Obviously I am. Bring it closer."

Charlotte did so. "How did you get back here with a broken leg?"

"I shouted until some yokel heard me and brought a cart." He bared his teeth at the memory.

The trip must have been horribly painful. Charlotte brought the single chair closer to the bed. "Tell me how this happened."

"I make a regular patrol," Merlin replied. "I climb trees at certain intervals for a better view."

"The same ones each time?"

"Because they have the best perspective," he answered impatiently.

"So anybody might be familiar with the pattern."

He scowled. "I suppose so."

"But that would mean someone was watching you," she said slowly. "And looking for an opportunity to hurt you."

"All the luck I have is bad luck," he muttered.

"But why would they be? Have you offended someone?" *Beyond just everyone*, Charlotte added silently.

"You don't try to kill someone over a minor offense."

This seemed an exaggeration. Though if he'd fallen wrong, he might have been killed, she supposed.

"It must be our murderer," Merlin declared.

"Our…"

"I'm sure Horton blabbed all over the tavern, and the wrong person eventually heard."

"But we were talking to him about the fire."

"Horton saw the ring. He most likely talked about that as well."

Charlotte nodded. "Still, I don't see why you should be targeted."

"Because I mean to hunt them down," replied Merlin impatiently.

"How would they know that?"

He looked away. "I might have told a few people about my plan to become a Bow Street runner."

"A few?"

"People find it interesting."

As they did not his customary conversation. "You talked about the investigation?"

"In general terms. I did not reveal any secrets, naturally."

Charlotte wondered about that. Had he said enough to draw an attack? If that was what had really happened. A thought suddenly struck her. "The rock that hit Glendarvon."

Merlin frowned. "What about it?"

"What if it came from the same source?"

"Things fly about on the hunting field. It is not the same at all."

"You don't find it a suspicious coincidence?"

"He is making a great deal over nothing."

Or perhaps Merlin wished to remain the center of attention, Charlotte thought, and he worried the marquess would usurp his place.

"These nobles care for nothing but their own selfish desires," Merlin said. "They will do despicable things to get what they want. A so-called lady made me think she loved me and then threw me away without a thought. Just to annoy her high-nosed family. She claimed it was all my fault, too."

Charlotte remembered aristocrats she'd met in London. Like the prince who'd tried to destroy Cecelia. There were many who were masters of disdain. And certainly selfish.

"Lord Glendarvon is not really interested in finding the truth," Merlin added.

"Why do you say that?"

"He could have tried to find it any time in the last decade. But he didn't lift a finger."

There were reasons for that. Merlin hadn't heard the marquess speak of that terrible night. He was not like those Londoners.

"He's only trying to ingratiate himself with you," the man added. "To cut a wheedle. He practically told me so."

"What?"

"He said one must make allowances for the ladies. And indulge their little foibles."

Charlotte stared at him, shaken. He did not meet her eyes. He had turned his attention back to the severed branch. "Foibles," she repeated.

"Or perhaps it was *foolishness*," he replied. "Some silly word. Those sorts of people respect no opinions but their own."

"I don't think that's quite fair."

Merlin shrugged. "They say all's fair in love and war. The winners, that is. Once they've been utterly ruthless and taken what they want." He fingered the branch again. "There can be no doubt this was sawn," he said. "We must preserve it as evidence."

"We'll take it to Lorne, where it will be safe," Charlotte said, only half attending. He started to protest, and she brought her mind back to the matter at hand. "It is the closest secure place. You must go there as well."

"No. I don't care to live under Tereford's eye."

"You cannot move around, even to keep the fire going," she pointed out. "And if someone does want to harm you—"

"I think that is all too clear!"

"They can reach you easily here. Alone."

Fear crossed his face. Charlotte was sorry for it, but she knew she was right. After a bit more argument, he conceded, and she rose to return to Lorne and summon people to move him.

"Hurry," he said as she walked out. Which was just like Merlin, to nag at her now that he had changed his mind.

The transfer was arranged. Charlotte sat with Cecelia and explained her reasoning as two men and a cart went to fetch him. She would think about that, and nothing else.

"Of course, he must stay here," Cecelia replied. "I always said so. But the rest of this—don't you think you are jumping to wild conclusions? Merlin has offended any number of people hereabouts. He…scatters accusations of stupidity. James's valet absolutely despises him."

"Enough to saw through a tree limb?" asked Charlotte.

The duchess snorted. "I would like to see Marston doing that. But no. I cannot imagine it."

"Merlin has always been annoying," Charlotte answered. "But just lately he has been bragging about how he will become a Bow Street runner through the finding of that ring. It makes a good tale. I'm sure it's spread through the whole neighborhood. And perhaps beyond."

Cecelia thought this over. "That does not seem wise."

"Merlin very much wants to succeed at something."

"And to be seen doing so."

Charlotte nodded, impressed by her friend's understanding.

"But do you really think Glendarvon's incident is connected?"

"What about me?"

Three men walked into the parlor where they were sitting—the marquess, the duke, and Charlotte's brother Henry—their tall figures making the room seem extremely crowded suddenly. Charlotte's first thought was how handsome they looked, and how at ease with each other. Her second was that the latter two had never made her heart pound in this dizzying fashion. Her third was fear that she was making a fool of herself.

"We have brought you fish," the duke said.

"In here?" Cecelia replied.

"Left with the cook, of course. What's going on? You look like conspirators."

Charlotte explained again, though she left out the part about Glendarvon.

But the duke made the connection at once. "Another attack. I *knew* there was something off about that stone. The angle made no sense."

The marquess looked thoughtful.

"This is too much," said Henry.

"If you see some flaw—" Charlotte began.

"Your reasoning is sound. As it always tends to be."

Charlotte couldn't help preening a little.

Until Henry went on, "So sound that you must drop this inquiry immediately."

"Henry—"

Her brother shook his head. "No. Looking for lost belongings is acceptable. Even the Shropshire 'treasure.' But this is going too far, Charlotte. Your school friends would agree with me if they were here."

"They would not!"

"Shall we write and ask them?"

"I will consult them, of course."

"Splendid. And when you hear their views…"

"That could be days! Weeks! I won't—"

"I propose we make a thorough search of Lorne," Cecelia interrupted in a carrying tone. "There can be no harm in that."

Everyone turned to look at her.

"We've been putting things in order, but we haven't looked in every crevice since the ring was found. Perhaps there is more to find. And shed light on the connection. There are plenty of us here right now to pitch in."

"Watch out, you clumsy oaf!" yelled a voice from the entry.

The duke looked at the duchess. "He couldn't stay in that hut with a broken leg," she said.

"Are you trying to break my other leg, you dolt?" Heavy footsteps started up the stairs.

"We could have paid someone a great deal of money to stay with him in the hut," said the duke.

"If someone is trying to kill him—" Charlotte began.

"One can understand the impulse," Tereford put in. At the duchess's frown, he waved a placating hand. "Only teasing, my dear."

"A joke too far, James."

"I beg your pardon." He looked sincerely sorry.

"So there's the cellar," said Cecelia, returning to her previous point. "I've scarcely been down there. The attics are small and look empty. Indeed, the house seems to have been cleared of any personal items. I've found no papers at all. No clothing or books."

"The 'nephew,'" murmured Charlotte.

Glendarvon heard her and nodded. "Begin at the top and work down?" he suggested.

"Why not?"

"Shall we divide our party or…?"

"Let us all go together," said Charlotte. She feared Henry might keep things from her if he thought them dangerous, though she couldn't imagine what such things would be.

They trooped up the stairs together. Merlin, lying in a bedchamber with his leg propped up and the door open, demanded to know what was happening. When he heard their purpose, he clawed at the coverlet in frustration. "You will report to me on what you find."

Charlotte, feeling sorry for him, said she would.

The attic was low and dim. Some light filtered in from two windows at the gable ends. Laurence could only stand upright in the center, where the roof peaked. He and Henry Deeping volunteered to crawl into the corners, taking lanterns to light the dimmest places. They ended up covered in dust, having found nothing.

The habitable floors were equally devoid of unusual items. The walls were plastered with no sign of secret openings. The furnishings consisted of large old-fashioned pieces and some small wooden tables. "I suppose we could rip up the upholstery," said the duke. "But I would prefer not."

∽

Laurence had decided the finding of the ring was a fluke by the time they came to the cellar stair. "More lanterns, I think," said the duchess.

These were fetched, and the party started down. The cellar extended beneath the entire remaining house. It was windowless, walled with stone. The floor was pounded earth and felt very solid. A leaning rack had once held wine bottles, Laurence thought. It was empty now. As were two banks of shelves against the wall that faced the burned stable wing. They moved around the space, shining their lanterns into corners, pushing on any stones that seemed loose.

"There's something behind here," said Miss Deeping. She pushed her lantern into the space between the shelves.

Laurence joined Henry Deeping in pulling the shelves

out of the way. The two of them were already covered in dust, so a bit more scarcely mattered. When the wall was exposed, it was clear that the stonework was different from the others.

"See here," said Miss Deeping. She set down her lantern, thrust her fingers into a crack, and tugged. There was a grating sound and a hint of movement. Laurence went to help her. He could barely fit his larger fingers into the crack. Together they managed to enlarge it. Henry Deeping stepped forward to grasp the edge, and with a good deal of effort, they pulled open a panel—wood faced with flat stones to match the wall. "It's a door," said Miss Deeping. She picked up her lantern and started forward into the pool of darkness beyond the opening.

"Wait a moment," said her brother. "We don't know what's back there."

"It must be the cellar of the old stable wing," she replied. "A secret passage!"

"Perhaps a priest's hole?" asked the duke. "This house is of an age to have one."

"That would be unusual in a hunting box," said the duchess. "Hardly a place to have a resident priest."

"A way station for traveling clergy?" suggested Henry Deeping.

Laurence knew some families had hidden Catholic clergymen during the turmoil that followed Henry the Eighth's takeover of the English church. There had been years of religious conflict.

"I'm going to see where it goes," declared Miss Deeping. "Yes, Henry, I will be careful." Holding her lantern well out before her, she stepped through.

Her light revealed more of the cellar they stood in, cut off by this newer wall. It extended forward about fifteen feet and then turned in an ell and ran off to the right.

Moving inside one by one, they examined the space.

"The stable wing was longer than this," said the duke. "Someone walled off the original cellar at each end." He went to look at the far end. Like the first, this wall was wood faced in stone.

"The workmen said nothing about a cellar when they cleared off the ashes to rebuild," said the duchess.

"So that entrance must be hidden as well," replied Miss Deeping. She walked along the new wall, lantern held high. "Here is another door like the one we came through, I think." She pushed. The panel resisted, then slowly scraped open.

They all crowded forward to look. Beyond was a square cellar room littered with bits of moldering hay. A ladder led up to a blackened trapdoor in the ceiling. "Not a good place to store fodder," said Henry Deeping. He stepped in to stir some of the hay with one foot. "That has been rotting for quite a while, I think." He pushed at the trapdoor. It didn't move. "Nailed shut," he noted, indicating a protruding point.

"I wonder if Horton knew about this?" asked the duchess.

"He said nothing when he was showing me the remains of the stable," replied the duke. "He did mention a hayloft, which 'went up like oily rags.' He is not a man who notices much that is out of the ordinary, I would say."

"But why was this done?" asked Miss Deeping. She turned to move around the blocked-off section of cellar, shining her lantern in the corners. "There's something here," she said.

They came to add their lights to hers and revealed a line of low chests along the back wall. Made of dark wood and covered in dust, they had faded into the general dimness.

Laurence bent to brush at the top of one of them. It was heavily carved. He couldn't make out the design.

Henry Deeping pulled at the top of another. "Locked."

"We'll have them carried upstairs," said the duke.

"But then people will find out they're here," said Miss Deeping.

"You think they should not?" Tereford gazed at her.

"Someone burned down the stable," she answered. "And attacked Glendarvon and Merlin."

He considered this. "Very well." He turned to his wife. "Do we have a ring of keys lying about?"

"No," replied the duchess. "The front door key was the only one given us."

"That is odd, in an old house."

She nodded.

"We'll have to break them open."

"Let me take a look," said Henry Deeping.

"Ah." In the flickering lantern light, the duke smiled. "I'd forgotten your larcenous talents." Seeing Laurence's puzzlement, Tereford added, "Henry can pick locks."

"And never would teach me," said Miss Deeping.

"These look possible," said her brother. "I'll need a few tools. And more light."

Laurence followed the duchess and Miss Deeping to fetch the needed items. "You are very good at uncovering secrets," he told the latter.

"I hate empty compliments," she said.

"That wasn't empty." When she said nothing, he murmured, "I wish you would tell me what is wrong."

"We agreed to investigate the mystery. Nothing more."

"But—"

"I must help Cecelia."

She hurried away. Laurence stood at the top of the cellar stairs with a hovering sense of unease.

Thirteen

HENRY DEEPING KNELT BEFORE ONE OF THE CHESTS, WITH lanterns set on either side aimed at the keyhole. His sister held another behind his left shoulder. He inserted a long slender knife and a bit of wire and began to manipulate them in the lock. Laurence wondered where he had acquired such a skill. "He made a study of this at Eton," murmured the Duke of Tereford. "Boys used to bring him locked boxes and such and place bets on how long it would take him to get them open."

"Not whether?" whispered Laurence.

"No, not that," replied the other man with a smile.

"Exaggeration," muttered Deeping. He leaned closer as if to listen to the carved chest.

It took him several minutes, but at last there was a click, and he withdrew the tools and raised the lid. As well as a good bit of dust.

The scent of cedar rose around them. Rich colors gleamed in the lantern light—crimson and emerald and gold. "That looks like silk," said the duchess. She leaned over and ran her fingers over it. "It is. Very fine stuff." She lifted out the crimson swath and held it up. It was a long coat-like garment with voluminous sleeves, edged with gold trim. "Beautiful," said the duchess. She drew out the emerald piece. It was a wide skirt, also embellished with embroidery.

"It looks like a wealthy woman's clothing from China," said Henry Deeping.

"Horton said Mr. Cantrell had objects from foreign places," said his sister.

"Was he involved in trade?" Laurence asked. "Or perhaps he was a collector."

"We know nothing about him," said the duke. "He left no papers behind."

"Unless there are some in here," said the duchess, indicating the line of trunks.

"Let us open them and see." Henry Deeping moved to kneel in front of the next one.

Over the next hour, he had them all unlocked. They found more rich clothing and jewel cases containing ornate earrings, necklaces, and haircombs. Another chest held some small statues and a number of oblong wooden tablets with vertical lines of script incised into them. A third was filled with bits of carved and gilded wood that appeared to slot together into a table or stand. The final chest was full of paper scrolls written in similar script.

"I'm fairly sure this is Chinese writing," Henry Deeping said. "I have tried to familiarize myself with different written forms from around the world."

Laurence remembered that this Deeping intended to work in the Foreign Office. In fact, someone had mentioned he started there in the New Year. "You can read it?"

"Oh no. Merely identify it."

"It is maddening," said Miss Deeping, who had unrolled a scroll and was staring at it as if meaning might emerge through the exertion of sheer will.

"I could find someone to translate," said her brother. "In London."

"Confidentially?" asked the duke.

Deeping looked at him. "I imagine so. Do you think that important?"

"The way they are hidden makes me curious. I think we would prefer to know what they say before the world discovers their existence."

"You worry your ancient relative was involved in something disreputable?" asked the duchess.

"I have no idea," her husband replied. "But I would like to be the first to know if so."

"Then we could try to make it right."

Tereford nodded.

"I will have to go up to town to make discreet inquiries," said Henry Deeping. "I can't do it by letter."

"No." The duke gazed down at the open trunks. "And the person you find must come here to look at them. We wouldn't wish to send off these scrolls on their own."

"Are you so concerned about what they may contain?" asked his wife.

"Only cautious," he replied. "I should like some control over who the translator can talk to."

"I wonder what this is?" said Miss Deeping. She had picked up one of the wooden tablets and was running her fingers over the carving.

She loved puzzles, Laurence thought. But she preferred those she could solve herself. "A poem or motto?" he guessed. "Or part of a game of some sort?"

She made no reply.

She was thoroughly engrossed in their finds, he thought. But she was also avoiding him, which was more and more annoying.

After a moment the duchess said, "The pieces are rather large for a game."

Despite all Laurence could do, Miss Deeping kept on

evading him. She stayed close to the duchess as it was decided that Henry Deeping would leave for London the next morning. And as he managed to relock the chests. Then the cellar was sealed up as it had been when they'd discovered it. They scuffed through their footprints in the dust outside the hidden door, though the duchess said no one was likely to come down here.

As a final straw, Miss Deeping refused to ride home with Laurence and her brother. She said she wished to consult the duchess on some private matter, but Laurence didn't believe it. She was snubbing him, and it wasn't fair. He'd done nothing. He turned and followed Henry Deeping toward the front door as an irate voice called down from upstairs. "Hello! Is anyone there? Where have you all gone?"

It was Merlin, and it wasn't his problem. Laurence closed the door behind them.

∽

"I'll speak to him," said the duke.

"Do you think—" began his wife.

"I said I would," said Charlotte at the same time. She had promised to report.

"I'll be perfectly polite," Tereford responded. "But I think it best that no one else knows what we found just now."

Charlotte watched him walk up the stairs, the picture of aristocratic elegance. He epitomized the sort of man who held the reins of power in society. And had never wondered if he deserved to. He had made all the decisions about their discovery without consultation. "It isn't fair to cut Merlin out now that he can't move around," she said to Cecelia.

"Let us go and wash our hands," her friend replied.

They were dusty, Charlotte noticed, as was the hem of her gown. Cecelia even had a smudge on her cheek, which was unprecedented. Charlotte also realized that she was cold. The cellar had been chilly.

They went to the kitchen and cleaned up. Cecilia said, "Some tea in the parlor, please, Mrs. Smith."

"I made scones, Your Grace."

"Oh, some of those, too. The duke adores your scones."

The cook flushed with pleasure.

Cecelia was always kind, Charlotte thought, but there was no question that she was the mistress and the rest of them were subordinate to her. She took her precedence for granted. "Merlin should not be excluded just because he's not of noble birth," Charlotte said as they sat before the parlor hearth. She held her hands out to warm them at the fire.

Her friend frowned at her. "I think it is more to do with his loose tongue than his rank. What made you say that?"

"He told me how he was treated down in Cornwall."

"Treated?"

"When a noble lady used him to annoy her family. And then tossed his love aside as if he was of no importance whatsoever. As if her status let her do anything she wished."

"That is not exactly the truth, Charlotte. It is a distorted version of what happened."

"How do you know?"

"Sarah told me. The lady in question is her husband's sister, and Sarah was there when they thrashed it out between them."

It occurred to Charlotte that all her school friends had

married into the aristocracy. For a forlorn moment, she felt even more separated from them.

"Tamara Pendrennon—that was her name—did flirt irresponsibly with Merlin when he was a tutor to a neighbor's children."

"And flirtation meant one thing to her and quite another to him," Charlotte responded.

"That seems to be true."

"Because she was of noble birth and could not be held to account for her behavior."

Cecelia shook her head. "She was reckless, rebelling against unreasonable parents, and she could have gotten herself into trouble."

"But she did not."

"Luckily not. But she did not tell Merlin she loved him or propose any future for the two of them."

"He was supposed to understand that she meant nothing," said Charlotte tonelessly.

Her friend gazed at her. "Does this conversation have something to do with the way you're acting around Glendarvon?" Cecilia asked.

"I don't know what you mean."

"There is a noticeable distance. Has he offended you? Acted the arrogant nobleman?"

"Apparently, his attitude is common in the upper reaches of society."

"What attitude is that, Charlotte?" The duchess's voice had gone cool.

Charlotte met her friend's eyes and remembered all the times Cecelia had proven her worth, all the good she did for those less fortunate. Even more now that she had the

Tereford fortune behind her. Charlotte knew she could trust her. "I'm afraid Glendarvon is humoring me for his own ends."

"And what are those?" Cecelia waited, then said, "Seduction?"

Charlotte shook her head. "Amusement?" she tried. "He told Merlin that men must indulge ladies' foibles. Their foolishness."

"Did he?"

Her tone made Charlotte frown.

"Merlin turns his own ideas and wishes into tales," the duchess continued. "Which then seem to him quite true. I have observed this on many occasions. He is not a liar, but a…fabulist. He believes."

Had he woven a tale about Glendarvon because he feared being excluded from their investigation? She looked at Cecelia again, seeing wisdom in her face. "My mother said men pretend to like what they do not, in the game of courtship." A game she'd never meant to play. Had she? Her thoughts were snarled into an intractable mass.

"Would you care to have a bit of advice from me?" Cecelia asked.

Humbly, Charlotte nodded.

Her friend gave her a sweet smile. "Retreating into hurt or offended silence solves nothing and gives worries space to grow like garden weeds. It is always better to speak to the other person and discover the truth. They may refuse to talk. And in that case, there's nothing to be done." Cecelia shrugged. "But if Merlin had confronted Tamara, he might have saved years of brooding solitude."

"He would have been hurt," Charlotte pointed out.

"In his case it was inevitable, sadly."

And what was her case? Charlotte wondered. Did she even have one? Did she have any idea what she was doing? Right now, the answer seemed to be no. She noticed the time on the mantel clock. How had it grown so late? She rose. "I must go home." She paused halfway across the room. "Thank you."

"My dear Charlotte, of course."

She passed the duke as she went out. He had taken the time to wash off the dust and change his coat. He looked his customary immaculate self. Charlotte raised a hand in farewell and departed without speaking.

❧

"Scones," said Tereford when he entered the parlor. He sat down and took one, biting into it with gusto.

"I didn't hear any shouting from upstairs," Cecelia observed.

"I promised Merlin we would tell him when we uncovered any new facts."

She gave him an ironic look.

"We have none of those so far," he added.

"Those chests are quite factual."

"But uninformative until we know what the documents say. It might be nothing but an art collection stored away for safekeeping."

Cecelia considered this as he finished the scone. "Do you think we are high-handed?"

"In this instance? Or…"

"In general. You have sometimes been arrogant and heedless of others' feelings and desires, James."

He acknowledged it with a nod. "I hope I become less so all the time. As I learn from you."

"Yes, but perhaps I am as well."

"No, Cecelia, you are not."

"You might not notice."

"Being so oblivious myself?" he asked with a lifted eyebrow and slight smile.

"Not that. But… Well, perhaps that." She gave him a rueful smile in return.

He reached out and took her hand. "After nearly losing my chance of happiness in life through my arrogance, I promise you I recognize such behavior. And you do not exhibit it, my dearest wife."

Cecelia squeezed his hand. "We have been spared so many of the harsh things most people suffer."

"We had our own pains and difficulties."

"No one escapes some of those. But we did not have to endure poverty or physical violence or constant societal injustice."

"No."

"We should do more to fight those things."

"You support a great many charitable causes."

"Not so very many."

"It seems so to me. My father insisted poverty was due to indolence, you know. And most other ills to a lack of self-control among the 'lower orders.'"

"He was mistaken about so many things," said Cecelia, who could not forgive her deceased father-in-law for his harshness toward her husband.

James laughed. "Nearly everything, I sometimes think."

"If we were to sell some of the Tereford properties, we could devote more resources to helping," Cecelia said.

"I am still reluctant to reduce the estate."

"None of the principal ones, of course. But places like this…" Cecelia gestured at the room around them. "Will we ever wish to stay at Lorne? You didn't know it existed until we made an inventory from the records. And yet it could make a comfortable home for someone once it is put to rights."

He looked around. "You make a good argument."

"I can be convinced if you disagree."

"Though, deep down, you are certain you know best about matters of estate business." He tempered the comment with a fond smile.

"No, James." Cecelia's answering smile was charmingly rueful. "Once, I did. That was my arrogance, if you like. But you have taught *me* that experience does not make one infallible, and how important it is to change and grow."

"Two heads are better than one?" he asked lightly, though the look in his blue eyes told her he was much moved.

"A partnership is best of all," she replied. "And I am grateful to have one." She leaned forward for a tender, lingering kiss, which no doubt would have led to more if Merlin had not chosen that moment to shout, "I need a chamber pot up here!"

James grimaced, then snorted a laugh. "I'll find him one, by God," he said and rose. But in the parlor doorway, he paused. "I do not know what I would have become without you," he said to his wife.

Cecelia's loving gaze followed him out.

જ⟶

Laurence received a packet from home the following morning. His estate agent had been busy with the questions he'd sent him about former servants and any connection to Lorne in their records. Leafing through the documents, Laurence noted several facts Miss Deeping would want to know, and this excited him more than the information itself. He missed their conversations acutely. Gazing at her across a crowded room was somehow worse than nothing.

It was not simple to find a time and place where they would not be interrupted. She was being kept busy by her mother on plans for the dance, and as there was no hunt scheduled that day, the house was full of family and guests going in and out on various expeditions. At last, in the late afternoon, he saw Miss Deeping walking outdoors. He hurried to get his coat and hat and go after her, only to find she'd disappeared. Cursing his slowness, he ranged around the gardens. Finally, rounding a clump of shrubbery, he saw her moving toward the paddock where the mares and their foals were kept. He walked swiftly in that direction.

Enveloped in a thick blue wool cloak, Miss Deeping leaned on the fence, observing the horses. It would make sense for Rigel to come over and greet her, Laurence thought, but the rescued foal never acknowledged them. Perhaps he'd been too young to remember being pulled from the muck. Now he was frisking across the field with the abandon of a happy, healthy youngster. He tossed his head and kicked out with his back legs for the sheer pleasure of it, it seemed. Then, suddenly, he skidded to a stop as if he'd hit a wall and jumped straight into the air, all four feet leaving the earth. As he came down, a large toad erupted from the grass and hopped away. The foal shied at the unexpected movement, whirled, and went running to his mother.

Miss Deeping burst out laughing. It was a lovely, musical

sound. The sort one would like to hear more often, Laurence thought. He had to join in.

She turned, saw him, and said, "I wanted to speak to you."

Just as he said, "I hoped to talk to you."

Laurence moved closer. The crisp air had turned her cheeks rosy, and she looked bright and intelligent and so very desirable. His heart turned over. He spread his hands to signify *Here I am*. He meant it in every possible way.

She looked at him as if she was uncertain how to begin.

"If I have offended you in some way—" he said.

"No. You haven't."

He was glad to know it, but even more puzzled about her recent coolness.

Miss Deeping took a visible breath. "Many people seem to think that a gentleman couldn't really be interested in a woman's ideas. They say that if he expresses any such interest, he must be…courting her."

Someone had said this to her about him, Laurence concluded. And he suspected *courting* might not have been the word used.

"I would hate it if you were using the…investigative process as an excuse to get in my good graces," she burst out. She grimaced. "I'm not certain I have any good graces."

"Can you think I would use my parents' murders as an excuse for a dalliance?" He wouldn't. He hadn't. Yet the old tragedy was undoubtedly a strand in the complex connection weaving between them.

"So your only motive is to pursue the investigation together." Her gaze raked over him, challenging, acute.

He couldn't say yes to that. It would be a lie. "I am honestly interested in solving the mystery. I would not pretend about that or try to deceive you." He wanted to add that he'd do almost anything to remain in her company. But she didn't want to hear that. That was her point. She didn't wish to be wooed. If he expressed any tender sentiments, she would turn away from him. There was a painful idea.

Laurence had never found himself in such a bind. He *had* learned, in London, to be circumspect and take care not to raise false expectations. Young ladies in town were on the lookout for any signs of interest, and many had mothers who were poised to pounce and maneuver a fellow into an offer. One learned to give them no excuse. Miss Deeping had turned this equation on its head. She was discouraging him, and he didn't *wish* to be discouraged. A pushing mama would be almost welcome just now! Did she really care nothing for him? He had been almost certain, on more than one occasion, that she did. How was he to find out if all mention of affection was forbidden?

⤸

"I'm glad that's settled then," said Charlotte. She was *not* disappointed at getting exactly what she'd wanted. How could she be? She should be pleased. She *was*. What she felt was not low spirits. It was calm satisfaction. "I'm sorry I was cool toward you." This was true. In fact, with the way he was looking at her now, she had a sudden urge to throw her arms around him.

No, she didn't. That was foolish. They were not enveloped in an aura of yearning so intense it seemed to make the very air thrum with longing. Charlotte blinked, shocked at this most uncharacteristic thought.

Glendarvon nodded as if she'd said something funereal. They stood beside the fence, placid mares and lively foals in the background.

"I should go in," said Charlotte. "Mama is buzzing with plans for the dance." She felt defeated by this awkward conversation. Cecelia would not be impressed by the way she'd used her advice. Realizing her hands were trembling, she folded them together under her cloak.

The marquess started like a man waking from a dream. "I wanted to tell you that I heard from my estate manager. He found some papers I wished to show you."

Charlotte's thoughts veered immediately into more familiar territory—a puzzle to be untangled. She was on firm ground there. It was like moving from teetering stepping-stones to a safe shore. "Is there any useful information?"

"Some, I believe."

"That's splendid." She itched to get her hands on it. "Bring everything to the morning room an hour before dinner. No one will be there at that time, and if we dress early, we can look over what you have while people are changing."

"Right."

He looked down at her as if he was trying to read some arcane message in her face. Was there some secret language of expressions? How did one learn that? And if she knew it, what would she wish to convey?

"I also enjoy your company," he blurted. "Greatly. I cannot pretend that I don't. That would be a lie." He turned and walked away.

She watched him go with a wistful delight that was quite foreign to her.

Later, as she waited in the morning room for Glendarvon

to appear, Charlotte was aware that she'd put on her most flattering gown and taken particular care with her hair. When she found herself pressing her lips together to add color, she had to acknowledge that Glendarvon's final words at the paddock had thrilled her. Experience had taught Charlotte that gentlemen did not enjoy her company. They found her disconcerting. *Prickly* was the irritating word she had heard far too often. But not from him. Never from him. She found herself blinking back tears and felt a twinge of horror. She wasn't some silly deb flaunting herself on the marriage mart. She would not give in to soppy sentiment. That went against everything she was. How could she trust these wild new impulses?

The marquess came in, very handsome in his evening dress, carrying a fat envelope. Business, Charlotte thought. This was not an assignation but a meeting to push forward their joint task.

He laid papers out on the table that usually held the bustle of breakfast in a laudably orderly manner.

Charlotte revived with a pulse of greed for the facts they contained.

"There are three former servants still receiving pensions," Glendarvon said, putting a hand on the first pile. "The others have died over the last twenty years."

"Do those three live nearby?"

He shook his head.

That was too bad. But one couldn't expect an investigation to be easy.

"My agent also found some correspondence with Mr. Cantrell at Lorne."

"Your parents wrote to him?"

"A few times." He indicated the second—thinner—pile.

Charlotte picked it up and ran her eyes down the page. "Your father thanks Cantrell for 'taking in' something."

"Perhaps he hosted some friends of theirs?"

"But why would he? They didn't live far apart. And your house is far larger."

"To hunt?" Glendarvon didn't seem satisfied with this idea.

Charlotte shook her head. She turned the page to look at another note. There were only two. "This assures Cantrell that the 'arrangement' is temporary." She frowned. "What arrangement?"

"I don't know. It is dated three months before they were killed," the marquess pointed out somberly.

"I wonder if it concerned the chests hidden in the cellar at Lorne?"

"That is a possibility."

"It seems an odd choice to give Cantrell anything for safekeeping. He was so much older, nearly certain to die before your parents. In normal circumstances," she added uncomfortably.

"And Lorne is part of the ducal estate," the marquess replied. "Not his to dispose of. We should find out more about Cantrell."

"I've heard Cecelia talk about him. They've worked out that he was a second cousin of the previous duke, who probably gave him leave to stay at Lorne. Unfortunately, the records were left in great disarray. They couldn't think of anyone to ask about him as that generation is all gone. Except for Tereford's grandmother Lady Wilton."

"The ogre of Almack's?"

"What?"

"Some of the younger men in London called Lady Wilton that."

Charlotte laughed. "I don't wonder. They don't want to attract her close attention. She exacts payment in juicy gossip." Guiltily, she remembered she had alerted the old lady to the marquess. Fortunately, Lady Wilton seemed to have forgotten about him.

Nodding, Glendarvon indicated the much thicker third pile of paper. "I asked him to send along copies of my parents' wills, in case they might contain anything relevant. I had never actually looked at them." He shrugged uneasily. "At first I couldn't read, of course. Later, there seemed no reason since I'd been told all the terms."

He hadn't wanted to return to the most painful episode of his childhood, Charlotte knew.

"They are simple because both of them were young," he continued. "Each left everything to me, with provision for my mother if Father should die before her. There is just this one odd thing in my mother's testament." He shuffled to the last page and pointed.

At the bottom, next to the deceased woman's signature, were Chinese characters like those they'd found on the scrolls in the chests.

Charlotte raised her eyes. They looked at each other.

"I hope Henry returns soon with the translator," she said.

"Indeed."

Sounds outside the room indicated people were assembling for dinner. "I should put these away for now," the marquess said.

"Yes." Charlotte watched the papers disappear into the

envelope with simmering impatience. The desire to *find out* was intense. Looking up again, she saw the same need in Glendarvon's blue eyes.

Fourteen

"IT WAS TOO BAD OF HENRY TO GO AWAY JUST BEFORE OUR assembly," said Charlotte's mother the following morning.

"We're hardly short of men to partner with the ladies," Charlotte replied. "In fact, we have a plethora."

"What a word!" Mama exclaimed. "Still, why did he have to leave just now? His position was not to begin until the New Year. I don't see why he should have any Foreign Office business to see to."

Sitting with her mother in her parlor, once again reviewing all the arrangements for the coming event, Charlotte was full of mental calculations. Henry had departed very early in the morning two days previously. He'd no doubt ridden hard and should be in London soon. Perhaps already, barring mishaps. He'd taken one of the carved wooden plaques from the cellar at Lorne as a sample to show potential translators. How long would it take to find the right person? All Charlotte's will bent to speed his errand. She was finding it very hard to wait. "He said he would be back soon," she said, as much to herself as to her mother.

"Well, we cannot worry about him. Has the champagne arrived from Leicester?"

"Yes, Mama." Charlotte was certain she'd told her this already.

"And the lobsters from the seaside?"

"Yes, Mama. Cook has them." She thought Mama was making an excessive effort over what was no more than a small neighborhood hop. But it was clearly more to her mother. They'd never held anything resembling a ball here at home. This did qualify, barely, and Mama seemed determined to make it memorable. "All is going well," Charlotte assured her.

"It's only a day away now."

"And everything is ready," Charlotte soothed.

"What gown do you intend to wear?"

"The lilac."

"I suppose that will do."

"It was made in London for the season." Charlotte had yielded to her friend Cecelia's advice and allowed a cascade of ruffles down the skirt. Everyone had said it looked well on her.

"You will only go off in a corner and sulk anyway," said her mother.

"I do not sulk!"

"Well, you never seem to have a good time at a ball. Sour faces don't help, you know."

"I don't—" Charlotte couldn't see her own expressions, of course. And she had felt sour at times. Gentlemen had not *flocked* to dance with her at society balls. If they were brought up and presented as suitable partners, they did their duty mostly in silence and hurried away after the set, since Charlotte had acquired a reputation for being sharp-tongued early on. She hadn't meant to. And she was certain she'd never said anything cruel or unfair. But her casual observations on life apparently inspired fear in the common run of young men. And so they avoided her when they could. Thinking of that happening in front of Glendarvon, even though he was *not* wooing her, Charlotte found she did not like the picture. She didn't wish him to see her being rejected, or reduced to dancing with her brothers.

An idea occurred to her. It was an idiotic idea, and yet it lingered in her brain, drifting back each time she pushed it aside. Through the day, it nagged until she was nearly reduced to scolding herself aloud. And after dinner that evening, when the gentlemen joined them in the drawing room, she found herself moving toward one of her brothers. Despite seething ambivalence over the plan, she ended up beside Cecil, eliciting an interrogative look. "May I ask you something?"

"Of course. But if you wish to know why our aunt has cockerel feathers in her hair, I can't tell you."

Charlotte smiled and still couldn't get the words out.

"Is something wrong?"

"No." She wanted to turn away and she didn't. This dithering was unlike her. "I just wondered if you might…"

He raised his quizzing glass to examine her. "You're beginning to worry me, Charlotte. What is it?"

"Would you look at my dress for the dance and see what you think?" she blurted.

Behind the magnifying lens, his eye widened. "You want my sartorial advice?"

"You are the most fashionable of us all," Charlotte replied.

"Which you never cared a whit about through an entire London season."

Her brother's gaze grew sharper. Charlotte felt uncomfortably exposed.

"What is different now?" he asked. "Why do you care?"

She started to turn away. "Never mind. This was a foolish—"

"No, no. You have asked, and I accept. You won't escape now." He let the glass drop and rubbed his hands together.

"Finally, a chance to deck out my only sister. I'll give you an entirely new touch."

Charlotte was already having second thoughts. "We had a first-class abigail to dress us in London." They'd paid a premium price for her services.

"She was competent, but much too conventional and prim," Cecil said. He pressed his lips together. "We can't have a new gown made in time, of course, but…"

"I've changed my mind." Her brother's focused glee was worrisome.

"Too late. The deal is struck."

"There was no deal, Cecil. I only asked you to look at my gown."

"Which was very wise of you. The leaders of society seek my opinion, you know. One of the patronesses of Almack's, who shall remain unnamed, swears I have a finer eye than her desperately expensive modiste."

Charlotte supposed it was Lady Cowper. This sounded like her. "I don't—"

"Don't wish to make everyone at our little ball gape in amazement?" Cecil interrupted archly. "Don't wish the gentlemen to fall at your feet in awed admiration?"

Though Charlotte knew the chances of this were vanishingly small, she found she couldn't resist the picture.

"Which gown do you intend to wear?" her brother asked.

"I thought… You may not remember my lilac crepe."

"I have an unerring memory for garments." Cecil pressed his lips together, considering. "That one does flatter you. But we might do better. Let us go and examine your wardrobe."

"Now?"

"We have very little time for this major renovation, Charlotte."

"Thank you," she replied dryly. "But I would prefer Mama not…join in. And if we disappear now, she will wonder why."

"She would limit our scope," Cecil acknowledged. "First thing in the morning, then. I will rise early just for you. We will lay everything out and see what we can do in a day."

Feeling oddly dilapidated, Charlotte moved away. Cecil couldn't make her wear anything she didn't wish to, she told herself. She would hear his opinions and make her own decision. Her gaze caught on Glendarvon talking to her brother Stanley on the other side of the drawing room. The thought of dazzling him had a curious appeal. She'd never wished to make a man's jaw drop in admiration before. Not any specific man at least. Not with this bone-deep longing. And why should she wish it? She'd practically *commanded* him not to court her.

❧

The Deeping house buzzed with preparations the next day, and Miss Deeping was kept fully occupied by her mother. Laurence followed the example of the household's sons and stayed out of the way. He looked over the documents his agent had sent more carefully, but discovered nothing new. He went out to the stables with Stanley and walked around the property. They passed the new stallion, Dexter, racing across a field, head high, tail flagging. "He's calmed down," Laurence noted.

"He's found his place in the herd," Stanley replied.

"How do you keep your stallions from fighting?"

"We give them each plenty of space, with mares and geldings in between."

Dexter turned and curveted. Laurence noted, "He is a magnificent animal."

"His line will be even more so," said Stanley with satisfaction as they walked on.

The day seemed long. Laurence began to suspect that any day when he couldn't exchange even a word with Miss Charlotte Deeping might drag. There had to be something he could do about that.

When he came downstairs dressed for the evening's festivities, Laurence found that some favored guests had arrived for dinner, including the Terefords and the Fralings, with Stanley's young lady, Felicity, very pretty in rose-pink. Laurence went over to speak to the duke. "Any word from Henry Deeping?" he asked quietly.

"None yet," was the reply. "He said it would take a few days to find a translator he could trust."

"Yes."

"But we hope not too many."

"I am eaten up with curiosity," Laurence said.

The duke nodded.

"It is very hard to be completely reliant on others to solve a mystery," said his wife.

Tereford smiled at her with fond understanding. She returned it with wry affection.

How did one get to that point? Laurence wondered. He'd seen happy couples before, naturally, but the Terefords seemed to have a particular harmony. There was nothing sickly-sweet about it, and it appeared to enhance rather than mute their personalities. Watching them made one want the same.

Which he was never going to find without some wooing, forbidden to him by the inimitable Charlotte Deeping. Most girls wanted to collect a string of suitors, but not her. She was... At that moment, she entered the room, and he lost his train of thought. Or any thoughts, really. His mind came to a full stop—dazzled.

Miss Deeping always looked well, but tonight she was... radiant. Like a Greek goddess, Laurence thought. Her slender form was draped in a swirl of color—lilac and amber and a frothy cream—teasing the subtle curves of her body as they flowed. Bands of matching ribbons set off her dark hair, with wisps of curls framing her face. He was riveted, entranced. Intercepting a glowing, vividly intelligent glance, he wanted to stride over to her and lay a claim. If he swept her into his arms and told her she was the loveliest creature he'd ever seen, a scandal would rise. Worse than that, all compliments were forbidden to him. He'd promised not to say such things.

Other men were staring at her, he saw. Even Stanley and Bertram Deeping looked amazed. Cecil, on the other hand, did not. His expression was smug. Laurence became conscious of a wish to warn all others off. Another impulse he had no right to act on. This was unbearable.

He was not seated beside Miss Deeping at dinner. A prominent neighbor received that honor, and Laurence had to watch the man flirt with her through the meal, though the fellow was fifty if he was a day and had his wife and two daughters with him.

More guests began to arrive as soon as they left the table. The hubbub grew as people shed wraps and made last-minute adjustments to their festive garb.

The Deeping house had no ballroom, but three parlors

along the back of the house could be joined by pushing back sliding doors. This had been done in the morning, and the furniture had been carted out, making space for the dancing.

Laurence pushed past the newcomers, skirting perilously near rudeness, determined to secure the first dance with Miss Deeping. But he missed out. A bumptious neighbor was there before him. Laurence begrudged him the smile he was granted and possession of her hand as the wretched fellow led her into the set that was forming.

"Going to ask someone to dance?" inquired Stanley, suddenly at his side. He had Miss Felicity Fraling on his arm and looked pleased with himself.

It was impolite not to. Looking around, Laurence encountered interested and calculating and hopeful gazes from the young ladies without partners. "Will you introduce me?" he asked his friend. He couldn't lean against the wall brooding, as Lord Byron was said to have done in his day. That would be a poor return for the Deepings' hospitality.

"Of course," said Stanley. "Who is your choice?"

He didn't care. "You choose for me."

Stanley gave him a sidelong look.

"Hannah Sidley," said Miss Fraling.

Stanley blinked, then smiled down at her with amused warmth. She twinkled back at him.

For a moment, Laurence feared a joke at his expense. But Stanley was not that sort, and Miss Fraling didn't seem to be either. They led him over to a young lady who looked a bit older than many of the others. She was calm and self-possessed rather than pretty, and she was not one of those who had been eying Laurence with eager speculation.

She seemed surprised when they approached her. He was

introduced and asked her to dance. She accepted, and they joined the set as the musicians struck up.

"You are a friend of Stanley Deeping's?" she asked as they moved into the first steps.

"Yes, we met at Eton," Laurence replied.

"He and Felicity Fraling make a lovely pair."

Laurence wasn't sure whether to agree. He didn't wish to betray Stanley's confidences. Although his friend's ardent interest was obvious in the way he looked at his partner in the dance. "Are you a friend of Miss Charlotte Deeping?" he asked instead.

"An acquaintance, merely," replied Miss Sidley. "I am several years older, and she was away at school a great deal, so we never spent much time together." She glanced at him as they turned and moved down the row of the country dance. "Are *you* a friend of hers?"

He wasn't sure how to answer that. He hoped he was. He wished to be. And more.

"Did you meet during her London season?" Miss Sidley asked.

"No, here." He was not coming off as a sparkling conversationalist, Laurence realized. "When Stanley invited me to stay for the hunting."

She nodded as they separated and processed up the lines. Laurence circled around, passing close to Miss Deeping as he stepped to his place. She smiled at him, and all other thoughts went out of his head.

The set went on. After an indeterminate time, the music ended. Laurence thanked Miss Sidley for the dance.

"You are most welcome," she said. "It was an unexpected pleasure."

He raised his eyebrows. Had she thought he would be a poor dancer?

"I didn't expect to be asked," she explained.

"Why not?"

"Well, everyone here thinks of me as the dowdy older sister. Quite on the shelf. You can see how they are marveling."

Looking around, Laurence did catch a number of puzzled gazes. To confound them further, he escorted Miss Sidley to the refreshment table for a glass of lemonade.

⁓

It felt odd to be attracting so much attention, Charlotte thought. Especially when she was wearing two of her London gowns taken apart and reassembled into a dashing confection under Cecil's direction. The fluttering draperies felt as if they might fall off at any moment, though they were sturdily sewn and only seemed to be revealing. She had twirled several times before a long mirror to be certain of that, and to get the full effect, which was, truthfully, stunning. It had been a distinct pleasure to surprise everyone. She thought Glendarvon's jaw might have actually dropped. The idea sent a tingle of triumph through her.

The marquess was coming toward her now. He'd been dancing with Hannah Sidley, which was interesting, when all the other girls in the room were obviously trying to entice him. Dancing very gracefully, Charlotte noted. But he was obviously headed toward her now. Charlotte didn't deign to examine the fact that she longed to dance with him.

A young neighbor came between them and requested a dance. She couldn't refuse him and then accept another partner immediately after. That would be rude. And far too revealing of her interest. So she allowed him to lead her away.

As she took her place, she saw her mother introduce the marquess to Anne Drake. Charlotte felt a moment of betrayal. Miss Drake was the loveliest and most vivacious girl here. Well, after Felicity Fraling at least. Had Mama *had* to pick her? But she'd undoubtedly insisted on being presented. Mama could hardly have refused.

Through the set, Miss Drake chattered flirtatiously and offered up dazzling smiles. Glendarvon responded. Naturally. He was always polite. Did Charlotte expect him to glower at a charming young lady? He was probably enjoying himself very much. She set herself to do the same, refusing to watch him. And then stealing glances when she couldn't help it.

But when that dance was over, Glendarvon bowed to his partner and moved swiftly to Charlotte's side. "May I have the next?" he asked.

Once Charlotte might have worried that he was doing it out of obligation or kindness, but not tonight. A sense of reckless triumph had come over her. She took his hand and walked into the set.

They faced each other. As she met his eyes, Charlotte felt as if light flashed from hers. The music began. She stepped, touched his hand, turned within his arm, glided down the row. She smiled, and he looked entranced. She could not be mistaken about that.

The set was like none she'd ever danced before, not at any grand ball she'd attended in London. Everything else in the room became a backdrop as their hands clasped. They whirled and dipped and passed under the raised arms of the other dancers. It was more intoxicating than the champagne her mother had stocked, of which she'd drunk more than her usual quota. She didn't wish it to end. She wanted to keep dancing with him forever. Dancing and what else?

And so, when the music stopped, Charlotte kept turning until they faced the far end of the joined parlors. She knew all the ins and outs of her own home. As the dancers milled about and returned to their starting points or reshuffled for the next set, she slipped behind a swath of drapery, pulling Glendarvon with her. There was a wide bow window behind it, leaving a sizable recess. The casement was slightly open, letting in a stream of cool autumn air.

The space was dim after the candlelit parlor. The curtains muffled some of the sound of the party. Charlotte had kept her hold on Glendarvon's hand. Now she shifted her fingers to his forearm and gazed up at him. He looked back, surprise giving way to a silent question. They were very close together. She was further intoxicated by his masculine scent. And there it was again, that inarticulate longing vibrating through her whole body.

Without giving herself time to examine her motives, Charlotte let herself fall into that flood. She stood on tiptoe and kissed him.

It was an amateurish, glancing kiss and might have been nothing had he not put his arms around her, pulled her close, and taken the embrace into another realm entirely. He was clearly no novice at kissing. His lips were an education, a gentle, insistent guide that took Charlotte step by step into spiraling arousal. And then his hands! They pressed her against him, kept her upright when her knees went weak, hinted at wild explorations. Charlotte felt as if she'd been dipped in fire. She laced her arms around his neck and arched up to meet him level for level as the embrace went incandescent.

She hadn't known she could feel so intensely. No one had explained—well, how could they? Mere words couldn't explicate passion. This storm of sensation was not susceptible to her familiar charts and analysis. She was whirling in unknown territory. And rather to her own surprise, she relished the plunge. Charlotte threw caution to the wind, melting against the hard muscle of his frame, urging him on with her whole being. All else disappeared. For a timeless interlude, the world was well and truly lost.

Then a girl's voice, seeming right next to Charlotte's ear, said, "I must have a dance with the handsome marquess."

Charlotte started and pulled dizzily back from him.

"I am determined," the voice added. "Where do you think he has gone?"

Someone must be standing right on the other side of the drapery, Charlotte realized. Just inches away, with no idea of their torrid embrace. She caught her breath and pressed her throbbing lips together. She wanted to laugh in crazy triumph. She wanted to climb out the window and run away with this man, never to return. She wanted to proclaim her revelations to the crowd.

It was hard to see in the low light, but Glendarvon seemed to be smiling down at her. He reached up to touch her cheek, and she trembled.

"There is Mrs. Deeping," said the voice. "Let us go and speak to her. She *must* present me." Footsteps moved off.

Mention of her mother brought Charlotte down to earth. Mama *would* be looking for her. And she knew the nooks and crannies of the house better than Charlotte did.

"We must go," Glendarvon whispered. "Much as I would like to stay."

The rough regret in his voice thrilled her. Charlotte gripped the cloth of his coat, yearning for another of those melting kisses.

"I don't want to cause trouble for you," he murmured.

She'd insisted she wanted no wooing from him. That had been a lie, Charlotte thought. Or it had become one in the past few minutes. One or the other. Both. Who cared? Now she knew she wanted so much more.

He let her go and moved away. For a moment, Charlotte felt bereft. Then she gave in to reality and stepped back.

Putting one eye to a crack in the curtains, she saw no one was nearby. Dancers passed at a little distance, like a moving screen. Holding up a hand to signal caution, she spread her fingers to indicate five minutes. When the marquess nodded, she peeked once again, found the coast still clear, and slipped out.

❧

Laurence stood in the dimness, recovering. He'd been aroused to the point of madness, and it wasn't easy to regain his senses. Her unexpected kiss and eager response to his touch had ravaged him. She was quicksilver and flame. Just thinking of her, he had to fight down desire once again. Lord, he wanted her!

The music was playing on the other side of the curtain. The dance went on. He would be missed. He had to get himself under control and go back. How could he watch her dance with other men after that?

Taking a deep breath, and then another, he checked the crevice in the drapery, chose his moment, and emerged. No one appeared to notice. He stood by the curtain for a while, as if he'd been loitering there, then made his way slowly around the edge of the room. He tried not to look for Miss Deeping, and failed. She was dancing with her brother Bertram. She was laughing.

Laurence's hands flexed involuntarily with the need to touch her. He wanted—everything.

The dancers wheeled to the right. She encountered his gaze, missed a step, and recovered with an assist from her brother. He was glad to see it. Perhaps she was feeling as dizzy as he was. She must be!

One thing was certain. A girl couldn't kiss a man senseless and then declare he wasn't to court her. That wasn't fair, and it couldn't be what she wanted. Every soft gasp, every eager response had shown that. He would make her his. And in that moment, Laurence realized he wanted Miss Charlotte Deeping for his wife. More than he'd ever wanted anything in his whole life. And he would do whatever was necessary to win her.

Fifteen

WORD CAME THAT HENRY DEEPING WAS ON HIS WAY BACK. He'd sent a fast courier ahead of the post chaise he'd hired, financed by the duke. Other than that, he sent little information.

"Why not tell us more?" Charlotte asked Cecelia, who had received the courier and passed along the message. They sat in her parlor at Lorne chewing over the news.

"I assume he didn't want to give any details as we wish to keep the matter confidential."

That made sense, though it was still frustrating. "He must have found a translator, since he is traveling in a coach," Charlotte said.

The duchess nodded. "He expects to arrive here tomorrow afternoon."

It had been decided that Henry would return first to Lorne, not the Deeping house. The visitor could thus be passed off as an acquaintance of the duke. Also this was where the scrolls were located. "I shall visit you again then," Charlotte declared.

Cecelia did not look surprised. "Will you bring Glendarvon along?"

Charlotte avoided her eyes. "Why would I?"

"Are you not investigating the mystery together?"

"Are we?" Charlotte's voice trembled, and she hated that.

"So I understood." The duchess continued to gaze at her. "It's obvious you are very taken with him. Why pretend? He is suitable and—"

"Because he has a title?" Charlotte interrupted with a snap.

"No," replied the duchess with exaggerated patience. "Because he seems honest and intelligent and kind."

She didn't mention he was dizzyingly attractive. Charlotte had figured that out through direct experimentation. And that was the problem. If she came within two feet of the marquess, her body started to yearn in his direction. Her mind went worryingly blank. She was thrown back into those moments when the world had melted into kisses. It was deeply unnerving. And impossible to make polite conversation with a man she'd passionately embraced behind a drapery. She'd been avoiding him since the dance.

"What's wrong, Charlotte?" asked Cecelia.

Something inside her gave way at this sympathetic inquiry. She'd lost her old friends one by one to the tides of passion, and now she appeared to be losing her very self. "Am I to let go of everything I am?" she blurted out. "I kissed him. And now when I'm near him, my thoughts whirl away like leaves in an autumn gale." Charlotte closed her hands into fists, gripping so hard her knuckles went white. "My brain has always been orderly. Do you remember the chart I made for Tom? In London?"

"I do. It was masterful."

"*That* is me. Everyone has always said so. Ada and Sarah and Harriet relied on my powers of analysis. Even my brothers acknowledge them." Charlotte lifted her fists to her temples. "But now I have become chaos."

Cecelia reached out, took Charlotte's hands, and pulled them down to hold them. Charlotte did not unfurl her fingers. A little silence passed. It did not bring calm.

"Do you think I have lost myself to marriage?" the duchess asked then. "You knew me before I wed, and now after."

Her attention caught, Charlotte paused and thought about this. "You seem the same. But I don't see what goes on in your mind."

"That is true. You can only trust me when I say it is not much altered. Even though I care so deeply about James."

"But…does he make your…senses reel?"

"Oh yes," replied Cecelia with a small secret smile.

Charlotte flushed and looked away. She'd begun to feel self-conscious.

"I saw a good deal of Sarah after her marriage, and she seemed much the same as ever."

"That's splendid for both of you, then." Charlotte sounded sullen. She heard it and couldn't help it.

"You haven't had much practice in romance," said the duchess.

"Because that's not the sort of person I am!" This was the point. Hadn't her friend understood that?

Cecelia bowed her head in acknowledgment. "You are the sort of person who likes to learn. I know that very well about you. You relish a new field of study."

That was true. But irrelevant.

"And love is a marvelous subject. Endlessly fascinating."

Love. She hadn't actually faced up to that word, Charlotte realized with an inner tremor. She wasn't quite ready to do so now. "Can one…investigate such a thing?"

"Continual learning and changing are vital in love, in my opinion. The rewards are rich."

This didn't seem to be quite what she'd meant. "But can it be organized?" Charlotte asked a little desperately.

"Well, I don't know about charts…"

Charlotte saw Cecelia hiding a smile and was suddenly overcome with mortification at her outburst. She wasn't certain what she'd actually said and what had only been running through her mind. She *was* certain she'd made a fool of herself. She pulled her hands away and folded her arms.

"What does Glendarvon have to say about this?" Cecelia asked.

"Because his opinion is more important?"

"No, Charlotte. I did not say that, and I assure you I did not think it. But it is equally pertinent. Is it not?"

Charlotte looked away. "I can't face him. Fortunately, he's been out on the hunting field a good deal." And her mother's rota had put her beside their other guests at dinner, though that wouldn't last.

"You should talk to him."

"How can I talk if I can't think?" Cecelia hadn't really understood. Possibly, Charlotte hadn't explained clearly, but she couldn't do better right now. "He must take care of himself."

"Perhaps he would like to take care of you."

"Because I have become incapable?" It sounded ill-natured.

"Not what I meant, Charlotte."

She knew that and was aware of her sulky tone. Cecelia had been characteristically gracious. Yet Charlotte couldn't bear any more kindness. She sprang to her feet. "I must go. I will see you tomorrow." And she rushed out before her friend could reply.

❧

Laurence received word of Henry Deeping's expected return through the duke as they trotted back toward the Deepings' after an energetic hunt capped by the taunting escape of the fox into another deep complex of burrows.

He was having similar success—or lack of it—in his pursuit of Miss Deeping. She was even better at diversion and evasion. Did she think he would catch her in his arms and indulge in more kisses? He pushed aside a surge of desire. All he wished to do was talk and ask her a particular question. Well, not *all*, Laurence admitted to himself. More kisses would hopefully follow if she answered as he hoped. But he'd begun to worry that she didn't intend to, that she regretted their encounter behind the draperies. He had to speak to her.

He knew she would be there for her brother's return from London. And so he kept an eye out for her departure to Lorne that afternoon. She somehow slipped past him, however, and he only caught up with her at the gates of the duke's house. "Miss Deeping," he called, spurring Ranger on. "A moment."

She had to have heard him, but she didn't turn. Instead, she went faster and was dismounting at the shed where Tereford sheltered horses by the time he reached her. "It's quite cold, isn't it?" she said as he came up. "A fire will be most welcome." She handed her reins to the groom the duke had hired and rushed away.

Laurence might have been annoyed, but he had to believe her haste signified some emotion. He was wild to discover whether it was inclined in his favor.

Inside, he and the duke found Miss Deeping seated next to the duchess, practically radiating a resolve not to be moved. He had to sit opposite her, burning with longing, and only a lifetime of hiding his true feelings let Laurence make light conversation in these maddening circumstances. That and a vow that he *would* speak to her on the ride back.

The post chaise pulled up at the front door of Lorne at two. They had been watching for it for some time and were looking out the windows when it arrived. Henry Deeping rode beside it.

All four of them hurried out and found him dismounting. Deeping nodded a greeting and went to open the carriage door. When he handed down two women, Laurence was surprised. He'd been expecting a bent, gray-haired old man to decipher their scrolls, he realized, amused at his own preconceptions.

They retreated to the parlor in a crowd. Once inside, Henry Deeping said, "Allow me to introduce Miss Daphne Palliser, who has kindly agreed to do our translating."

The older of the two women nodded. Stocky and brown-haired, with a bookish air, she appeared to be in her thirties. She was attired in a plain pelisse and wore spectacles that magnified her gray eyes, making her look owlish.

"And this is Miss Kate Brown," Deeping added, his tone stiff.

The second young lady seemed a decade or so younger, but she had an assured air and dress that suggested her position was not that of a servant or hired companion. She was as tall as Miss Deeping, square-shouldered, with honey-colored hair and violet-blue eyes. "Good day," she said in an accent like cut glass. Deeping named the four of them to complete the introductions. Both women's gazes shifted from one to the next as he did so.

The newcomers shed their outer garments, and everyone sat down. The small parlor felt crowded with so many in it.

"Would you like tea?" asked the duchess.

"I do not drink tea," said Miss Palliser. Miss Brown looked ambivalent.

"Something else?" The duchess's mind was clearly working. "A glass of wine? Or cider?"

"Cider," Miss Palliser agreed.

"Splendid. And you, Miss Brown?"

"Tea would be welcome," the other woman said, as if confessing a weakness.

"Miss Palliser is the daughter of an English diplomat," said Henry Deeping. "She has traveled all over the world."

"Unlike others of us who were never taken along," Miss Brown muttered.

Miss Palliser gave her companion a sidelong glance. "I encountered Chinese writing when I was eight years old and became fascinated," she said. "I have had the opportunity to study it in a variety of places"

"You were fortunate," said the duke, who leaned elegantly against the mantelpiece.

"Not particularly."

Tereford raised one dark eyebrow.

"My father believes in suiting himself. It was simply easier for him to let the servants pack me up and haul me along than to pay any attention to me. And so I did as I pleased."

She didn't seem bothered by this. Indeed, she was one of the most phlegmatic people Laurence had ever encountered.

"And your mother?" asked the duchess.

"Died in childbirth," Miss Palliser replied with startling composure.

"I am sorry," said the duchess, blinking. "And you, Miss Brown, are…"

"My grandfather was a friend of Miss Palliser's father. That is how I found her for you."

"You found her?" the duchess asked.

Everyone looked at Henry Deeping. Laurence thought he seemed disgruntled. "Miss Brown was kind enough to introduce me to Miss Palliser when she…discovered I was seeking a translator," he said.

"You weren't very subtle," said Miss Brown.

"That is exactly what I was!" replied Deeping, glowering. "I heard you."

"You were hidden behind a potted palm!"

"I was happy to hear of the project," said Miss Palliser.

"Miss Palliser's abilities are proven," Deeping added as if someone had questioned his choice.

"So you are not friends?" asked the duchess with less than her usual aplomb. She looked from one of her new guests to the other.

"We met for this journey," said Miss Palliser.

"I came to bear her company," said Miss Brown. "So that she needn't travel alone with a strange man."

"Not as strange as you," Henry Deeping muttered. Laurence didn't think anyone else heard him.

"And because you were intensely curious," said Miss Palliser with a slight smile.

"Who would not be?" asked Miss Brown.

This remark struck Miss Charlotte Deeping, Laurence noticed. Indeed, she seemed quite interested in the newcomers. "Your family did not object to your coming?" she asked Miss Brown.

"My grandfather died some months ago."

"I am sorry."

Miss Brown turned away as if the subject pained her.

The refreshments arrived, and Laurence was glad of it. He thought the conversation was growing awkward. Miss Brown received her cup of tea as if it was mildly shameful, which Laurence found odd. Miss Palliser sipped the cider appreciatively.

"Miss Palliser understands our wish to keep this matter private," said Henry Deeping. "She is not connected with any official organizations."

Their guest smiled ironically. "I am, after all, a woman. What 'official' connections could I have?"

Miss Deeping made a huffing sound, while Miss Brown frowned.

"Are you tired from your journey?" asked the duchess. "Would you like to rest for a while?"

Miss Palliser shook her head. "I am eager to look at your documents. I'd rather dive straight in."

Lanterns were fetched and lit. The whole party trooped down to the cellar and into the secret room. "Well hidden," commented Miss Palliser.

The chests were opened. She walked along them, now and then turning over an object or holding up a garment. "These are beautiful things from China," she said. "How did they come to be here?"

"We don't know," said the duke. "Perhaps these will tell us." He indicated the scrolls in the final chest.

"Ah." She bent to lift one out and carefully unrolled it. Laurence and Henry Deeping brought their lanterns closer to illuminate the paper but not close enough to risk igniting it. Time ticked by. "This appears to be about trade in Canton," said Miss Palliser after a while. "It speaks of the hongs—the merchant groups there." She looked around. "A table to spread it out on would be helpful. And I have brought some notes and sources to help me."

"Of course, you cannot be expected to work down here," said the duchess. "We must think how to set up a proper place." She pursed her lips. "Unfortunately, the house is small."

They closed the hidden door and went back upstairs. Laurence became aware of shouting as he reached the top. "Hello," called a man. "Is anyone there?"

Laurence recognized Merlin's voice reverberating down the stairwell from the upper floor.

"I'm going mad from boredom in this place," he yelled. "Where is the crutch I was promised? What's going on?" A thump echoed. It sounded like a fist hitting a tabletop. More of the same followed.

The duke's sigh was audible. The newcomers looked puzzled.

The duchess was right, Laurence thought. Lorne was a cramped place, particularly since the fire. He didn't see how it could accommodate the two new guests as well as a room for Miss Palliser to work on the translations. Merlin would undoubtedly be sticking his nose in at every opportunity. And perhaps talking too much again. The Deeping house was even worse, full of people with no knowledge of their discovery. There was no help for it. "They should come to my house," Laurence said.

Everyone turned to look at him.

"Miss Palliser and Miss Brown," he went on. "And the scrolls. There's more space." He turned to Miss Palliser. "We think the writing may be linked to my family. We could set up a study for you."

"Has everyone gone deaf?" shouted Merlin. "Or gone away?" The pounding resumed.

Laurence gave in to the inevitable. "Merlin could come as well," he said.

The duke brightened.

"Merlin?" asked Miss Brown and Miss Palliser in unison.

"It's a long story," replied the duchess.

"You intend to keep the translation results for yourself?" asked Miss Deeping coolly.

Something in her tone seemed to alert all the females in the parlor. They perked up like a pack of hounds hearing the view halloo. Their heads swiveled toward him. It was a bit uncanny.

Looking at Miss Deeping—sardonic, intrepid, lovely, fascinating—Laurence realized he cared more for her than for anyone else in this room, than anyone else in his life. *Wooing* was such a pallid word. He wanted to slay dragons for her. He wanted to lay her heart's desire at her feet. If he could discover what it was. If he couldn't *be* her heart's desire. How did a man manage that?

People were staring. He could at least show her he was serious about the investigation she'd initiated. "All of you are welcome to come along," he said. He would change the habits of a lifetime to have Miss Deeping near.

"We are a bit cramped here," said the duchess.

"The post chaise is still outside," said Henry Deeping.

"Where is your house?" asked Miss Brown. "Mr., er…"

"Lord Glendarvon," said Miss Palliser, who clearly did not forget anything told to her.

"Not too far away," said Laurence. "A few hours by coach."

"I can order a cart for Merlin," said the duke. "He can lie down in the back. Best he goes separately."

"Merlin?" repeated Miss Brown.

"It's a nom de guerre," said the duke.

There were some smiles. But not from Miss Brown. "Which war?" she asked.

"Er, *la guerre de l'amour*?"

This earned Tereford a resigned look from his wife.

Miss Brown looked from one to the other, probably wondering if she was being mocked.

"You seem to be interesting people," commented Miss Palliser.

Laurence stifled a laugh.

After a bit of debate, his suggestion was adopted. The newcomers' luggage was put back on the chaise, and the chest holding the scrolls was carefully transferred as well. The duke took it upon himself to inform Merlin of the move. And also urge him to keep quiet about developments, Laurence assumed. A cart was produced and filled with bedding to cushion his ride.

Laurence sent off a messenger with instructions to his housekeeper. Riding cross-country, the man would get there well before the carriage. Laurence would do the same. It was his duty as host. But he refused to leave until he had tried once more to speak to Miss Deeping. He used the excuse of retrieving some of his things from the Deeping house.

But the opportunity he had expected did not emerge. Henry Deeping joined them on the ride, and he filled the entire journey complaining about Kate Brown. "She treated me as if I were some sort of blackguard," he said. "She insisted on a character reference. I was forced to go to our uncle, who thought it very odd, I can tell you."

"Well, Henry, she knew nothing about you, after all,"

replied Miss Deeping. "If a stranger showed up and asked me to go off with him..."

"That is a different thing entirely! You are my sister, and—"

"Miss Palliser is someone whose skills you require. So she is to do as you say."

Prickly, thought Laurence as her brother made an exasperated sound. He'd come to enjoy her astringent quality, particularly when it was directed at someone else. She always gave a conversation zest.

"I was *glad* to have a female companion for Miss Palliser," said Deeping. "Of course. I would have hired someone to accompany her on the journey. I made that quite clear. There was no need to act as if I intended to kidnap her."

"I'm sure Miss Brown was simply being careful," said Miss Deeping.

"She was offensive. And someone else can escort them back to London. I've had enough!" Henry, usually so calmly urbane, scowled at the lane before them.

"Perhaps the marquess will do so."

"I will?" It was one of her verbal ambushes. Laurence rallied his faculties for a joust.

"You seemed to find them interesting," she added.

"Who would not? A young lady who can translate Chinese writing."

"Miss Brown is not interesting," said Henry Deeping. "She is insolent." He seemed pleased at the juxtaposition of words. His lips moved as if repeating them silently.

"You seemed interested in them yourself," Laurence said to Miss Deeping.

"And so you hurried them off out of my reach," she snapped.

She was angry about that. "It made sense if we want to get the translation done as efficiently as possible," Laurence pointed out.

"Oh, efficiently," said Miss Deeping, as if he'd named some irritating eccentricity.

"You should come as well."

"It is not so easy as that, as you *must* know."

"It was a good idea to offer them rooms at your home," said Henry. "Lets us all steer clear of Miss Brown's sharp tongue."

"It's splendid that you have settled everything between you," responded his sister. "My opinions are clearly not wanted." She urged her mare to a gallop and raced away.

This was not an auspicious moment for his important question, Laurence noted. He was not a fool.

"I am sick to death of carping women," said Henry Deeping. "I shall spend the coming days hunting. Without a lady in sight."

Laurence said nothing. His mind was with the graceful figure disappearing around the bend in the lane before them. His wooing was not going well. It had been a debacle, in fact. And now he had to leave her to see to these visitors. He'd boxed himself in there. He'd imagined her joining them, without thinking things through. It occurred to him that it would be wise to consult the duchess.

～

Reaching home, Charlotte went straight to her room to change out of her riding habit. She nearly threw it on the floor when she took it off. And she pulled a gown from her wardrobe completely at random. She was wildly frustrated with everything in her life at this moment, and the maddening Marquess of Glendarvon was at the center of it all. Maddening Marquess, she thought. It was the perfect label for him. He was driving her mad.

She could not believe Miss Palliser and the mysterious scrolls had been snatched out of her reach. The idea that the puzzle would be worked out and solved far away from her was insupportable. She had meant to take part in the unraveling. She'd imagined sitting with Miss Palliser, poring over the papers, and learning about their significance. Hadn't she been the one who began the whole endeavor? Wasn't that the point? She'd also been drawn to those two women. She would like to get to know them better.

You should come as well, the Maddening Marquess had said, as if it she could just hare off to a man's home whenever she liked. He knew—of course he knew!—that a young lady required permission and idiotic encumbrances like chaperones. Except Miss Brown and Miss Palliser apparently had the freedom to travel. Perhaps no one cared where they went or what they did. She didn't wish for that, of course. But she felt a twinge of envy nonetheless.

Now she was in the uncomfortable position of scheming for a visit to Glendarvon's home. People would assume she was pursuing him, setting her cap at a title as the gossips vulgarly put it. When all she wanted was to solve an old mystery.

No, not *all*.

Charlotte walked over to the window and looked out at the autumnal garden. She had to be honest with herself. There was the matter of passionate kisses. Her skin heated at the memory. Her breath quickened. She…wanted. She yearned for more of his intoxicating touch. *And* she was determined to retain her grip on logic and good sense. She refused to lose herself in a daze of desire. But she longed to kiss him again, to feel his arms around her, with an intensity she'd never experienced before in her life. She gripped the edge of the window and wrestled with the aching tide. The conflict was insupportable. What was she to do?

Glendarvon had ridden off to make certain his visitors were "suitably settled." He hadn't said when he intended to return. Or if he did. She'd avoided him since their incendiary embraces, and now he was gone. Charlotte was simultaneously bereft and filled with an anger she knew to be unreasonable. She fought both. She would *not* be at the mercy of a storm of feeling. If only she knew how to quell it.

Her brothers gave her a wide berth that evening, not wanting to feel the sting of her acerbic wit.

When the gentlemen gathered for the hunt the following morning, Charlotte was summoned to the drawing room to greet Cecelia, who had come along with her husband. Charlotte welcomed her with some surprise.

"Glendarvon stopped at Lorne on his way home," the duchess told her. "As you know there is no hostess at his home, which makes the ladies' stay a bit improper. I am going along to fill that position while the scrolls are translated."

Charlotte nodded.

"I'm eager to know what they contain, of course. As soon as may be."

"Of course. We all are."

The duchess nodded. "James is arranging for us to drive up tomorrow. I wanted to let you know." Her tone suggested that Charlotte should understand more than she was saying.

And then she understood and readied herself to pounce on the opportunity. But before she could speak, Cecelia added, "I hoped you might come along and bear me company."

With a gift dropped on her before she could ask, Charlotte met her friend's steady gaze. Cecelia's blue eyes were not guileless. On the contrary, they brimmed with guile. To what end? "Did he say anything else?"

"Glendarvon?"

"Yes, Cecelia. The Madd... I mean, who else?"

The duchess's delicate eyebrows went up at her slip of the tongue. "Nothing of consequence. That I recall."

"He didn't mention me?"

"No. Should he have?"

"No," Charlotte said. Her friend's gaze was...speculative? "I want to keep on with the investigation," she couldn't help but add.

"I knew you did. Such a great opportunity."

Charlotte found she couldn't care about Cecelia's arch tone. "Yes, thank you, I would like to come. I must speak to my mother first."

"Shall I come along?"

"No." Charlotte preferred to manage Mama herself.

"Very well." Cecelia rose. "I shall expect you to join us unless I hear otherwise."

Charlotte nodded, saw her out, and went in search of her mother. "Cecelia has agreed to serve as hostess," she told her when she had explained the invitation.

"I don't understand," Mama replied. "Why does everyone wish to go to Glendarvon's?"

This was a difficulty, since Charlotte couldn't explain the true reason. "Not everyone. It will be a bit of variety for Cecelia, and you know neither she nor I care much for hunting."

"The duchess is a suitable chaperone," her mother allowed. "Though I had thought them settled at Lorne for the hunting season."

"Cecelia says their work there is nearly done. They have decided to put Lorne up for sale."

"Have they?" Her mother looked intrigued. "I wonder what they will ask. Surely not an excessive amount, with the damage from the fire."

Remembering Mama's interest in properties for her younger brother, Charlotte said, "I will inquire if you like."

"Not just yet." Mama was clearly diverted by the idea, however. So much so that she seemed to have forgotten Charlotte's request.

"You've urged me to go to house parties before," Charlotte suggested.

"This isn't..." Mama examined Charlotte with care. "Such a visit might be seen as a marked sign of preference."

"It is just an outing. A country diversion."

"Is it?"

"Yes, Mama." Charlotte made her tone firm and uncompromising. She tried to look thoroughly sensible.

Her mother sighed. "Well, I suppose you may go. The duchess is responsible and trustworthy."

Charlotte felt a surge of triumph, which had to do with the knowledge that she would be in on the solving of the mystery. Not with her proximity to Glendarvon. Or opportunities to be alone with him. Not at all.

Henry expressed no interest in coming along. He had remained uncharacteristically touchy since his return from

London and told Charlotte he intended to concentrate on hunting as that was why he'd come to Leicestershire in the first place.

Charlotte went to pack her things and prepare to visit the home of the Maddening Marquess.

Sixteen

THE TEREFORDS' TRAVELING COACH HAD BEEN SUM-
moned back, and the party used it to reach Glendarvon's
home the following day. The marquess welcomed them
at the front door with a harassed expression, which was
explained when Miss Kate Brown came out after him, followed by Merlin on a set of crutches.

"Where is Mr. Deeping?" Miss Brown demanded amid
their greetings.

"Henry is not coming," said Charlotte.

"What? When he is the one who set all this in motion?"

This was not quite true, but she didn't wish to argue. "He
wanted to do some hunting."

"Hunting!" Miss Brown said the word as if it described
an outrage.

"Has Miss Palliser made any progress on the translation?"
asked the duke.

"She is working on it. She has not reported to me," Miss
Brown replied.

"I strongly object to the fact that I was not told about
these documents from the beginning," said Merlin. "I feel I
have been very ill-used in this matter."

"Do come in," said the marquess like a man seeking
rescue.

They filed past him. Charlotte reacted to his presence
like iron to a lodestone. He drew her. She couldn't help but
go closer.

But Merlin stumped up and planted himself between

them. "We had agreed to work together," he complained to Charlotte. "I considered it a promise. And then I was set aside like an old boot."

"Hardly that," she replied. She moved on, following the Terefords and Miss Brown through the entry hall.

"Exactly like that," said Merlin, swinging along beside her. He had already become adept with the crutches.

"You were brought here to be part of the investigation," Charlotte pointed out.

"After days of deception!"

She stopped and faced him. "You talked too freely about your ambitions to be a Bow Street runner. We didn't wish to attract any more attention. And it did not seem you could be trusted to keep quiet."

Merlin rocked to a halt and stared at her. Several expressions crossed his face. "You're saying I blabbed?"

She shrugged, letting him draw his own conclusions.

"And so it is my own fault that tree branch was sawn through?"

That didn't seem fair. "The person who did it is responsible. Have you any more ideas on who it might have been? As you...kept watch, did you ever notice anyone watching you?"

"Me?"

"Or trying to draw you out? Make you say more than you meant to?" Charlotte had thought about this, and it seemed likely. Merlin's prowling about the neighborhood of Lorne had been quite noticeable. "You lived alone for such a long time in Cornwall. Perhaps you became unused to...conversation." More than that, the stories she'd heard about Merlin suggested he was not a man who picked up subtle signals.

He bristled. "I did not tell any secrets!"

"Did you hint that you knew things?" Charlotte asked. She would have laid odds that he had. "Suggest buried truths would be coming out?"

Merlin's silence was answer enough.

She had a good deal of sympathy for him. She had often misinterpreted people's reactions when she was younger. And she was familiar with the temptation to hint at special knowledge. "I have often wondered how the Bow Street runners do their work," she went on. "Gathering information from those who may not wish to give it. That can't be easy. Especially when they have no official position and cannot force anyone to answer. I think they must be experts at blending into the background. In all sorts of different places." An errant thought struck her. "I have an acquaintance rather like that. He is an actor in London."

"An actor?" Merlin looked insulted. "Prancing about on the stage and spewing nonsense?"

"No. Well, he does prance a bit when he's in a play. But he is amazingly unobtrusive at other times."

"I don't want to disappear!"

This heartfelt cry moved Charlotte. She understood it all too well.

"And I won't," he added. "No matter how much anyone would like me to. You can count on that!" He moved through a doorway on the right, in the wake of the Terefords and Miss Brown. The sound of his crutches on the wooden floor gradually faded.

Laurence closed the front door and enjoyed an instant of blessed silence. His unplanned house party had been getting out of hand, and he was exceedingly glad to welcome new allies. The duchess's calm responses to Miss Brown had been a relief. And Miss Deeping had been her usual masterful self with Merlin. Laurence was filled with admiration and gratitude, along with delight at seeing her again. He wasn't sure why she remained standing with her back to him, now that the entry had emptied.

Before he could ask, she turned. Her eyes caught his and rendered him momentarily speechless. She was so…vivid. Everything grew more alive for him in her presence.

"I thought I might speak to Miss Palliser," she said. "Can you tell me where to find her?"

Fleetingly, he couldn't. His faculties had deserted him. He scrambled to recover them as her eyebrows drew together, and he just managed it. "She has a workplace set up in a parlor near her room."

"And that is?"

"Upstairs in the north wing." Laurence shook his head. "She is not very forthcoming so far. Perhaps you can find out more than I did. As you are not an instrument of masculine oppression."

"An…?"

He pointed to himself.

"What did you do?"

"I exist. I am male and titled. Therefore, I oppress. Apparently."

"I suppose you took some prerogative for granted," said Miss Deeping.

Laurence didn't think he had. He'd been trying to be a

good host. And a gentleman. Miss Palliser appeared to find him silly. And Miss Brown seemed primed to take offense. Like a cannon waiting for a match. She had exploded several times already. But he couldn't think about her when Miss Deeping was standing right here, bright and lovely. "Let me show you the portrait gallery," he said. "There are some fine pieces. You didn't have the chance to see it when you visited before." He offered his arm. "Miss Palliser will make a report at dinner."

She raised her eyes to his face, dropped them again.

"A bit of a stroll after your carriage ride," he added. "Work out the kinks. It's too cold to walk outside."

After what appeared to be an inner debate, she put a hand on his arm. He felt it as a triumph.

He led her to the gallery and talked for a time about his ancestors. Not too tediously, he thought. When he felt her fingers begin to relax on his arm, he said, "Just to be clear, I am doing my best to be charming because I am wooing you."

She pulled her hand away. "We agreed that you would not."

"Our…encounter at the dance changed the terms of our agreement. Don't you think?" Surely she must. It had altered everything for him.

She met his eyes. There were volumes to be read in her dark gaze, if he could only decipher them. They weren't quite as obscure as the markings on the mysterious scrolls. He thought he could see uncertainty, stubbornness. And— was it possible?—yearning.

"And so I intend to do a bit of courting," he continued with a flicker of hope.

"Indeed. And what will this entail?"

Laurence was delighted at the irony in her tone. This was the intriguing young lady he had fallen for. Also it was not a refusal. That was the key thing. "Pleasant conversation," he replied. "Exploration of your...interests."

Her cheeks flushed.

That last had not come out right, Laurence thought. It had sounded suggestive, which he hadn't meant. Kisses were not to be mentioned. And so, of course, the memory of them burned through him. "An occasional compliment," he added quickly.

"Such as?"

"Ah." He fumbled. "I have not prepared any."

"And they do not simply spring to mind in my presence?"

Was she teasing him? That had to be a good sign. Didn't it? She didn't sound angry.

"That seems to show a lack of foresight," Miss Deeping continued.

"I wasn't certain when I would get an opportunity to speak to you in private."

"And yet you were determined to find one?"

"Yes." He was off-balance. And willing to remain so for the rest of his life.

"And so you might have thought ahead."

"I will do so in future."

"Do you think there will be a future?"

She still spoke lightly, but he took the question as deadly serious. "Miss Deeping, do you have any objection to my character or appearance?"

"No."

"And have I done anything to offend you or give you a lasting distaste for me?"

She hesitated, then shook her head.

He had hoped for a bit more, but he noticed her eyes looked softer, inquisitive. "Will you grant me a chance to convince you?"

"Of what?"

"We'll see at the end of it, eh?"

"End of what?"

She had moved closer, like a wild creature enticed by a treat. Laurence leaned toward her and murmured, "The courting."

He bent his head. She raised her chin. The kiss fell into place as if it had happened many times before.

It started soft and sweet, one pair of lips confiding in another. It grew compelling, demand and response dancing back and forth between them. Laurence's fingers flexed as it veered into wildly arousing. He pulled her against him, felt her body soften and yield to his touch. Her hands laced behind his neck. She arched up, urging him on. Desire raged through him. The world was about to go up in flames.

But it couldn't. He couldn't sweep her away to bed, no matter how much he might want to. He had to take great care. He could not risk marring the most important endeavor of his life.

And so he let the kiss go and stepped back. The small disappointed sound she made filled him with triumph. The fact she stared, wild-eyed, then turned and rushed away was satisfying. She had clearly been shaken as deeply as he. He felt as if he'd won a crucial contest.

❧

After dinner that evening, when the servants had left the drawing room and only their party remained, Miss Palliser called for the group's attention.

"I have some things to tell you," she began when they turned to her.

Everyone gathered around her in a circle of sofas and chairs.

"I have looked through all the documents you gave me and divided them into three categories," she continued. "The largest has to do with operations of the hongs in Canton."

Charlotte called her thoughts to order. They tended to drift back to her recent encounter with the Maddening Marquess if she gave them the least opportunity, and now she took care to keep her gaze off Glendarvon lest she lose herself again. She would not lose herself! This was a moment to think, to apply her established skills. She was not a creature of whirling fire. She was Charlotte—sharp and analytical and organized. And she was about to learn information important to her investigation. "What are hongs?" she asked.

"The word refers to both a building and a type of Chinese merchant...intermediary," replied Miss Palliser. "Do you know how foreign trade works in China?"

Most people shook their heads. The duke made a so-so gesture. Merlin's crutches clattered as he moved them a bit.

"The emperor does not want trading ships landing wherever they please in China," explained the translator. "And so he decreed they can only trade in Canton, overseen by the hongs."

"They are middlemen," said the duke.

"Yes. All trade is to flow through them."

"Could old Mr. Cantrell have been a trader?" wondered Cecelia.

The duke shrugged his ignorance. "It seems unlikely."

"Who is that?" asked Miss Brown.

"The old man who used to live in the house where the scrolls were found," Charlotte told her.

"The second category is the will of a Chinese woman," said Miss Palliser. "Along with an inventory of the items she left. She must have been well off. It includes clothing and jewels and other precious things."

"The contents of the chests in Lorne's cellar," suggested Glendarvon.

The sound of his voice sent a thrill through Charlotte. Her body wanted to vibrate with it. She commanded it to stop.

"Those chests would not hold all the items listed," replied Miss Palliser. "It was the disposition of a great fortune. The third category of documents seems to be a personal narrative. I have only glanced at that one as of yet." She gazed around the room. "I think it best I translate all the first sort to begin."

"Why?" asked the marquess.

"Because from what I have seen so far, the information those contain may be dangerous."

"How so?" asked the duke.

"I have seen mention of corruption in the operations of a hong and of opium. You know about the disgrace of the opium trade?"

Miss Brown made an exasperated sound. "Of course they don't. No one pays attention."

"I am somewhat aware," replied the duke dryly. "Henry would be more so."

"And it is extremely irresponsible of Mr. Deeping not to be here," snapped Miss Brown. She glared around the circle as if his absence was their fault.

"He did his part in bringing Miss Palliser here," Charlotte could not help but say. She didn't like to hear her brother criticized. Not by anyone other than herself.

Miss Brown's violet eyes locked on her. Charlotte expected to see anger in them. But that was not the impression she gathered. Strain, she thought. Miss Brown looked like a person pushing herself to complete a mission and worried she might not succeed. The other woman looked away and said, "We English are practically addicted to our tea." Miss Brown looked at the teapot with obvious ambivalence. "Which comes from China. You must know *that* at least."

"I believe I have heard that," murmured the duke ironically.

Cecelia gave him a look; Miss Brown gave him a scowl.

"The English drink so much tea that we are running out of money to pay for it," said Miss Palliser. "The Chinese government requires silver or gold in exchange. They are not interested in our trade goods."

"And so traders have turned to darker means," said Miss Brown. "They are selling opium in China to get the money."

"Opium is illegal there," said Miss Palliser. "The emperor has banned it."

"But traders get the drug in India and smuggle it into China for gold in order to buy tea." Miss Brown scanned the group again. "The British have bribed officials and distributed opium freely to people to get them addicted."

"That is appalling," said the duchess.

"It is why I will not touch tea," said Miss Palliser.

"You mentioned corruption," said the duke. "Do you mean the hongs are involved in this illicit trade?"

"Phrases in the scrolls suggest one at least may be," replied Miss Palliser. "If they offer proof, this could cause great trouble in Canton."

"There is already trouble," said Miss Brown. "Politicians are all venal fools. It will end in war."

"We must hope it can be avoided," said Miss Palliser. She did not look hopeful.

"What does this have to do with the fire at Lorne and the ring I found and the events here?" asked Merlin, gesturing at the room around them. "We can do nothing about politics half a world away."

"Perhaps we should try," murmured Cecelia.

Glendarvon nodded. "As for the connections, when we see exactly what we have, we can draw conclusions." He looked at Miss Palliser. "How much time do you need?"

"Probably more than one day. There are a good many documents, and sometimes I need to consult sources or think about the translations."

"I would be happy to be of assistance in any way I can," said Charlotte. She was gratified when Miss Palliser accepted the offer with a nod.

The party broke into smaller groups. Charlotte went to sit beside Miss Brown, who interested her. Here was a young lady even more prickly than Charlotte usually dared to be. "You live in London?" she asked.

"At present."

"You moved there from elsewhere?"

"Yes," said Miss Brown.

Charlotte waited for her to elaborate. She did not. "Your family is there?" she asked.

"I am staying with an...aunt."

For some reason, Charlotte felt this wasn't true. She abandoned tact. "Were you really hiding behind a potted palm to eavesdrop on Henry?"

"It is not eavesdropping if you happen to overhear something."

"And then you just walked up and told him about Miss Palliser?"

"An opportunity must be grasped," Miss Brown replied unhelpfully.

Charlotte approved of this sentiment. "Where was the potted palm?"

"At a...reception."

Miss Brown didn't want to say, Charlotte noted, becoming even more curious. "Henry is starting a position in the Foreign Office after Christmas."

"So he said."

"Did you think he was lying?" Charlotte wondered.

A sigh escaped Miss Brown, and her mood seemed to shift. "No. Not really. I could see he was..."

"Sincere?" Charlotte asked when she did not go on.

This made the other woman smile. But the expression didn't last. "More fortunate than some," she answered.

Charlotte waited until it was clear she was not going to elaborate. "Why do you say so?" she asked then.

"Because a man has the power to do things."

Miss Brown met her eyes, and they had an instant of perfect understanding.

Glendarvon chose this moment to join them, taking a

chair opposite the sofa they occupied with a warm smile. A devastating smile.

Charlotte felt as if the room spun a little, the balance disturbed and realigned by his large handsome figure. She could resist this. Of course she could. Would. Did. Except a traitorous part of her didn't wish to.

The marquess's smile faded when Miss Brown frowned at him. "I hope I'm not interrupting," he said.

"And if you are?" she asked.

"I will take myself off at once." He started to rise.

"No need. I'll go." Miss Brown stood and walked away.

He shook his head. "She doesn't like me. And I can't work out what I've done to offend her. Do you think I should apologize?"

"For what?"

"I don't know. Your brother said—" He sighed. "Never mind."

"Which brother? And what did he say?"

"It is of no consequence." They watched Miss Brown sit beside Miss Palliser. "I don't like to feel I've offended a guest."

"I don't think Miss Brown was offended. She just didn't want to talk to you. And she doesn't bother to pretend." Charlotte rather admired that.

Glendarvon laughed. "You are always forthright."

"If you don't like it—"

"I do like it," he interrupted.

His tone was like a caress. Almost exactly like one. It seemed to brush across Charlotte's skin and ruffle her innermost depths.

"I count on it," he added. "I don't know what I'd do without it."

The look in his eyes left her silent and breathless.

Seventeen

After meeting with his agent the following morning, Laurence stayed on in his estate office and plotted how best to court Miss Charlotte Deeping. The usual sort of activity—a drive, a walk—seemed woefully insufficient. Also a cold snap had descended. Freezing rain had coated the bare branches and garden paths with a skim of ice, and the outdoors was not enticing. He doubted that even the most ardent hunters would be out today.

Just now, the object of his affections was holed up with Miss Palliser and Miss Brown, poring over rows of Chinese writing that Charlotte found fascinating. Laurence knew that if he showed up at that parlor, he would be pinned by three pairs of impatient female eyes. And three acute minds would see through any excuse he offered for the interruption. They didn't want his help either. He'd asked. Laurence shook his head. He wanted to impress her, not be seen as a diversion from more important work.

But she would emerge at some point. Not just for meals, he hoped. Should he show her around the house? Heat rolled over him as he remembered their visit to the portrait gallery. She'd kept her distance since then, though he'd caught her giving him piercing looks. He wanted to stand up well under her scrutiny.

He could ask her opinion about a horse. That was her family business after all, and she was an expert. He reviewed the animals currently in his stables. There was none that deserved special attention. She might think he was being patronizing.

Laurence sighed. None of that was any good. And then he saw his mistake. He hadn't been thinking straight. That was difficult to do when you were dizzy with longing and every topic wandered off toward desire. But if he looked at things from her point of view, the answer was obvious. Miss Deeping was immersed in the scrolls because the investigation was her chief interest. She would welcome, and admire, any contribution to the process. They'd even agreed to work together to solve the mystery.

He sat and thought and reviewed all that had occurred since he'd first arrived at the Deeping house. Then he went in search of Merlin.

He found the Terefords first. They were sitting together in a firelit parlor surrounded by papers and correspondence. The scene was both busy and cozily intimate. "Have you seen Merlin?" he asked.

"Not since breakfast," replied the duchess.

The duke did not look up from a page filled with columns of numbers.

"He said something about finding a book to read," she added.

Laurence nodded his thanks and withdrew.

❧

"Our host looked like a man on a mission," the duchess said to her husband.

"Um," he replied. "Did you notice this charge for sandstone blocks in London? It seems off to me."

She leaned forward to look, her eyes luminous with tenderness.

❧

Laurence found Merlin stretched out on a sofa in the library, his crutches laid on the rug beside him. He held an open book on his chest, but he closed it when Laurence entered. The man looked less sulky than usual, even glad to see company. Perhaps he was lonely. "I want to talk to you about the ring," Laurence said, sitting nearby.

This brought a return of his usual scowl. "I'm not giving it to you."

"I'm not asking you to. I wanted to discuss how you found it."

"I was poking about in the ashes of the fire," replied Merlin as if this was a stupid question.

"Yes, but in what way exactly?"

"What do you mean? In the way one does." He waved a hand. "Desultorily. Like a man who has no purpose."

Laurence ignored the complaint. "Why that particular day?" he asked.

"Eh?"

"You'd been at Lorne for a while. What moved you to explore the ashes just then?"

"Oh." Merlin took the ring from his waistcoat pocket. Apparently, he carried it with him always. He turned it in his fingers. "The builders were starting their work. I knew they would clear everything out."

"Yes."

Merlin frowned again, more thoughtfully. "I wondered if they would find any interesting bits in the ashes. And then I just thought I'd look for myself. I don't know why that occurred to me."

"So how did you proceed?" Laurence asked.

Hitching himself into a sitting position, Merlin said, "What is this about? I have told everyone the story."

"I know. But I…learned recently that one can recall more details by reviewing a set of actions step by step."

The other man looked interested. "Learned from who? The duke?"

Laurence shook his head. "An experienced source. I found the method quite effective."

"You did?"

"Yes." He didn't wish to elaborate. "So, having decided to look, you then…"

Merlin stared at him for a long moment, then answered, "I got a long stick and started to stir the ashes. I felt foolish after a while, but I didn't have anything else to do, did I?"

"How did you move about the burned space?" Impatience made Laurence want to go faster, but he resisted.

"Systematically," Merlin replied. His eyes went distant. "Up and down the length. I found some charred pieces of harness, a blackened bit, and the corner of a woolen blanket. Plenty of cinders. And then the stick struck something hard, embedded in the ashes. I tapped at it and dug a little. Something gave, and a small object flew up and hit the stone foundation. There was a clink." He turned the ring and repeated, "Clink."

"How deep down in the ashes?" asked Laurence.

"Several inches. It wasn't sitting on top." Merlin marveled. "It was a great piece of luck that I found it, really."

"As if it had been buried?"

"Not so deep as that. It was in the compacted ashes, not in the earth below."

"I don't suppose there were floorboards in the stable," said Laurence.

"There were at that end," Merlin replied. "The builders said there had been rooms for the stablemen there. The duke is having them restored."

"Which end?"

"Er, north?"

"If your book is the burned wing of Lorne, where was the ring lying?"

Merlin looked down at the closed volume. He shifted it in his lap, bit his lower lip, then placed a fingertip.

Laurence reviewed the geography of Lorne in his mind. He thought the location Merlin had chosen was near the blocked-off trapdoor to the cellar. He stood and fetched paper and pen to note this down. "Can you recall anything else?" he asked.

"Once I'd rubbed off the soot and saw I had a gem, I went inside," Merlin replied.

"And the builders went to work soon after."

"Yes."

There had been no mention of the trapdoor. Merlin hadn't seen it, as he hadn't come into the cellar. Perhaps Tereford had told the workmen to ignore it. Laurence would ask. "Well done," he told the other man.

Merlin looked surprisingly gratified.

Laurence caught Miss Deeping as she was going down to dinner that evening. He fell into step beside her and said, "I have some information."

"Information?"

"About the ring." Succinctly, he told her what Merlin had revealed. "So I wonder if whoever dropped the ring was either using the trapdoor or trying to get through it," he concluded.

She had stopped at the head of the stairs and was frowning in concentration. "A thief or a conspirator?" she wondered.

"Precisely."

"Merlin didn't mention any of this before."

"He didn't recall until I reviewed the discovery with him, inspired by your methods."

"My…" She gazed up at him, her dark eyes wide, her lips a little parted. "Inspired?"

A surge of desire erased every trace of logic from Laurence's brain. He was at the mercy of his body for a moment, burning.

As if she felt it, her cheeks flushed, her breath caught.

They were like two people swept away by a mighty flood, flailing for handholds in the tumult. Laurence nearly grabbed her hand.

Miss Deeping took a step back. "Inspired?" she repeated.

He had been. He was. He suspected he always would be. But right now, he needed to get hold of himself. With supreme effort, Laurence gathered his wits. He had to look away from her to manage it. "The…the way you took me step by step through the details about the wardrobe," he explained.

The echoes of that intimate occasion vibrated in the air between them.

Laurence pulled a sheet of paper from his pocket and unfolded it. "I made a chart," he said.

"You what?"

"I made a chart. That is another of your practices, isn't

it?" He held out the page where he had plotted the location of the jewel in the ashes.

She took it. "This is not a chart. It is a drawing."

But from the way she was looking at him, Laurence dared to hope he was making progress. His heart pounded. And even though the Terefords came to join them and interrupted their tête-à-tête, his spirits were buoyant as they walked down the stairs together.

❧

The following afternoon, Miss Palliser came to Laurence in the estate office and said, "I have finished. I have some curious things to tell you."

He sent word to the others, and within half an hour, they all gathered in the room, extra chairs having been fetched. Miss Palliser was settled at the desk, with the scrolls and translations spread out before her. He'd left orders that they were not to be disturbed.

Miss Palliser waited until they had settled and were watching attentively. Then she put her hand on the largest pile. "These represent the first category of documents I mentioned to you," she said in her prosaic voice. "They give detailed evidence of a hong's involvement in the opium trade. Including names. Someone compiled enough details to get these men executed if the Chinese government found out."

People around the room exchanged glances.

"As I told you, this information is very dangerous. I have no doubt they would kill to suppress it."

"We must get it out of our hands," said Miss Brown. "To the proper officials."

The duke nodded.

"Why is it here?" asked the duchess.

"That shall become clearer." Miss Palliser exchanged glances with the two young ladies who had been working with her and probably knew the outcome. Laurence gazed at Miss Deeping's profile, the most compelling sight in the room despite these revelations.

"The will is simply that," Miss Palliser went on, placing her hand on the second pile. "It belongs to the mother of one of the merchants mentioned in the first batch and sets out the disposition of her possessions."

"Why would those things be together and here?" wondered the duchess.

"I believe the personal narrative explains," answered Miss Palliser, moving her hand to the third pile. "It is the story of a woman who came from Canton to England." She picked up a sheaf of paper. "You can read my translation for yourself. I found it most enlightening."

"Perhaps you can tell us the main points," said the duke.

Miss Palliser nodded. "This woman was the daughter of an important hong merchant and a Portuguese lady. Her father's name suggests he was related to one of the corrupt traders, though not one of them himself. The woman did not know how her mother came to be with him. Whether she'd been taken from a ship or sold as part of a trading exchange."

"Sold!" exclaimed the duchess.

"Such things happen," said Miss Brown. Miss Deeping looked stony.

"Her mother was a concubine, you understand, not an official wife, so the writer of this story was not strictly legitimate to Western eyes. Somehow, she met a European man who had come to Canton on a trading ship, though he was not a trader." Miss Palliser gazed at the papers. "That was most unusual. A rich merchant's daughter would have been watched and guarded."

"Even if she was half Portuguese?" asked the duchess.

"Yes. But she managed to steal time with him somehow, and she and this man fell in love and wished to marry. Her father refused, of course."

"Why 'of course'?" asked Merlin, who was looking fascinated by the tale.

"Her father would wish to…dispose of her for his own advantage. Very like an arranged marriage between families here. His word was law. She was forbidden to leave her rooms. Yet somehow she did. I can't imagine how. She must have had help from the servants in the house. She gathered up a cache of treasures."

"That had been bequeathed to her in the will we found," Miss Deeping added.

Miss Palliser nodded. "Her name was there. She thought of them as her rightful dowry, and I believe she brought the will as proof of ownership. She also took the documents showing the corruption of hong officials, some of them her relatives, as protection. And she fled with her love."

Laurence was feeling strangely disoriented, as if perilous ideas were spinning inside his head.

"They were married according to his rites and came to England to live at his home. But this lady was very worried about pursuit. She knew her father was a vindictive man, and his relatives even more so. She hoped the evidence she'd brought would hold them off. She had left behind a note saying it would remain hidden as long as she was left alone."

"That seems a dangerous choice," said the duke.

Miss Palliser nodded. "I think it would have been better to simply disappear. But she'd taken the valuables as well. Which might have meant more than the loss of one girl."

"And they would not have trusted her to keep their secrets," said Miss Brown.

"Particularly if her new husband had been sent to find such evidence," murmured the duke.

Miss Palliser looked at him with approval. "I wondered about that. But why then didn't they turn the scrolls over to the English authorities?"

Tereford nodded.

"Maybe they decided they didn't want to be embroiled in politics," said Merlin.

"I think it was more of a desperate gamble," said Miss Deeping. "And they were afraid."

Something twisted in Laurence's insides.

"All those may be true," agreed Miss Palliser. "In any case, they found a hiding place for the things they'd brought with an acquaintance of her husband's. She did not think the connection would be suspected as they were not known to be friends. I think they paid this person to keep the things, though she does not say so directly. They agreed it would be a temporary measure. They intended to find a better place in time. She placed her story there with them as she didn't dare keep it in her home."

"In the cellar at Lorne," said the duchess.

Miss Palliser nodded.

Silence fell as everyone contemplated the story.

Moving like a sleepwalker, Laurence rose and retrieved his mother's will from a drawer. He placed it before Miss

Palliser before turning to the final page with the Chinese character beside the English signature. She bent over it, then looked up at him in astonishment. "It is she. The same name as in the story."

Laurence dropped back into his chair, his legs suddenly weak.

"What is?" asked Miss Brown. "What are you talking about?"

Miss Palliser had gone back to the beginning of the will. "Your mother?"

Laurence nodded.

"She is the one who came from Canton?" asked Miss Deeping.

"So it seems." His own voice sounded faraway to Laurence. An inner roaring obscured it.

"So your parents were probably killed to get these documents," said Merlin. He hobbled over to examine them more closely.

"Merlin," said the duchess repressively.

"But shouldn't the murderers have forced them to hand them over before they—"

"Merlin!"

He blinked and looked mildly mortified.

Laurence was conscious of a battery of eyes focused on him. He needed to think. He strode out of the room, heedless of people calling his name, and went outside to walk. It wasn't enough. He didn't want to be found and...comforted. Or spoken to at all. Not just now. He hurried to the stable and had Ranger saddled. Relieved when no one appeared to question him, he galloped away into the cold countryside.

The tale of love and escape from Canton whirled through

his mind—romantic, alien to all he'd thought he knew about his parents. They hadn't told him. Not a hint.

He'd been too young, Laurence acknowledged. He wouldn't have understood, and he couldn't have been trusted to keep their secret. Surely they would have confided in him later. If there had been a later for his family.

His whole body clenched, and Ranger shied at the unexpected pressure of his knees. Laurence made himself relax.

The thunder of hooves sounded behind him. Laurence wondered if he'd strayed into the path of some foxhunting. Before he could turn and look, four riders came up, two on each side of him, jostling far too close. He shouted a protest even as Ranger tossed his head and bellowed his own strong objections, offering to kick and bite the interlopers.

A stunning blow struck the back of Laurence's head. As he reeled in the saddle, a bag was pushed over his head, followed by another blow. The world went black.

∽

"Glendarvon ought to be back by now," said Charlotte. She'd come to the duchess's chamber to speak to her friend. The party was dressing for dinner as if nothing had happened. No one had seemed to know what else to do.

"He had a great deal to think about," replied Cecelia. She clasped a pendant around her neck.

But Charlotte was worried. The days were short at this time of year, and the skies had grown dusky. It was cold. There would be no moonlight.

"This is his home country," Cecelia added. "He knows his way about."

"His horse won't like the dark." They didn't. They liked to be able to see where they were setting their hooves. His mount might refuse to go on. Or toss him off in protest if he urged too hard. And though the marquess was a fine rider, he would be distracted by all that had happened. Obviously. She despised the understatement.

Cecelia sighed. "I don't see what we can do. If he must wait until morning, I'm sure he'll find some shelter. It is his land all around here."

Charlotte conceded the point, but she was deeply uneasy. Glendarvon had looked so stricken when he'd gone out. His life had been turned upside down. Why hadn't she run after him? Now he was gone, and she had no idea how to find him.

Her mind filled with pictures of him lying on the cold earth—his limbs twisted. His neck broken! She'd seen a man brought back from a hunt after such an injury. Dead. She sank onto a chair.

"Are you all right?" asked Cecelia.

She'd just sat there, even though she knew more about his tragic history than anyone else in the room. And cared more? Her head began nodding before her thoughts could catch up.

"What is it, Charlotte?"

"I let him go. Alone."

"I think he wanted some solitude."

"Would you have let the duke go after all that?" Charlotte saw in her friend's eyes that she would not.

"Is the case the same?" the duchess asked gently.

"He is not my husband, you mean. Or anything to me."

"Clearly, he is something."

"I didn't want to attract attention," Charlotte said with

contempt for her own cowardice. She'd been afraid to reveal how much she cared. Had she even known?

She brushed this rationalization aside. Somewhere in the depths of her being, she'd known. She'd just refused to admit it, mired in her fears and hesitations. But it was foolish to keep denying that she loved the man with all her heart. She wanted to rush out and find him and tell him. She was desperate to throw her arms around him and offer comfort. Now that it might be too late.

Cecelia came and put a hand on her shoulder. "I'm sure it will be all right," she said.

Charlotte wished she could be.

Eighteen

LAURENCE WOKE LYING ON HIS SIDE, DIZZY AND SICK. THE
bag was still on his head. He moved and had to fight not
to vomit inside it, which would be extremely unpleasant.
Reaching for the bag, he found his hands were tied in front
of him and secured with another rope to his bound ankles.
His head was pounding. Worse than it had after the thrown
stone. Not a sensation he would have cared to repeat.

He waited a few minutes, and then managed to sit up, battling nausea again.

He heard a door open and shut.

"You are awake. Good," said a masculine voice. "My apologies for the sack. It is unlikely that we would ever meet, but
if we should, I would prefer not to be recognized."

The man sounded educated, with a slight accent Laurence
did not recognize. "Who are you?" he asked.

"That doesn't really matter. We need to reach an agreement about the documents in your possession."

"How do you know about those?"

"Please. Their existence has been known in Canton for
years. And even who took them. Their location was the
problem, despite a truly exhaustive search of your house."
He sounded aggrieved.

"Search?" Laurence tried to gather his wits through the
acute pain.

"Servants were inserted to look for them."

"In my home!" Laurence struggled to take this idea in.
And then wondered if he had felt this secret scrutiny in

some way, giving him another reason not to be at ease in the house.

"They meant you no harm. They were there simply to find the items. Which were somewhere else entirely, it seems." The man sounded disgusted. "I was summoned from London to retrieve them as soon as their presence became known."

"From your spies." It seemed they hadn't kept the secret from his household. People saw things, Laurence acknowledged.

"That is their function." His captor sounded indifferent.

"And now you will kill me as you did my parents?"

"*I* certainly did not. That was a stupidly botched attempt." The man's contempt was clear in his tone. "Emotions were high back then, you understand. The lady's father was furious. Matters are easier now that he is dead."

The fellow was speaking of his grandfather, Laurence realized. He felt nothing. Except the pounding pain in his head and chafing of his wrists.

"His rage drove people on to retrieve the documents and the woman," the voice continued. "I was told the confrontation got out of hand because they fought back much more fiercely than expected. The man to protect his wife, the woman like an absolute Fury. The attackers defended themselves, as was their instinct. Too well. They were badly slashed themselves."

"I find I don't care," said Laurence.

"Well, I thought you might like to know they were not meant to kill your mother."

"And my father?"

There was a short silence. "He, of course, had to be punished for his theft."

"Of the documents?"

"Of a woman from her family. The men were killed for their failure, of course."

Despite everything, Laurence was shocked.

"And there the matter rested. You were too young to know anything. The servants seemed ignorant. A watch was kept while informants were found and inserted into the house."

"Inserted." The thought still revolted Laurence. "It has been years."

"In China one learns to take the long view. I tell you all this so you understand we are quite serious. We will not go away."

Laurence was still thinking about members of his staff watching him and rifling through his possessions.

"We will trade you for the papers," the man went on. "A simple exchange, and then you needn't worry any longer. The…persons on your staff will be gone."

"How many?"

"That is irrelevant."

Not to him. "I'm surprised they didn't just steal them."

"That was considered, but they were well guarded. And I would prefer to avoid violence. I do not wish to attract more widespread attention. Exaggerated tales have already spread too far. A robbery would make that worse."

He didn't want the story to reach official channels, Laurence saw. But he must know they would report what they'd learned. Tereford and Henry Deeping would know the proper people to tell. And in that moment, Laurence realized he couldn't remember any of the foreign names Miss Palliser had mentioned. Not even his mother's. Miss Palliser would though.

"This can be of little importance to you," the man said. "You need only do as I say."

"You will kill me if I refuse, I suppose."

"That would not be useful. I hope to convince you."

"Convince!"

"Indeed. For example, if we were forced to invade your house, your friends might be hurt." The threat was calmly spoken, but clear.

Laurence's heart started to pound, multiplying the pain in his head until it was almost unbearable. Charlotte Deeping was there, under the eyes of this man's spies. If they hurt her... Terror filled him at the idea. He loved her. He had to keep her from harm. And the others as well, of course.

He decided to play for time, perhaps find some chance to escape. "Might I have some water?" he asked. As soon as he said the word, his parched throat cried out for liquid.

"Water will be brought to you. And food. When you have written the letter I require."

Laurence jerked his bound wrists. "How am I to do that?"

There were rustling sounds. "I have left paper and a pen and ink beside you," the man said. "As well as the precise wording you are to use. Copy them exactly." A small knife was pressed into Laurence's hand. "You may free yourself."

He heard the door open and close again, along with bolts being shot.

Hunching over, Laurence reached for the bag on his head. He jerked at it and found it was tied around his neck. He couldn't get it off, hog-tied as he was. He began to saw at the rope connecting his wrists and ankles. The position was awkward, and it took him quite a while to cut through it, but at last he did. After that he was able to loose his feet and, more torturously, his hands. As soon as he did, he sliced through the string securing the bag and finally got it off. It was a vast relief to breathe freely, though he was dizzy with the pain in his head.

He sat on the pounded-earth floor of a basement storage room, lit by a small lantern sitting nearby. He didn't recognize the place. Two walls were stone and two were wood.

It was cold. He'd begun to shiver. Seeing he was sitting on a ragged blanket, he moved to pull it around him, then held his hands over the lantern. His fingers were stiff. His whole body ached.

The room was empty except for a lidded bucket in one corner. There were no windows. The wooden walls and door were thick timber.

He turned to the paper and pen left beside him. Picking up the note he was to write out, he read the words. They were stark and simple. He didn't see how to slip in another message. He couldn't warn his friends of the spies around them or hint at his location. He didn't know where he was. When his captors opened the door to take the page from him, perhaps he could overpower them. Laurence flexed his legs to restore circulation and wished his head would stop throbbing.

A sound made him turn. A narrow horizontal opening appeared at the bottom of the door. A bit of wood had been cut out of it there. A hand slid a small glass of water forward and then quickly withdrew. The opening was shut again.

Laurence crawled over to the offering. He drank it down in one gulp. "More," he croaked.

"When you write the letter," said the hated voice of his jailer.

Only then did Laurence realize the door would not be opening. They had arranged things so it needn't be. He would have no chance to fight his way out.

～

The ransom note was brought to the Duke of Tereford as he dressed the following morning. His valet handed it over, a nervous footman standing behind him. "We thought this had best come to you, Your Grace," said the former.

The duke read it, frowned, and asked the footman, "Where did this come from?"

"It was slipped under the front door during the night, Your Grace."

Frown deepening, the duke said, "Ask all the houseguests to gather in the breakfast room as soon as may be."

"Yes, Your Grace."

Half an hour later, their group was sitting at the breakfast table. The servants had been dismissed. Tereford held the open page before him. "I'll begin by saying I compared the handwriting in this note to samples in the estate office. I'm confident it was written by Glendarvon."

Charlotte's pulse began to pound. She clasped her hands tight.

"It reads as follows," added the duke. "I will be released when all the scrolls are brought to the Knipton village church. They know the exact number. Miss Palliser is to deliver them, along with all her translations, tomorrow morning at ten."

"No," said Miss Brown. "We are not sending her." When the others turned to her, she said, "Obviously, they mean to take her."

A hubbub of voices arose as Charlotte's mind raced. "How do they know so much?" she asked.

"I suppose they made Glendarvon tell them," replied Miss Brown.

The picture this presented made Charlotte's blood run cold.

"How will they be sure we gave them all the translations?" asked the duchess. "We can make copies."

"Without the Chinese original, they will mean nothing," said Miss Palliser. "I might have made them up." She seemed remarkably calm.

"We will take all the men of the household and surround the church," said the duke.

"Are they all to be trusted?" asked Merlin.

"What do you mean?"

"How many scrolls are there?" Merlin asked the group.

Tereford shrugged. "Twenty?"

"I'm not certain," Merlin answered. "Are any of us?"

People shook their heads. Charlotte remembered a pile of cylinders. She could not have said exactly how many. She didn't think the marquess could either.

"Except Miss Palliser, of course," Merlin added.

The translator looked at him. "If you are accusing me of being in league with the kidnappers, I can only say there would have been many easier ways for me to take the documents. I might have fled with them before any of you arrived."

"Of course you are not in league with them," snapped Miss Brown. "I will go in her place and hand over the wretched things."

"And then they will take *you*," said Miss Palliser. "And be very angry when they discover the deception." She shook her head. "I will not allow that."

"We have a day to form a plan," said the duke. "We must think of every contingency. I think we can rely on the staff here to help."

Conversation went round and round for much of the morning. After a while Charlotte noticed her ideas were not receiving much credence. Tereford was beginning to act like a commanding general. He appeared to feel that as the only unimpaired male present, he was the natural person to be in charge.

Finally, when another suggestion she made was brushed aside, she slipped away. If her old school friends were here, they would plot something together. But they were not. However, she thought she might have possible substitutes. Miss Palliser and Miss Brown had abandoned the discussion some time ago.

She found them in the study chamber where they had all worked together. They were still arguing about who would go to the church, but they fell silent when she entered. Under their inquiring gazes, Charlotte abandoned caution and plunged in. "It seems to me that these kidnappers assume only the men are important," she said.

"Rather like our friend the duke," said Miss Brown dryly.

Charlotte nodded. "I believe they must be the ones who attacked the marquess during a hunt. And sawed through the branch to injure Merlin. But they seem to take no notice of females."

"As who does?" murmured Miss Palliser.

"Except they want to get their hands on Miss Palliser," replied Miss Brown.

Charlotte nodded again. "But what if there were other women wandering about the church at the time they set?

Nattering on about the stained glass or some such thing, would they see that as a threat?"

The other two women stared at her.

"I don't think they would," she continued. "I think such women might get quite close to them." The stares were growing uncomfortable. "I can shoot," Charlotte said. "My brother taught me. I'm quite good. And I don't lose my nerve at the sound of gunfire."

Miss Palliser examined Charlotte even more closely. She looked at Miss Brown, back at Charlotte, and then she picked up a penknife from the desk, the sort used to sharpen quills. With a flick of her wrist, she threw it. The blade embedded itself deeply in the wall beside the fireplace.

Charlotte jumped in surprise and delight.

"I can do better with a larger knife," Miss Palliser commented calmly. Seeing Charlotte's admiring expression, she smiled. "My father hired a rather disreputable fellow as a bodyguard once. I persuaded him to teach me. I thought it a useful skill for a girl."

Miss Brown frowned. "I can fence a bit," she said. "But I don't see how I could carry a sword to the church. It would be too visible. And I'm not terribly good." She seemed disappointed in herself.

Charlotte pressed on. "I think Merlin made a good point. If the solution were as simple as surrounding the church with men from here, the kidnappers would not have proposed the meeting."

"You think they have informants in the house?" asked Miss Palliser.

"That would explain how they knew the scrolls were here," said Miss Brown.

"Money can buy information," said Charlotte. "The person might not have seen any harm in sharing some gossip."

"Or they might be deeper into the plan and help the kidnappers escape," said Miss Palliser.

"With you in tow," replied Miss Brown.

Pleased to find them as quick-witted as her old friends, Charlotte said, "But that wouldn't matter if they were prevented from leaving the church."

The other two gazed at her. "How?" asked Miss Brown.

"What do you propose?" asked Miss Palliser at the same time.

Charlotte gathered her thoughts. She'd been thinking this through very carefully. "Miss Brown and I could hide in the church quite early. In the darkness. Before anyone noticed." She glanced at the other woman. "It would be a long cold wait."

Miss Brown brushed this caveat aside.

Turning to Miss Palliser, Charlotte continued, "When you enter with a bag or some such thing, their eyes will be on you. And then we will appear around a corner twittering about the beauties of the church." She pointed at Miss Brown and then herself.

"While they are distracted, I set down the bag and bring out my knives," said Miss Palliser.

Charlotte nodded. "I will pull out a pistol. Miss Brown will have one as well." She looked at the other woman. "But only to hand to me if I need it. Wild firing will ruin everything."

Fortunately, Miss Brown accepted this with a nod.

"We must be prepared to wound," Charlotte told Miss Palliser. "If we merely threaten, they probably won't believe us and they will keep coming. We cannot allow men to get too close. If we engage hand to hand, we will be overpowered."

Miss Palliser nodded. "I will not kill anyone," she said.

"Nor will I," Charlotte assured her. "Let us agree not to. I propose leg wounds. I can fire very accurately."

"So can I."

"I can tie secure knots," said Miss Brown as if remembering an accomplishment.

"A good thought," said Charlotte. "We should have rope. But our hands can't be encumbered."

"Wind coils around our waists under our cloaks," suggested Miss Brown.

"Good idea."

"You have pistols?" asked Miss Palliser. She looked prepared to admire Charlotte if she did.

"There is a gun room here. I can get them."

"If you ask—" began Miss Brown doubtfully.

"I shall not," interrupted Charlotte. "Because if anyone else finds out about our plan…"

"We will be stopped," finished Miss Brown.

"Because we must not risk our delicate selves," said Miss Palliser.

"Except you, whom they care nothing about."

"That is not quite fair, Kate. And you know I am quite able to defend myself."

"We mustn't let anything slip," Charlotte added. "Not to a maid or anyone."

They both nodded.

"So we are agreed?"

The second nods were resolute.

Charlotte had to wait until very late before making her way to the gun room. The household was understandably agitated, and it took time to settle. She was conscious of nerves as she crept down to the estate office and opened the cupboard containing tidy rows of keys. They were not labeled, but the marquess had shown her his system during her last visit, and she'd understood the principle of organization at once. She felt a pang as she took the gun room key. Where was he? What was happening to him? Her hands trembled as she prayed his captors were treating him well.

When she came out of the gun room with two pistols, the narrow beam of her dark lantern revealed Merlin lurking in the shadows, leaning on his crutches. "I thought you'd be up to something," he said. "So I followed you."

"Shh," said Charlotte, wondering how he had crept after her so silently on his crutches. "I'm not..." He was staring pointedly at the cloth bag she'd brought to hold the guns. Their outlines were visible.

"I want in on your scheme," Merlin said.

"I don't—"

"Or we can just go and speak to the duke about whatever it is," he interrupted. "I imagine it would annoy him to be wakened."

"Do speak quietly," Charlotte muttered. She stood very still. "What I intend can only be carried out by women," she said finally.

This silenced him.

"These people disregard women," she went on. "They attacked Glendarvon and you, but they paid no attention to me at all." This rankled, though she did not wish she'd been targeted.

"Ha." Merlin leaned back against the wall as if his broken leg might be hurting. "The duke's plan is foolish," he said. "He believes that if servants have worked in a house for a number of years, they must be loyal and trustworthy." He made a contemptuous sound. "Devoted to the interests of their employers."

Charlotte nodded. Tereford had his failings.

"Some of the men he plans to post are in the pay of the villains," Merlin continued. "I feel sure of that."

"And so the kidnappers must not leave the church," she dared to say.

"Are you going to shoot them?" The idea seemed to please him.

Charlotte said nothing. She was holding pistols, however.

"Have you ever fired a gun?"

"Often. My brother Henry taught me."

"Ah, the sharpshooter." Merlin seemed to come to a decision. "I will tell the duke what you're doing."

"But…"

He held up a hand. "Unless you swear you will make him write a letter on my behalf to the Bow Street runners."

"I can't promise to *make* him. How would I?"

"You can be very persuasive."

Charlotte struggled with an urge to throttle the man. "I vow to do my best. And to ask others for recommendations as well. Glendarvon."

"If they haven't killed him," said Merlin.

"Killed!" Realizing she'd cried out, Charlotte lowered her voice. "Why would you say such a thing?"

"That often happens, in kidnappings."

Her heart pounded with fear. "Not this time."

Merlin shrugged. "Three letters."

Charlotte pushed back her anxiety. She could manage that. She would enlist one of her brothers. Of course a letter from her, a female, was useless. "Agreed."

He hesitated, still obviously frustrated, then stepped back and let her pass. Charlotte returned the gun room key and crept up to her room. She thought it unlikely that she would sleep at all.

And in fact, she did not.

But when she met Miss Brown and Miss Palliser in the predawn darkness, she didn't feel tired. She was too agitated for that.

"It was decided that I am to carry the actual scrolls into the church," whispered Miss Palliser. "The duke thinks that if I do not have the real thing, they might grow violent."

"He means to take them on their way out, with evidence of their crime," murmured Miss Brown.

"And so they shall," said Charlotte. "You are ready?"

Miss Brown exhibited the rope wound around her waist. Charlotte had one as well, on top of layers of her warmest garments. The bag holding the pistols was hung on it. They put on thick cloaks and gloves.

"Luck," said Miss Palliser. They clasped hands briefly and parted.

It was very dark and cold when they slipped out a side door that locked behind them. The village church was less than a mile away by local footpaths, though farther by road. Charlotte had plotted the route on a large map on the wall of the estate office, and she carried a small dark lantern to show the way. When they had moved out of sight of the windows, she cracked it open, and they walked faster.

"I feel crazily reckless," said Miss Brown.

"Yes." The sensation was familiar to Charlotte from other adventures, though this one exceeded all those she and her school friends had dared.

"What if the kidnappers have come very early?"

"They probably will. But I think they will wait at least until first light. We should be silent, however."

"What if we encounter someone?"

"We are ladies on the way to the bedside of a dying friend," Charlotte improvised. "Or perhaps a lying-in. Yes, I think that. Women's affairs. No man wants to inquire too closely about *those*."

"You are very crafty," said Miss Brown.

"Thank you."

"You really think we can do this?"

"Yes," Charlotte replied as a bolster to her own confidence.

They moved in silence after that, and encountered no one in the frigid countryside. Walking warmed Charlotte a little. Behind all else ran worry for Glendarvon. Where was he and in what condition? Would he be with the villains when they arrived? She doubted it. They would want to be sure of their booty before releasing him. She refused to think of any other outcome.

They reached the edge of the little village. She closed the lantern, and they crept along in darkness. Finally, the church loomed. They ghosted up to the door, opened it a crack, and slipped through.

Inside, it was even darker, though not quite so cold. Charlotte pushed a bit of her cloak into Miss Brown's hand, then put her fingers on the stone wall and began to feel her way around the edifice. She'd looked at this church briefly on her previous visit, and she had made a plan.

Slowly and carefully, she led Miss Brown to the low door of the church tower. Charlotte opened it, noting with gratitude that the hinges did not creak. They went through, felt their way up a few steps, and sat down. "Now we wait," she breathed.

"And try not to freeze," was the whispered reply.

⸎

People talked of going mad from frustration, but Laurence wondered if he really had. This was the day set in the note they'd made him write, and all sounds had gone from his prison. He felt he'd been abandoned in his cold, primitive cell.

He'd experimented with scratching at the door and then kicking it. He'd shouted. There'd been no response. His captors had gone. It would have been the moment to escape, if escape had been possible, but he could make no impression on the heavy door. He knew from sounds he'd heard and the blank panels that it was bolted shut rather than having a lock he might pick, and he suspected it might be barred as well. It didn't move an inch when he put his shoulder to it.

He was tired from the cold and gnawing hunger. They'd given him only a bit of bread. He'd gotten the impression that their supplies were limited. But thirst was the worst torment. His mouth and throat were parched, and he dreamed of a long drink. The little water they'd given him had tasted musty, however, and he feared for its quality. If he fell ill, that would crown this wretched interlude.

The silence seemed to grow heavier. The shadows seemed to close in. He had no reason to trust his captor's word. He might take the scrolls and leave Laurence here to starve.

And then the small lantern Laurence had been allowed from the beginning went out.

Real darkness descended. He could see nothing.

A wave of panic rose in Laurence's breast. He'd just managed to tolerate being locked in this cramped storeroom. He'd reasoned with himself and performed calming exercises. Now, in the blackness, alone, memories of being shut in a dark wardrobe as murder was committed a few feet away flooded him. He was trapped. He was helpless. Anything might come at him, and he would have no defense.

Laurence completely lost his composure then. He raged around the small space, beating on the walls, tripping over the lantern, falling hard and rising again, yelling curses and pleas. Finding the door with groping hands, he battered himself against it over and over until his shoulders screamed.

The uncaring universe made no response.

He fell to the earthen floor and dropped his face in his hands. Tremors shook him. Tears threatened. He couldn't stand this. He was going to break.

And then the image of Charlotte Deeping rose in his mind. Intrepid, he thought. She had been completely self-possessed after he'd almost ridden her down. She had been ready to jump into a fen to save a struggling colt. She inspired courage. And she was a link to light and life, an anchor in a sea of fearful recollections. He clung to the memory of her rather than those ancient tragedies.

Gradually, painfully, he fought the panic down. It was like a house-to-house battle in a long-ago war. Inch by agonizing inch, he clawed his way to balance.

Even if he was abandoned, his friends would scour the countryside to find him, Laurence told himself. They would search every structure for miles around his home. He could not be terribly far from it. There hadn't been time to travel much. Someone would come. He had only to wait. Alone. In the deep dark. Where time seemed to have stopped.

He began to shudder with cold. He crawled across the dirt floor to find the ragged blanket and huddled into it. He could feel his hands bleeding. He wiped them on the wool.

He must think of pleasant things, happy times. Charlotte Deeping's face when she smiled up at him, their stimulating conversations, searing stolen kisses. Those warmed him. She was his lifeline.

Nineteen

IT SEEMED FOREVER BEFORE THE FIRST LIGHT BEGAN TO filter down through the windows in the upper part of the church tower. Every few minutes, Charlotte flexed the muscles in her legs and arms to keep the blood flowing. She opened and closed her hands inside her gloves. She didn't want to find she'd stiffened into immobility when the time came to spring up.

As soon as they could see better, they adjusted their position, crouched right next to the door panels. Charlotte took out the pistols and laid them at her side, ready to hand. The growing morning seemed endless. Charlotte listened with all her might, but there was no sound other than the winter birds waking.

And then, at long last, there was something. The door scraped on the stone floor and soft footsteps entered. Charlotte put her ear to the door. "Search the place," said a muted voice.

Charlotte looked up and met Miss Brown's grim gaze. No more waiting. It was beginning. She took hold of the door latch. As they'd planned, Miss Brown joined in. They had to make this door seem locked. Everything depended on it.

After what seemed an eternity, as her hands were becoming cramped, the latch trembled and tried to move. Charlotte held more firmly. Miss Brown grimaced. The door shook as if someone had kicked it. And then nothing.

Charlotte did not let go. She wasn't stupid. But there was no further trial of the tower door. They must have decided it was locked, as she'd hoped. Still, she kept hold, as footsteps shuffled on the other side. She longed to know how many men were out there, but she could not look. Her fingers trembled with strain, and she relaxed just a little.

Another eternity crawled past. Charlotte didn't see how she could stand much more, and then a slammed door made them jump.

"Here I am," said Miss Palliser, speaking very loudly as they'd agreed. "Standing in the middle of the church with the scrolls as you commanded." She meant to let them know her location.

Feeling curiously light-headed, Charlotte let go of the latch, picked up a pistol, handed the other to her companion, and stood. Holding the gun at her side under her cloak, she stepped out of the tower onto the church floor. Moving toward the middle of the building, and Miss Palliser, Charlotte said, "Thirteenth century," in her best silly, twittering voice. "So very historic."

"Oh yes," said Miss Brown, sounding suitably brainless. "Romantic indeed."

There were four men in the church, confronting Miss Palliser. All of them had turned to stare incredulously. Three looked like English workingmen. The fourth was darker in complexion, perhaps Italian or eastern European.

They were close enough. Charlotte revealed her pistol. Miss Brown did the same, though she was not to fire.

The men sneered, one and all. Two started toward them. Charlotte did not wait. Knowing threats would be ignored, she shot, hitting one of the men in the calf. He went down, clutching his leg, and the other stopped short. She traded pistols with Miss Brown and aimed the loaded one.

A knife flew from Miss Palliser's hand into the side of one of the other men. Blades already protruded from the shoulder and thigh of the fourth, but he didn't seem deterred. He lunged forward with bared teeth. Suspecting he was the leader, Charlotte shot him in the posterior. He fell with an enraged shout. Miss Brown traded her gun for a reloaded pistol.

The door of the church burst open, and men flooded in, the Duke of Tereford in the lead. "What the devil?" he shouted when he saw them.

"Rope," ordered Charlotte, holding her pistol steady on the leader.

Miss Brown set down the empty gun and unwound the coil around her waist.

There was a certain amount of chaos as the kidnappers were secured. Pistols were discovered deep in two of their pockets. They hadn't had time to draw them. Finally, they were tied up, their wounds roughly bound. Charlotte went to stand over the one she thought in charge. The duke made no objection, she noticed. "Where is Lord Glendarvon?" she asked the man.

"Women," he said disgustedly. "I don't believe it."

"Where is he?" she repeated.

"I don't think I will tell you."

Charlotte raised the pistol that still held a bullet. Miss Palliser knelt at the man's side and put a knife to his throat.

"You wouldn't dare," he sneered.

"What were you going to do with me, I wonder?" asked Miss Palliser. "When you took me away from here?" The blade moved a little. A trickle of blood ran down onto his neckcloth.

"Can't you stop these lunatic females?" the man asked the duke, who stood off to the side.

"They ask a very pertinent question," Tereford replied.

"If you let me go, I'll answer it."

The duke shook his head.

"You won't kill me."

"You'll all hang as traitors," said Miss Brown.

Charlotte didn't think this was true, but it had the desired effect. One of the other men writhed in his bonds. "I ain't done nothing so bad," he cried. "Just what I was told. The feller you want is in an empty house about three miles north of here."

"Shut up," said the leader.

"I ain't going to hang!"

The two others began to protest that they had been following orders. The quartet was bundled up and taken away to be held for questioning. Charlotte scarcely noticed. She was immersed in a flood of relief that the marquess was alive.

When they emerged from the church, it was discovered that two of the servants had slipped away. They were not seen again.

❧

After the passage of numberless eons, Laurence at last heard sounds from outside his prison. He didn't care by this point if it was his captors or someone else. He rose from the floor and began to shout into the darkness.

He heard a series of thumps and then a crash. Blessed light appeared under his cell door, bouncing in the crevice as if a lantern swung nearer. "Here," he called.

Voices, footsteps, the bolts shot back. The door opened, and his dark-accustomed eyes were dazzled by sudden illumination. He saw only black figures against painful yellow light.

Someone flew at him. Laurence raised his hands to fend them off. In the next instant, he found his arms full of a desperate, fragrant figure. "You're all right," cried Charlotte Deeping in his ear. She clutched him. "You're all right."

Laurence lurched and nearly went down.

"*Are* you all right?" she asked. Her hands patted over him, searching for wounds.

"Cold and half-starved," Laurence said. He did not admit to the half-mad part of it. "How did you…? What are *you* doing here?"

"Miss Deeping and her, er, cohort captured the villains who took you," said the Duke of Tereford from the doorway. His tone was rueful, but he didn't seem to be joking.

"Cohort?" replied Laurence, bewildered.

Miss Deeping stepped back. "Did no one bring blankets?" she demanded. "Or a flask of brandy?"

"Not for me," Laurence said. He'd be tipsy on a sip with his empty stomach. "Can we just go out?" He managed not to babble it.

They helped him up some rickety stairs, through a house that showed signs of rough camping, and into a November day that seemed utterly glorious to Laurence. He did not care that rain drizzled and a cold wind blew. The land rolled away in all directions. The sky was wide. No walls closed in on him. And there was Ranger, looking better fed and cared for than Laurence had been. The horse nosed him when Laurence approached, as if to say *Where have you been, man?*

He clutched the saddle, mounted clumsily, and then bent over, dizzy.

"What's wrong?" cried Miss Deeping.

"Nothing." He straightened slowly. The vertigo had passed. "Have you any water?"

"Did no one bring any?" She gazed around the group as if they were incompetent. "Why didn't I think of that?" she added.

There were quite a few people here with her, Laurence noticed. The duke, several of his own servants, Miss Brown. In his current state, this seemed confusing. What was she doing here? "Never mind." Laurence looked up and opened his mouth, letting the rain fall into it. It was delicious and tantalizing and not enough.

"We must get him home," said Miss Deeping.

They were giving him dubious looks, Laurence saw. He supposed it was odd, but he kept trying to swallow the rain.

They set off. It felt like a long ride, though he came into familiar country almost immediately. And with that he realized his prison must have been the old Torbert house, in the process of being sold by an old man's heirs. He couldn't understand how the gang had found it. Until he remembered. He urged Ranger toward the duke's mount, which neither horse appreciated. "Some of my staff are in the pay of those people," Laurence told him. He frowned suspiciously at the ones in their party.

"Not any longer," Tereford replied. He looked bitter about this for some reason. "They've taken to their heels."

It appeared that a great deal had happened during his captivity. He would insist on hearing it all when he felt more himself. Ranger snapped at Tereford's horse. Laurence dropped back.

At the house Laurence was welcomed with gratifying acclaim. He was furnished with a hot bath and fresh clothing, and plied with food and drink. He strove to keep up with the chorus of voices explaining the day's events to the duchess, but the fatigue he'd been fighting in the dark descended upon him, and it all seemed very confusing. When he nearly put his face into a bowl of soup, he was hustled off to bed. The mattress and lavender-scented sheets were wonderful, and with all the draperies open, Laurence was able to plunge into sorely needed sleep.

అం

"I wish you would stop pacing, Charlotte," said the duchess the next day. "You are like a caged lion."

"Why is Glendarvon not awake?" Charlotte replied. "He never sleeps through the morning."

"He has been through an ordeal. Of course he needs rest."

"Yes." Charlotte reproached herself silently. Naturally, he had to recover. But she needed to see him. She needed to be in his arms again, as she'd been when she flew at him in that cell. The duke had seen it; no doubt he'd told Cecelia. She didn't care.

"I am still annoyed with you," the duchess went on. "It was too bad to leave me out of all your plans."

"We thought we might need to lie to the duke." As it happened, this hadn't been required, because no one had expected the ladies to act, Charlotte thought acidly.

"I see," said Cecelia. "I would not want to do that." She sighed. "I don't suppose I could have helped much in any case. Miss Palliser can really throw knives?" She had been particularly impressed by this skill.

"With amazing accuracy," replied Charlotte.

Sounds from outside took her to the window. "It's a post chaise," she said. "Two of them, actually. And Henry." Her brother was riding beside the first vehicle. It pulled up. She counted the figures descending from the carriage. "And four other men. Strangers." No one got out of the second one.

"From the Foreign Office, I'm sure," said Cecelia. "Your brother must have sent for them when the marquess was taken."

So it proved when the newcomers were ushered in and Henry introduced them. He ended with "This is John Bexley. He has been to China and knows a great deal about it."

Mr. Bexley murmured some caveat.

The duke came in, followed by Merlin on his crutches, and then Miss Brown and Miss Palliser. Henry began more presentations.

But Mr. Bexley interrupted him. "What are you doing here?" he asked.

He was staring at Miss Brown, Charlotte noted. And she had flushed bright red. "I came up with Miss Palliser," she answered. "To bear her company."

"She has been very helpful," said the duke. "As has Miss Brown."

"Brown?" Bexley frowned. "What are you playing—"

"That is of no consequence," interrupted Miss Brown. Or perhaps *not* Miss Brown, Charlotte thought, but some other name entirely. There was a new mystery here.

Henry was staring at the now-nameless young lady as if he'd seen a ghost. "Castlereagh's reception for the Russians," he said. "I saw you there. I knew there was *something* about you."

Charlotte hadn't thought of Miss…whoever…as one who moved in the foreign secretary's exalted circles.

Miss Brown ignored Henry as if he hadn't spoken. "I suppose you have come to take charge of the scrolls," she said to Bexley. "And the man who wanted them enough to kidnap a peer?"

Mr. Bexley nodded, his expression gone blank. Or perhaps diplomatic, Charlotte thought.

"I don't know what you'll get out of him," she went on. "He hasn't even told anyone his name."

"Miss Palliser and I will return to London with you," said the putative Miss Brown. Her tone was suddenly commanding, as if she was accustomed to obedience. "We should pack, Miss Palliser."

"You assume they are going back at once?" asked Henry.

"Naturally," she answered. She looked at Bexley, raising her eyebrows. He nodded, his blue eyes watchful and possibly amused. Miss Brown pulled at Miss Palliser's arm. "We aren't needed here any longer."

Definitely amused, Miss Palliser allowed herself to be hustled out.

"Who is she?" Henry demanded of the newcomers. "*Miss Brown* isn't her real name, is it?"

"Why would you say so?" asked Mr. Bexley.

"Because you were obviously surprised to hear her use it," Henry responded.

"You should ask her."

"As if she would tell me anything," muttered Henry.

Bexley let this pass. "I should like to gather up the papers and the prisoners and start back as soon as possible. We can make some miles today even though the team isn't fresh. Miss Palliser and I can discuss her translations."

Charlotte slipped out of the room on a mission of her own.

She found the Miss Not-Brown folding garments into a portmanteau in her bedchamber. Charlotte shut the door behind her and sat in an armchair.

"I am rather occupied at the moment," said the other woman.

"Fleeing the scene of your…ruse?"

"What? What do you mean?"

"What is your real name?" Charlotte was interested, and she thought Henry *really* wanted to know.

"Did Bexley—" She bit off the words.

Charlotte waited. When the silence had grown long, she said, "We faced the villains together. Are we not comrades?"

The other woman sighed. "I wanted to come here to do something of significance, which I have had little chance for in my life. I think I have done so."

Charlotte nodded. She knew all this. It was sheer stalling. She conveyed this opinion with a look.

"My name is…rather well-known."

"In diplomatic circles," Charlotte guessed. The signs pointed in that direction.

Now Miss Brown bowed her head in acknowledgment. "I did not wish it mentioned."

Another silence fell. "You are not going to tell me," Charlotte concluded.

"It is irrelevant. The matter is resolved. We will go back to London."

"So I am not worthy of your secret?" Charlotte was rather hurt by her attitude.

"I don't wish anyone else to know."

This didn't help, really. "My brother is entering the Foreign Service quite soon. Don't you think he should know?"

"It has nothing to do with him. And I forbid you to tell him anything."

Charlotte stiffened in the chair. She was not accustomed to being ordered about so imperiously.

"I mean, I beg you not to," said the other woman.

"He is my brother."

"And I am your comrade. You said."

Piqued, dissatisfied, Charlotte rose. "I don't seem to have anything to tell him."

"We did a brave deed together. Is that not enough?"

"So I should not expect to hear from you in the future?" She had thought she'd made a friend. Apparently, the feeling was not mutual.

Her companion looked nonplussed. "I…I suppose not."

"I see." Hurt and angry, Charlotte walked out of the room. She did not slam the door. That would have been redundant. She'd already had an opening shut in her face.

Twenty

LAURENCE WOKE FROM A CONFUSED DREAM TO FIND THE sun setting. He'd slept the clock around, which he'd never done before in his life. He felt much better for it.

He dressed for dinner, though it would be some time before the meal, and went downstairs. The house felt oddly empty as he moved slowly through it, and he wondered where everyone could be.

But he forgot all the others when he came upon Miss Deeping in the drawing room, standing at a window and looking out. She turned when he entered, and the very air seemed to flare with excitement. For a moment Laurence thought she would throw herself into his arms again, as she had at his rescue. He waited in hope, but she didn't move.

"There you are," she said softly. "You slept so long."

His spirits sang at the quiet beauty of her face. He moved toward her. "I was worn down, apparently. What has been happening?"

"Henry arrived with people from the Foreign Office," she said. "They took the scrolls and prisoners and set off for London. Miss Palliser and Miss…Brown went too."

"Ah," he replied, still lost in admiration of her.

"We didn't want to disturb you. The duke agreed it was the best solution."

She seemed concerned that he would feel they'd usurped his authority. Laurence was simply glad the matter had been resolved and the villains removed. All his attention was reserved for just one person. "What did Tereford mean when he said your cohort captured the villains?"

"I have no cohort," she replied with obvious bitterness.

"But Tereford did say that?" He had been dazed, but he was certain he remembered correctly.

"Miss Palliser can throw knives" was the odd reply.

"Can she?"

"And Henry taught me to shoot, you know."

"I remember. Now you have me agog to hear the details."

She smiled a little, and he was cheered. "Well, when your note was delivered…"

"The one they made me write," Laurence put in.

"Yes. How did they do so?"

"They threatened to hurt you…my friends if I refused."

She looked at him. Laurence looked back. He felt as if his heart and soul were in the long gaze they exchanged. He was sorry when it ended.

"The duke made a plan to surround the church with men from your household and catch the gang that way," Miss Deeping continued then.

"They had informants here in the house," Laurence told her. He still hated that idea.

"That is what Merlin thought. He is rather clever." She frowned. "Oh, I have to get letters for him. Will you write one?"

This was a non sequitur, but it didn't matter. "I will do anything you ask," Laurence said.

Miss Deeping flushed. She looked down. "I had another idea of how to catch them."

As she told him what the three ladies had done, Laurence grew more and more amazed. "You are a wonder," he said when she finished. "I am speechless with astonishment. And admiration."

She looked gratified.

"And yet not entirely speechless. Obviously." He smiled at her. "Or surprised either. Haven't I seen many times that you are intrepid?"

"You are not humiliated to have been rescued by women?"

He didn't know what she meant. "Why should I be?"

"Isn't it always the gallant hero and the maiden in peril?" Miss Deeping made an impatient gesture. "A girl standing about and mewling over her fate. Oh, poor helpless me. Alas, alas. I will just stand here and let them tie me to a rock to be the monster's dinner." She grimaced. "Why not learn archery or javelin throwing? Pick up a stout stick at least?"

Laurence burst out laughing. "You would never mewl, would you?"

"I think not!"

The indignation in her tone was a delight. Words burst out of him. "When I was shut up in the dark, shuddering with cold and terror from the past, I thought of you. Your example gave me the courage to hang on."

Her lips parted as she gazed at him. "Mine did?"

"Yes. And it sustained me. Got me through the worst. I think you could always get me through. Anything."

Emotion moved in her dark eyes. "I do not have to lose myself," she murmured.

"What?"

"I was worried... But it is not so with you."

"I don't understand."

"Exactly." She shook her head as if marveling. "When I heard they'd taken you, I was terrified."

"No, you weren't."

"I was."

"You marched into that church and shot the blackguards," he pointed out.

"I was terrified for *you*," she replied, her voice vibrating with feeling.

Laurence's breath caught on a sudden surge of hope and longing. "I love you," he said. And then was enchanted to realize she had said it, too, at the same moment.

Now she threw herself into his arms. He caught her eagerly. There followed an interlude of searing kisses and increasingly passionate caresses.

He was panting when he had to draw back. It was that or carry her off to his bedchamber and tear away all this irritating clothing.

He led her to a drawing room sofa, where they nestled together. There was just one more very important thing. "After all the talk of not wooing—" Laurence began.

"I think I am most thoroughly wooed," she interrupted.

This very characteristic sentence filled him with exultation. "Miss Deeping," he began again.

"Charlotte, surely," she said. She put a hand to his cheek.

The simple touch thrilled him beyond measure. "Charlotte," he amended. "But you must let me speak."

"Must I?"

Her tone was fond. He savored it. "Unless you would prefer to do so? I have no objection."

"Why, whatever can you mean, my lord?"

"You will marry me, won't you? Wait. That was inept. I should get down on one knee and propose in form." He started to rise. She pulled him back.

"Kneeling is not required. I will marry you."

The delight he felt then was indescribable. He kissed her, and reveled in the knowledge that he would be doing so for the rest of their lives.

"I warn you I intend to make some changes here."

"Please. Create a revolution in the house, as you have in my heart." Under her command, the place would become a home to him at last, he thought.

"Pretty speeches, Laurence?"

How could he feel such a thrill at his name on her lips? "Truth," he answered. "Only and always."

"Only and always," she repeated. Like a vow.

Happiness such as he'd never expected to feel flooded through Laurence. He pulled her close for another kiss.

And Merlin stumped into the drawing room on his crutches, stopping in front of them. "Ah, you're awake," he said to the marquess.

"You have the least tact of any man on earth," replied Charlotte as they reluctantly drew apart.

Merlin ignored this. "You haven't forgotten my letters, I hope. Tereford is talking of leaving."

"I have not."

"Good." Instead of taking himself off, he dropped into a chair facing them. "I've been trying to work out how that ring got to Lorne," he said. "And who the nephew was who cleared out the place."

Charlotte actually was interested in these questions, though his timing was annoying.

"The killers must have taken the ring," he went on. "But after that—"

"They were killed in turn," said Glendarvon. "For

botching their mission. They were supposed to retrieve the papers and my mother."

Charlotte and Merlin gazed at him.

"The leader of that gang told me," he added.

"So the ring was handed along to their bosses, I suppose," said Merlin. He considered. "I think they must have heard later that your parents had visited Lorne. And so, when the old man died, they took the opportunity to steal everything."

"Carrying the ring along?" wondered Charlotte.

"A kind of memento perhaps?"

Glendarvon shivered. Charlotte leaned closer to him.

"But they lost the ring and didn't find the hiding place," Merlin concluded.

Charlotte nodded. It made sense, though they would never know for certain.

"I can sell you the ring now," Merlin said to the marquess. "I don't need it anymore."

"Need it for what?" asked Charlotte.

"Assurance that I would not be excluded from the investigation," he replied. Turning back to Glendarvon, he said, "Shall we say five hundred pounds?"

"What?" Charlotte's jaw dropped. "That's an outrageous amount."

"The jeweler in Leicester said it's a fine gem," Merlin retorted. "And who can put a value on a family heirloom? Priceless, eh?"

"You are shameless."

"I need the funds to set up in London. I won't be able to join the runners until my leg heals. That'll be weeks. Maybe months."

"Four hundred," said the marquess.

Charlotte turned to him. "That's still too much."

"Done," said Merlin.

Glendarvon nodded. "And now, do go away."

"You shouldn't let him cheat you," said Charlotte as Merlin levered himself up and stumped out.

"The sum is agreed," said Merlin over his shoulder. "No drawing back."

"Really," Charlotte said when he was gone. "You might have gotten it for less."

"But I have better things to do," he answered, pulling her close and into a blazing kiss.

"Much better," she agreed breathlessly after a time.

~∞~

Three days later an enlarged party gathered outside Laurence's house. The entire Deeping family had come to celebrate the engagement, and there had been a fine dinner and quite a few toasts to future happiness. Everyone but the happy couple had been surprised to be called outdoors into a frosty night. And even more startled to be led to what appeared to be a perfectly ordinary wardrobe brought down from one of the bedchambers. It sat in the middle of the graveled drive. Wood and kindling had been piled around it. Flammable materials could be seen inside the open doors as well.

"Do you understand what this is about?" the duke asked his duchess as they watched Glendarvon approach with a flaming torch. "Guy Fawkes Day is well past."

"I don't," the duchess replied. "Only that is it quite significant to Glendarvon and, thus, to Charlotte."

"The wardrobe turns clothing moldy? It is cursed? Haunted by a malevolent ghost?"

"When did you grow so fanciful?" she asked.

"When I was invited to watch a common piece of furniture immolated."

The marquess set the torch to the kindling. Flames sprang up immediately and crackled upward.

"Though I would have liked to set fire to Great-Uncle Percival's hoardings," the duke added.

"That would have caused another Great Fire of London." The Terefords moved back from the increasing heat.

∼⌖∼

"It is like a Viking funeral," said Charlotte on the other side of the flames. "A send-off for a heroic warrior."

"Warrior?" Laurence had thrown the torch into the fire, and now he stood with his arm around her. He would like to stand so for the rest of his life, he thought.

"The wardrobe," she replied. "It saved you. It was your shield and protection. And we revere it for that. But it is time for every reminder of that day to be gone."

"To Valhalla?" he asked, enjoying the workings of her mind as he always would.

Charlotte grinned at him and nodded.

"So the dead heroes in—what is it, Odin's hall?—will hang their swords inside? Put their helmets on the upper shelf?"

Charlotte laughed with sheer joy. "Oh, I do hope so!"

The wardrobe collapsed in on itself in a shower of sparks. Bertram Deeping gave a cheer and capered about waving a burning stick. "This is *better* than Guy Fawkes," he shouted.

"You do realize Bertram is to be your brother now," Charlotte said to Laurence.

"Will he put vinegar in my tea?" Laurence sounded rather taken with the idea.

"Or worse. And all four of them will stick their noses into your affairs. In their various ways."

"There is nothing I want more," he answered. "Except you."

Right in front of everyone, she kissed him.

⤎

"This is a happy outcome," said Cecelia on the other side of the fire.

"The last of your friends is settled," replied the duke. "Er, Miss Deeping is the last, is she not?"

Cecelia gave him an impish smile. "I have all sort of friends."

"Because you are so utterly charming."

She relented. "Charlotte is the last for now."

"And it is time we were on our way to London," the duke said as they moved farther back from the blaze.

"It is a pity to cut your hunting short."

"There will be other years," he replied. "And other places now that we have sold Lorne to the Deepings."

"A good solution," Cecelia replied.

"At a very low price," he pointed out.

"Well, we liked the idea of one of their sons settled there."

He nodded. "And the town house requires our attention."

He said *our* so naturally and strongly. All the changes they'd been through were in that word and tone. It warmed Cecelia's heart. "I have some news for you, James."

"Yes? Not some fresh disaster at the far ends of Britain, I hope?"

"No." She put a hand to her midsection. "I am with child."

The joy that flooded his face made her cry as he pulled her into his arms.

Read on for a sneak peek at the next in
the Duke's Estates series from *New York
Times* bestselling author Jane Ashford

THE DUKE'S BEST FRIEND

KATE MEACHAM MOVED THROUGH THE ORNATE ROOMS
of the Austrian embassy like a tiger patrolling its territory,
she thought, or a fierce, sleek sea creature sliding unseen
through the depths. Her grandfather had introduced her to
gatherings like this glittering St. Nicholas Day reception, and
she had learned to use them to soak up tidbits of useful information for him. Grandfather, an illustrious diplomat loaded
with accolades and honors, had taught her that few people
in the realms of power took much notice of a young woman,
except perhaps to admire her face and form. They gazed
right past a youthful lady to discover someone of actual significance. And sometimes they revealed secrets that they
thought she wouldn't understand.

A pang of grief shook Kate. Her grandfather had died
almost a year ago. She still missed him terribly.

Kate scanned the crowd for one particular tall, handsome
figure. She'd been wanting to speak to Jerome Delaroche for

some time and was surprised he had not contacted her when he'd returned to London.

At last, she found him, chatting with a circle of young attachés in one of the back parlors. His dapper, square-jawed figure stood out even in this impeccably turned-out group. She joined them and gradually, subtly, separated him from them. When they were far enough away for private conversation, he said, "What are you doing here? I thought you'd been banned from diplomatic receptions."

"What? Nonsense. Who told you that?"

Jerome shrugged. "I heard it somewhere."

A way of saying he would not tell her. Her attendance had been discouraged since her grandfather's death, Kate admitted to herself. But there had been no formal protest. Yet. "Of course I haven't been banned." She still had the support of some of her grandfather's friends. "I expected to see you as soon as you returned to London, Jerome."

"I've had a great deal to do."

"What sorts of things?"

"This and that."

Kate frowned. He must know she wanted all the details of his recent overseas journey. "I gave you the information that led you to Gibraltar. And won you a commendation, I expect. I should like to know how it went."

"I cannot tell you. It is a confidential Foreign Office matter."

"Which never would have come to light without me."

"How *did* you find out that fellow was spreading dangerous rumors?"

"I hear things."

"By venturing into places you should not go. And doing things you shouldn't."

"What are you suggesting?"

"Nothing."

"There's no need to hide your teeth. We've known each other since we were infants."

"I'm not certain infants can be said to be acquainted."

"Do you suppose I seduce my way to secrets?"

Jerome looked away. "Of course not."

"That's fortunate. Because I do not."

"I never thought so for a moment."

But she thought perhaps he had. Or had heard others speculate on the idea. Some people's minds went immediately in that direction. As if a woman had no other resources.

"Who is looking after you, Kate? Now that your grandfather is gone?"

This was chancy territory. She stifled her irritation at the idea she required looking after, like a child, at the age of twenty-four. "You needn't worry."

"As you said, we've been friends all our lives."

Kate nodded. As children, they had run wild during visits to the country. On school holidays, they had pored over globes and atlases and had imagined being sent to the ends of the earth on adventures. They'd mourned together when all four of their parents had died in a shipwreck at the Cape of Good Hope. A location that had been grossly mislabeled, Kate thought.

"I shan't be able to help you," Jerome went on. "I shall be rather busier in future."

"Do you have a new position?" Her information, and his admittedly clever action on it, had probably brought him a promotion. Kate tried to be simply glad and not envious. A young lady—no matter how well-born and educated and talented—could not go on diplomatic missions. As the world saw it, she could be an ornament in embassies, companion to a man, and little else. "Happy to have helped," she said with only a hint of sarcasm.

Jerome moved from one foot to the other in uncomfortable silence. Kate wondered what could be the matter with him. Jerome was the smoothest fellow she knew.

"The thing is, Kate, I've offered for Emma Lisle. We're to be married in March."

"Emma Lisle? That ninny?"

He looked pained and offended. "She's a gentle, sweet girl who cares about *me* rather than my missions."

"And will be of no help on them."

"I don't require help! Nor do I wish to be a counter on the board of your ambitions." He frowned and lowered his voice. "We are not compatible, Kate."

Kate stood there, confused, until she realized that Jerome had assumed she'd been angling for a proposal. As if a woman could not associate with a man, offer him aid, for any other reason than the hope of marriage. "You can't think that I…"

"I'll work hard and devote myself to diplomatic work, argue the cases, hammer out the agreements, but when I finish and come home, I want a peaceful place. Emma will give me that."

"Peace is not brainless," Kate replied. At once she regretted it—the words and the acid tone.

Jerome's jaw tightened. "Unfair, Kate. Very nearly cruel."

She bowed her head. He was right. Emma Lisle was a kind, pleasant girl. She shouldn't have said that. "I know. I'm sorr—"

"You must admit that you are at all not suited for diplomacy."

"What?"

"Such work requires tact and patience and…a convivial nature. You possess none of those."

"How can you say that? I do."

He raised a skeptical eyebrow.

Patience was hard to master, Kate admitted silently. "Grandfather said I had a quick mind and plenty of courage."

Jerome nodded. "Indeed. But you are also abrasive and foolhardy. You don't think before you speak. And you… smolder."

"Smolder?"

"You're doing it now. You shouldn't look at a man that way. It makes people think you're no better than you should be."

Kate was stunned. She had thought that Jerome liked her.

"Coming here, pulling me away from everyone else." He looked around uneasily.

"I didn't pull you!"

"People will assume an intrigue. Especially now that you are…unsupervised." He shook his head. "You would be a disaster in an overseas embassy, rouse all the wrong sorts of attention. You must find something else to do with yourself. I'm sorry that I cannot help." Jerome turned and walked away. His departure seemed oddly final.

There had been quite a few such terminal moments in the last year since her grandfather's demise.

Kate raised a hand to her forehead. The movement was echoed in a long mirror on the wall. Jerome had been standing in front of it. Now Kate faced her reflection—a tall, square-shouldered woman, with honey-colored hair and violet-blue eyes, a reasonably fashionable gown. Judged quite pretty by those who were supposed to know. She looked angry, as well she might after that exchange. Is that what Jerome had meant by *smolder*? She didn't think it was. Not at all. He'd practically called her a lightskirt. How dare he?

She gazed into her own burning eyes. *Had* she considered marrying Jerome? On some deep level where plans were hatched, ambitions weighed? Kate shook her head. She'd thought of him as a surrogate brother, sometimes annoying but loyal and reliable. Clearly she'd been mistaken.

Her reflection in the mirror wavered a little, shaken by her misjudgment and his accusations. While her grandfather lived, she'd had a place. His mere existence had opened gatherings like these to her, even though he rarely attended himself. She'd revered and loved him. She missed him acutely. But he was gone. And with him, seemingly, had gone her social standing. Over this last year, it had felt as if her life was melting away like snow in a lingering thaw.

Jerome's words echoed in her mind—find something else to do with herself. How was she to do that, exactly? Grandfather had given her a most unconventional upbringing. She had none of the accomplishments of young ladies of her background and class. Girls like Emma Lisle, for example.

The image in the mirror stared back at her. Kate straightened like a soldier coming to attention. She hadn't wanted those skills. She would not be judged by them. She would think of something. She always did.

An older couple appeared in the glass beside her. "Hello. Miss Meacham, isn't it? We met at the Castlereagh ball."

Where she had not been invited, Kate thought, any more than she had been tonight. Getting in there had been a bit of a coup. She groped for a name. These were the Grindells, she recalled. He was a minor functionary in the customs office.

"Are you here all alone?" asked Mrs. Grindell.

"Oh no." Technically, it wasn't a lie. There were people all around her.

"Very sorry to hear about your grandfather," said Mr. Grindell. "A marvelous man."

"Yes, he was."

"We didn't see you at the Russian gala," he added.

"Of course, it was full of foreigners," sniffed Mrs. Grindell.

Hardly a surprise at a foreign embassy, Kate wanted to say. But she did not. Despite Jerome's insulting opinion, she was capable of tact. "I was out of town for a while," she replied instead.

"Visiting friends?" asked Mrs. Grindell nosily.

She had been supporting a friend. An acquaintance. A newly met connection. They had helped foil a dastardly plot involving long-lost documents, a ruthless foreign agent, kidnapping, and a cunning trap in which she had played a crucial part. It had been extremely invigorating and would remain one of her most cherished memories. She longed to hear about the aftermath. If she hadn't given a false name in the matter, she could inquire. But if she *had* used her own name, she could not have joined in.

"Where are you staying now that your grandfather is gone?" Mrs. Grindell had the look of an inveterate gossip.

Kate had no suitable answer to that question. It was time to slip away. She wouldn't accomplish much in her current mood. Kate looked around. "Oh, there is the Austrian ambassador."

The Grindells turned eagerly, as she'd known they would. She was unimportant in the scheme of things, a mere diversion until someone of significance came along. She used the distraction to slip behind a larger group of guests and then around them to the edge of the room. Casually she made her way down it, her gaze distant but purposeful, as if she was on her way to meet someone unexceptionable. Her chaperone, perhaps. The imaginary older female who made Kate's existence socially acceptable.

Hiding a sneer, she slipped into a hallway and through a door into the back premises. She knew the geography of all the major diplomatic residences—how to insert and extract herself without the bother of front entries and invitation cards. Lower servants didn't question a lady walking with assurance. As long as she kept moving. And major domos could be evaded. Sneaking made things like cloaks and bonnets awkward, but she'd always found a place to leave hers until she returned for them.

What could Jerome have meant—that she'd been banned? How would they? They wouldn't dare. She would not be dropped into oblivion simply because she was an unattached female!

❧

Henry Deeping leveled his pistol, aimed, and fired, putting a bullet dead center in a disc hanging at the opposite end of Manton's Shooting Gallery. He enjoyed the precision of the action, the pleasure of exercising his skill. He was a crack shot, and he savored the sense of control that gave him, the thrill of action in a humdrum morning. Life might pull him in inconvenient directions. People might behave capriciously. Circumstances might bore or disappoint. But here he could always succeed.

Henry waited while an attendant changed out the row of perforated wafers. When the man had moved away, he shot again. Bullseye. Bullseye.

He had planned to be with his family for Christmas, enjoying the festivities of the season, only returning to London in the New Year to take up his first post in the Foreign Office. But the capture of a dangerous agent near his family home in Leicestershire, and the discovery of potentially explosive documents written in Chinese—incredible as that adventure now seemed—had brought him back to town early.

He had found the translator, helped corner the agent, escorted the captive to town, and now he was kept kicking up his heels at others' convenience, occasionally summoned to answer questions about the sequence of events that had already been covered in written reports. On the one hand, he was pleased to have attracted the attention of his new Foreign Office superiors. He'd been commended for his deft handling of the situation. On the other, he was sorry to miss the family holiday. All of his friends and connections were far away.

Yet as soon as he thought this, he was proven wrong.

A tall, athletically built man strolled into the room, his pale pantaloons and exquisitely cut long-tailed blue coat proclaiming him a Nonpareil. "I thought I might find you here," said the Duke of Tereford. "Putting every other shooter to shame, as usual."

There were no other gentlemen present, but Henry appreciated the spirit of the compliment. He had known James since they were twelve-year-olds arriving at school, facing a new place with a mixture of bravado and trepidation. Henry had sat with James in classrooms and run beside him on playing fields. They'd had adventures as young men on the strut in society and plunged into deeper waters on several memorable occasions. When James had come into his inheritance and assumed a dukedom, Henry had been glad for him and only a little envious. Well, perhaps more than a little. In one stroke James had acquired title, fortune, and a life's work. Not that he had wanted the latter at the time.

He felt a familiar sense of eclipse as James came closer. The duke was known as the handsomest man in London. Henry was aware that his own tall, thin figure, pale skin, and dark hair and eyes were not nearly so striking. He looked well enough, but he was no Adonis. "I'm surprised to see you back in town at this time of year," he said.

"The townhouse is cleared and repaired at last," Tereford replied. "It's ready to be furnished and made ready for next season and for Cecelia to spend a great deal of money."

"Are you actually posing as a put-upon husband whose wife overspends?" Henry asked.

Tereford smiled. "No. It's more likely to be me overspending."

"As everyone knows." James's inheritance had come with a flood of responsibilities that had threatened to overwhelm him, but had instead been the making of him, Henry thought now. Through a very fortunate marriage.

"Not everyone, surely?"

Henry gave him a satirical look and received a grimace in return. "Cecelia is certainly the more sensible one," Tereford said.

"You know, from what I have observed lately, I think you work together as a very efficient team."

A tremor of emotion showed on the duke's face and, as quickly, disappeared. "Thank you."

Feeling that he should say more, Henry added, "I was wrong to doubt the wisdom of your marriage. I'm sorry for anything I might have said that…"

"I know, Henry."

The look they exchanged spoke volumes without the need for actual words. It encompassed years of friendship, good-natured teasing, and many occasions when they stood up for each other. That history let Henry see that something was bothering the duke. He raised his eyebrows, indicating an openness to confidences.

"I am to be a father next year," Tereford said.

"Congratulations!"

The duke's answering smile was wry. "Thank you, but I'm terrified. What do I know about fatherhood? My own was not a good example."

"You aren't like him," Henry said. James's father had been a cold, sarcastic person, and his biting criticisms had been particularly hard on his heir. Henry had never observed the least sign of softness in the man, and he'd often pitied his friend when he endured one of his parent's thundering scolds.

"Not like him anymore?" the duke asked.

"You never were."

"Was I not?" Tereford looked uncertain. "I've been called selfish and arrogant."

Henry couldn't deny it. James had shown leanings in that direction. Henry himself had pointed them out a time or two. "Not since you married, I daresay."

Tereford's expression grew tender, then uneasy. "When I am presented with a child—"

"What's become of that family you had living in the townhouse?" Henry interrupted.

"The Gardeners?" Tereford asked, surprised.

"Right." Henry had been astonished when he'd discovered that Tereford had taken in an indigent family to watch over his London townhouse as the detritus of decades was cleared away.

"Mrs. Gardener is making ready to move to the country," the duke replied. "It is what she wished."

"There were several children."

"Ned and Jen and Effie. Ned is an apprentice tailor at Weston's now."

"You get along quite well with them."

"I do?"

Henry nodded. He had seen it and been startled.

"Well..." The duke still looked uncertain.

"You'll do very well. Wait and see."

Tereford bowed his head, abandoning the topic more than agreeing. "Are you in town for Christmas?"

"Yes. It's taking a great deal of time to resolve the Leicestershire matter."

The duke nodded. He had been involved in that as well, an anomaly in a somewhat motley crew.

"I think the Foreign Office feels that my job has started," Henry added. "And my time is no longer my own."

"A memorable beginning."

Henry nodded. He should count himself fortunate. He needed to make his way in the world, and his uncle had very kindly volunteered to help him. It was true that Henry had expressed no desire to be a diplomat. Such things happened when one was quiet in a noisy family. Someone popped up to tell you what to do. And he hadn't refused. Diplomacy was a respected profession. It offered sensible, practical possibilities. Quite unlike his own grandiose dreams. He shoved that thought into the oblivion where all its fellows lay.

"We're here so that Cecelia can see the best doctors," said the duke. "You must spend Christmas with us."

"That would be pleasant." Henry felt his mood lift. The Terefords were very good company as well as friends. "Perhaps the duchess can advise me. My uncle says I need to find a proper wife if I wish to succeed in diplomatic circles."

"We've given up matchmaking," Tereford replied.

"We?" Henry smiled at the thought of James doing any such thing.

"I was…drawn into the courtships of your sister and her friends. But no more. Cecelia agrees."

"Don't I deserve as much assistance?" In fact, Henry was not eager to marry for the sake of his career. That seemed a cold, sad endeavor. But he enjoyed teasing James.

"Do you really require it?"

"I was joking."

Tereford examined him with benign curiosity. "Have you heard anything from Miss Brown?" he asked.

"What? No." Henry had not been able to forget the acerbic young lady who'd pushed her way into the Leicestershire affair while seeming to disdain them all. She'd had some undefined connection to the Foreign Office and almost certainly was not actually named Brown. But he didn't see why James would mention her now. "I wouldn't expect to do so."

"Ah, well, I suppose you could find her again."